THE WILDCAT DEN

THE WILDCAT DEN

A Book of Fiction

Mark W. Royston

Author of *The Spout Spring & (As a Bonus)*
Too Poor to Paint Too Proud to Whitewash
(The Early Years)

iUniverse, Inc.
New York Lincoln Shanghai

The Wildcat Den
A Book of Fiction

iUniverse books may be ordered through booksellers or by contacting:

iUniverse
2021 Pine Lake Road, Suite 100
Lincoln, NE 68512
www.iuniverse.com
1-800-Authors (1-800-288-4677)

Because of the dynamic nature of the Internet, any Web addresses or links contained in this book may have changed since publication and may no longer be valid.

Certain characters in this work are historical figures, and certain events portrayed did take place. However, this is a work of fiction. All of the other characters, names, and events as well as all places, incidents, organizations, and dialogue in this novel are either the products of the author's imagination or are used fictitiously.

ISBN: 978-0-595-47688-6 (pbk)
ISBN: 978-0-595-91952-9 (ebk)

Printed in the United States of America

CONTENTS

THE WILDCAT DEN

Too Poor to Paint Too Proud to Whitewash The Navy Years

The Wildcat Den

A Book of Fiction
By
Mark W. Royston

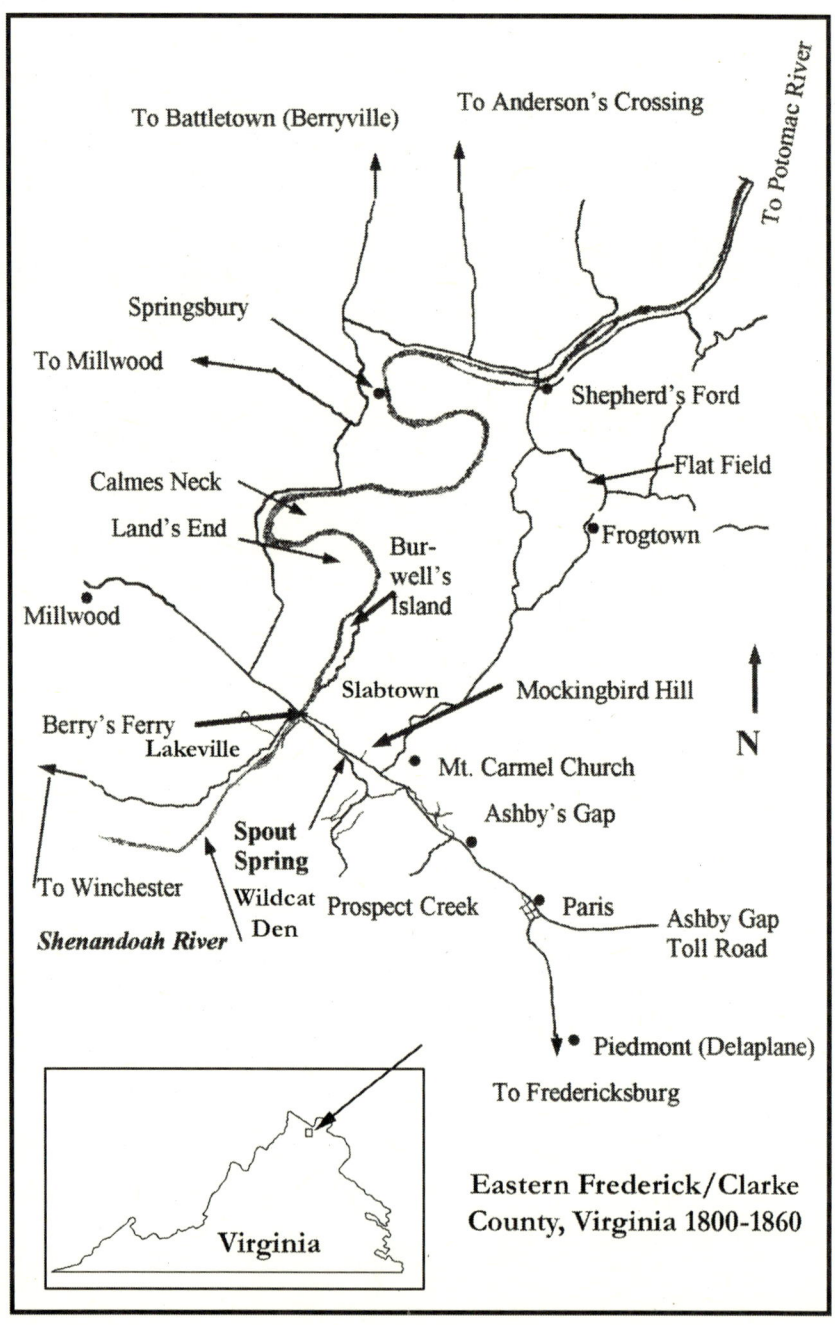

To Battletown (Berryville)

To Anderson's Crossing

To Potomac River

Springsbury

To Millwood

Shepherd's Ford

Calmes Neck

Flat Field

Land's End

Frogtown

Bur-
well's
Island

Millwood

Slabtown

Mockingbird Hill

Berry's Ferry
Lakeville

N

Mt. Carmel Church

Ashby's Gap

To Winchester

**Spout
Spring**

Wildcat
Den

Prospect Creek

Paris

Ashby Gap
Toll Road

Shenandoah River

Piedmont (Delaplane)

Virginia

To Fredericksburg

**Eastern Frederick/Clarke
County, Virginia 1800-1860**

PREFACE

This is not the story of extraordinary people living in ordinary times. Rather it is the story of ordinary people living in extraordinary times. It is a family to whom war came. They did not seek it out, it came to them. Most survived. Devastated lands and a ruined economy were a part of their daily lives. Living in the Blue Ridge Mountains shielded them from some of the effects but not all. Mountain people were known for taking care of their own problems. The myths of some of their solutions helped to keep out the intruder.

Peter Kemp Royston (He was known as P.K. to reduce the confusion with his father's same first name.) lived from 1819 to 1898, his wife, Mary Ann Adams Royston, from 1829 to 1906. They saw the railroad come as well as kerosene lighting. Neither ever rode in an automobile. Electricity was something that many of the towns in the Valley had by the turn of the century, but the mountains had to wait until after WWII to be able to turn a switch.

They never saw a "movie" but did have their picture taken. They lived through the Civil War, the Reconstruction Period and the battle for the Recovery of the South. There were sixteen nephews who fought in the War, three did not return.

Many of the characters are created to try and give a picture as to how things may have happened. Many of the stories are mountain lore passed on by the author's mother. They may be fiction but as lore goes, there is always a modicum of truth in the telling. Only one in the family itself is a "created" person and the reader will be left to his own devices to figure out which character.

Dates don't always gibe but neither do the facts on tombstones. The drownings at the Shenandoah and the shelling of the Royston house were real, but not necessarily as described. Many details of other family members are given short shrift so as not to confuse the reader.

The book is the next generation of the family whose story was first told in the *Spout Spring*. Don't look for classic prose, just look for the personalities and the times in which they lived and how they may have reacted.

Acknowledgements

Writing a book is the putting together of details that were given to you by others. My thanks to those who were generous with sharing their knowledge of that area known as Clarke County in Northwestern Virginia.

Special thanks go to Cousin Don Royston whose genealogy details of our family give anchor to the fiction which I have produced.

The Clarke County Historical Society has published many booklets on early Clarke County and these details help to put life to those days of yore. Mary Thomason Morris, their archivist, is always generous with her time and encouragement. Her book, *Connections and Partings*, gives great references for marriages and deaths in Clarke County from 1857 to 1884.

Val Van Meter provided the prod that kept the book going when ideas began to fail. Val's love for the Shenandoah Valley and the Blue Ridge is reflected in her own writings as she follows the stories in Clarke and Frederick Counties for The Winchester Evening Star and before that as editor of the Clarke Times Courier.

The people of Clarke County and especially those who make the mountain their home are always generous in their reflections of my endeavors. While the details are put on paper sitting at a chair in

Southern California, it is the thought of these friends that keep alive the vision of the area of which I write.

Thanks also to my wife, Doris, who not only proofs my writings but is never critical of its quality. One does learn to judge the sections that are weak by the level of enthusiasm she gives that particular part.

And finally thanks to those who pick up this book and read it. May it give you the desire to learn more about your own ancestors who lived in times where difficulties were faced without the "advantage" of instant media analysis and the availability of modern conveniences that now allow us to spend time in leisure pursuits such as writing a book.

Dedication
To My Father
Luther Lee Royston

Dad was an "old man" when I was born. My recollection of him and my writing about him over the years have reflected this. I never knew him as a young person, full of the energies that he had before physical setbacks cost him the vigor of youth.

It is only after I have spent time reflecting on the life of his father, grandfather and great grandfather that I have come to realize how limited my view was of Dad. My writings reflected this limited knowledge and with that the unfairness to which he was treated in my thoughts.

The available facts about his early life are limited and I may never get the opportunity to write extensively about him. Because of that I take this opportunity to redress any mistakes I have made in my past reflections of his life.

To summarize his life and physical person, he was born in 1871 and died in 1941 (when I was eleven). In his young manhood, he was a "giant" of those times, being 6' 8" tall and weighing around 265 pounds. He had great physical strength, and it was only after some serious injuries that he became an old man before his time.

He had five boys and one girl from his first marriage. He married my mother, thirty years his junior, in 1923 after being widowed in 1918. His second marriage produced two children of which I was the youngest.

He was a very religious man and was the Sunday School Superintendent of Mount Carmel Church for a number of years starting around 1900. He lived most of his life in the Blue Ridge Mountains with a formal education that stopped in the fifth grade.

To my father, I dedicate this book

Prologue

It was a perfect day for a special chore. The thunder rolled across the sky and heat lightening made its threatening gestures. One would have thought it was an August day rather than late March. *No one will ever identify the sound of dynamite over this aerial display of nature,* P.K. thought.

He walked with the stride of a farmer who had spent many hours with one foot in the furrow of a mold board plow. What at one time was a mile-consuming gait now was more of a slow amble. He left his house near an area locally known as Slabtown and made his way down by the spring and the pond into which it flowed. Following the exiting stream he went toward the Ashby Gap Turn Pike. Crossing it, he headed south over the hill toward Wildcat Hollow.

Turning upstream when he reached the trail that paralleled Prospect Creek, he slowed to insure he was the only one in the vicinity. Just after reaching a turn in the creek, he looked for the granite outcropping and finding it, he crossed the creek. A few yards into the woods he found what he was seeking. The shale turned abruptly into granite and a small ledge protruded over the pile of shale.

He paused and let his mind go back over the years. Only he and his wife Mary Ann knew that this was the location of the wildcat den that had given the hollow its name. He was sure no one knew that the outcropping was the cover for a medium size cave that had allowed these wild animals a large area in which to live and bear their young. It had even been large enough for an overweight man to take refuge in trying times.

He thought, *Old Cave, you have served your purpose well. The wildcats have moved on to more remote areas and there is no need for man or beast to use your spaces for a lair or a sanctuary. It is time to take away any vestige of your past life and any evidence that might show that you ever existed.*

Reaching into his coat pocket he brought out a full-stick of dynamite and a coil of fuse. He mentally sized a length of fuse and with a practiced movement bit off a length and attached it to the dynamite cap. Reaching under the ledge he felt for the rifle and ammunition that he knew to be there. Satisfying himself that no one had stumbled on to this spot, he lit the fuse on the dynamite and leaned as far into the crevice as his ample size would let him. He tossed the dynamite back onto the ledge behind the opening and glancing around, started to make his way back to Prospect Creek. He counted as he walked and just as he neared the creek he turned and listened. A muffled explosion that could scarcely be heard a few hundred yards told him the deed was done. Just to insure it had worked to his planning, he walked a few yards back toward the cave. What had once been an outcropping was now a depression. A wisp of dust escaped from the spot but any evidence that this was once a wildcat den was gone.

He returned to the creek and made his way back to his house near the old slab mill, now with the slightly derisive name of Slabtown. A bead of sweat on his lip was the only evidence of any exertion. His son, Buck, looked up from washing his face and hands from a basin near the kitchen door and greeted his father, "I was wondering if you were going to be back for dinner. Where have you been? I thought you were going to finish dynamiting those postholes down near the MacDonald line."

"I've done all the dynamiting that I'll ever do," P.K. answered. "It's time to give that job up to someone with better teeth than I. Biting off fuse cord is getting to be too much for me."

"Don't know if I have anyone who can take your place. You may have to hang on for a while longer," Buck responded. "It's getting toward sundown. Even with this thunder storm there is enough sunlight for your evening thoughts with Ma."

P.K. washed up and dried his face and hands on the common towel supported on a rod near the wash bucket. He moved out to the front porch which faced east but had a special spot where one could sit and see the sun set in the pond's reflection. Here as always, his wife of over fifty years was waiting for him.

"Hard day?" she questioned.

"No, but a special day for getting chores done that should have been done long ago," P.K. answered. "I told Buck that he needed to get someone else to dynamite his post holes. I've lit my last fuse."

"That sounds sort of final," said his wife, Mary Ann. "Especially when I get the musty odor of the Wildcat Den. Have you been visiting your old rendezvous?"

It had been some time since he had told Mary Ann of his times spent at the den. The story of the rifle had come out, as well as the burial of the Union soldier at the Royston Graveyard. They had both agreed it was best to let the secrets die with them.

"But let's not worry about tomorrow. It's time to catch the sun's reflection as it peeks through the thunder clouds and say our evening prayers for the children." The usual routine was for P.K. to call out the children's names and for Mary Ann to petition God for their safe delivery from all dangers real or otherwise. Occasionally a snort would be heard from P.K. if he thought the request was too outlandish.

"Thomas," intoned P.K. Thomas was the oldest and one who looked much like P.K. P.K. used the given name of Thomas rather than the nickname of "Toad" given him at his birth by P.K.'s father.

"May God bless Thomas and Lucy Ellen and their children. Keep them close to you and to us as they grow old."

"Charles," P.K. continued. Mary Ann always called Charles, "Dink" as he was much smaller than the oldest son.

"Continue to bless 'Dink' and Martha and the nine children. Another is due to be born just now. Protect Martha in these trying days. Take care of their little Lilly Margaret. She is always so frail and sickly," Mary Ann asked fervently.

"Fanny." Fanny was the next oldest and was married to Hubert Trussell. They and their five children lived in the old home place near Wildcat Hollow.

"Fanny, we see often. Keep her always near. Keep Hubert safe as he works on building Mount Carmel School. Let Fanny bring that new baby by as she brings dinner to Hubert at Mount Carmel School."

"John Franklin," P.K. called the name of the fourth child. John carried the nickname of 'Augie' and many thought this was from another name, Augustine, that was dropped somewhere along the line. Augie had been born prematurely and if anyone would have bothered to count, it was the month of August that played the role in his nickname. Mary Ann would look at P.K. and shyly smile, remembering the conception month.

"He was our August baby," she would remind P.K.

"God, please take care of my Baptist kids, Augie, Julia Ann and their family. We don't see them much but keep in touch as they live across the river. Their little Fanny is only a year old and I ache to see her."

"Buck," said P.K. loud enough to carry through the house. Buck, if he heard, knew the scenario and didn't try to respond.

"Walter Settle" said Mary Ann calling him by his given names. "Thank God for Walter. He has been so good to us in our declining years. Take care of Virginia and her babies, Marcus and Peter Kemp, who are now with you in Paradise. I try my best to take care of the rest of the children."

"Nimrod and Pammie," P.K. named the twins together, even though Pammie was the only one who survived.

"Nimrod? I wonder what he would be like as a man. He would be in his late thirties now. Life hurts so much when you lose them so young. Pammie is single but we pray for him to find someone who truly cares for him," Mary Ann's voice grew soft as she recalled the hurts gone by.

"Jim," added P.K. *Jim was born during the war and was lucky to survive as the shells were very noisome when he was being born*, P.K. thought.

"God, you really need to take care of Jim. He has so much trouble being straight up with things. Seems he wants to tell stories even when he has nothing to gain," Mary Ann pleaded for her son who's nickname was 'Twister' because of how he twisted the stories.

"Daughter Mary," P.K. said softly as he thought of the one born so many years ago and who only lived a month.

Mary Ann's eyes misted. "Consumption they called it. T.B. was what it was. How can it take someone so young? She would be thirty four now and have children of her own." Mary Ann's voice was almost accusatory as she let God know what she thought.

P.K. interrupted her thoughts as he continued his litany. "Mary Ann," he added bringing the namesake of his wife to the front.

"Oh yes, Mary Ann, we are so much alike, Never could get along without arguing, Marrying Jack Longerbeam was the best thing that happened to her. She is about ready to have her sixth. We ask you God to take care of her," Mary Ann implored, thinking that it wasn't fair to think about birth so close after she had remembered losing one of her own.

"Robert," P.K. said next.

"Robert Winter, he is the smart one in the family. Don't know where he got all those brains. We ask that you help him to use them wisely, now that he has just married. I wonder how smart his children will be?" she said, sounding like maybe she expected God to speak and answer her.

"Elizabeth," P.K. continued down the list of their many children.

"Elizabeth," mused Mary Ann. Elizabeth was married to Henry Smallwood, brother of Augie's wife, Julia. "It sure helps keep the family together," she noted to God as she seemed to think he needed an explanation.

"Edward," said P.K. in a somewhat labored voice, sliding by the twins who died at childbirth and were laid to rest without the benefit of even a name.

"Edward," Mary Ann looked skyward as if wanting an explanation for the reason her son moved to West Virginia. "I guess the boys normally go where their wife lives, even though that didn't happen to me."

"Sarah Kirsten," said P.K. in a voice almost a whisper. His thoughts went back all the way to the Civil War and wondered how close he came to killing a man. If he had, Sarah's husband would not have been born.

"Dear beautiful Sarah. Give her the fortitude to survive in an alien land," Mary Ann could think of no other way to describe Oklahoma.

"Harriett," P.K. finished.

"My lovable Harriett," Mary Ann sighed. "She died so young. She would be a full blown woman by now and would have children of her own. Thank you Lord for the few years you gave us with her."

As they finished the prayers for their children, the sun's light flashed across the pond as it set behind a stand of oaks to the West. Mary Ann turned toward P.K. expecting the usual smile. His chin had dropped on to his chest and it appeared he had fallen asleep. She rose and went to the kitchen to start supper for Buck and his children, leaving P.K. apparently sleeping as he routinely did after prayers.

Peter Kemp (P.K.) Royston was buried at Mount Carmel Methodist Church under a favorite tree on April 2nd, 1898. Mary Ann Adams Royston would follow him in death on January 6th, 1906.

INTO THE WILDCAT DEN

What a summer day! eleven year old P.K. thought as he headed up Wildcat Hollow. What had been just a trail a few years ago was now almost a road, with ruts worn by the steady stream of wagons that used the Ashby Gap route west, but who didn't like the steepness of the Fox Trap Hill. It added a few hundred yards to the journey but took some of the danger out of the descent on the west side of the Blue Ridge. Now the road was just about abandoned as the immigrants were using other routes to cross the Blue Ridge. The grass was growing between the ruts but there was sufficient local traffic to keep the ruts ground to dust.

The road followed Prospect Creek and P.K. would stop and put his feet into the creek. It was sticky hot and he ground his toes into the dust making little balls of mud from his wet feet. Once in a while the creek would make a slight bend and eddies would carve out a small hole large enough for swimming. The trees growing on the edge of the creek would have the dirt washed out from their roots and small aquatic mammals would take refuge under these tendrils. P.K. saw a movement in the water and looked over to see a water moccasin snake as it swam across to the other side. By now he knew how to recognize and distinguish between a poisonous snake and a non-poisonous one.

When you went swimming in the creek, it was best to avoid the root area.

The June Bugs were bumbling around and the gnats made their facial attacks. Using his arm and hand as a fan in front of his face, he tried to keep the bugs at bay. *One of these days someone will invent something to control these bugs*, he thought.

His reverie was interrupted by the meow of a cat. Following the sound, he saw a small kitten caught in the roots of one of the trees dipping into the creek. *Why that little fellow is about to drown*, he thought. P.K. made his way to the kitten and gently extracted it from the roots of the tree. I wonder who owns this one, he mused, knowing that no one lived anywhere close to the area.

The only thing around here is the wildcat den. It then dawned on him; he did not have a house cat but a very small wildcat. The idea startled him and he dropped the kitten. To his surprise the kitten didn't run away but came and rubbed against his leg. He picked it up again and the kitten purred and snuggled against the crook in his arm.

P.K. had always wanted to find out exactly where the wildcat den was. At times he had glimpsed movements in a rock formation in the area, but there were a number of outcroppings in the vicinity. Any of them could be the wildcat den. Maybe now he could find the den itself. Then a sobering thought came to him. The mother and father wildcats might not like him handling their kitten. He started to drop the kitten but its claws came out and grabbed his shirt sleeve. *Oh well, I will take it to the area of the den and drop it off*, he thought. As he came to the junction where Passage Creek joined Prospect Creek from Ashby's Gap he neared the site of the rock outcroppings. The kitten was gently purring as it continued its free ride. *I really would like to see that wildcat den*, he thought. *Maybe the baby kitten will take me to it.* Just as he turned toward the largest rock pile, there was a snarl from an adult wildcat. The mother was not at all happy with someone holding her baby. P.K. started to throw down the kitten and head for a safer place. The kitten, however, hung onto P.K.'s arm and in a purring tone must have been trying to tell its mother, "I have a new friend and he saved my life." The mother's snarl turned softer and soon it, too, was rubbing against P.K.'s leg. It appeared he was accepted into the family. Now the kitten wiggled to get down as if anxious to show his new friend his abode. P.K. followed both as they made their way close to the bottom of a large granite boulder that was setting on what appeared to be an outcropping of shale. With a leap, the kitten disappeared underneath the shale. *This must be the den*, P.K thought. He stepped down between the rocks and almost disappeared into the collection of leaves and debris from ages past. He pulled away some of the leaves and gave a whistle. *There is a small cave under these rocks. Who would ever have guessed?* He pushed his way into the opening and there was the kitten, its mother and two other small cats. Each seemed to accept him as a friend of the first kitten. In time they rubbed his legs and licked his hand. Viewing his surroundings he thought, *There is room enough here for a full grown man to stretch out. No wonder no one has ever found the wildcat den. It would be the perfect place to hide out.*

It dawned on him that the hour was getting on and he should head for home. Reluctantly he extracted himself from his new found playground and headed down the trail. He waded into the creek and attempted to divest himself of a peculiar smell. He wanted to tell the news to his mother but knew that it wasn't the wise thing to do. Once the word got out about the exact location of the den, everybody would want to go see it and it would be ruined. It would be his own little secret, he decided.

As he headed home he passed the path going over to the Spout Spring. He got a glimpse of his father, two buckets in hand, walking toward the spring. *Pa sure loves that spring*, he thought. The thought was a happy one. The more Pa went to the spring, the less P.K. had to carry water. His water carrying responsibility was pretty much limited to hauling wash water from the creek for clothes washing and in drought times to keep the garden from dying.

As he entered the house, his mother called to him in a strident voice, "P.K., where on earth have you been? I need wood cut for the supper fire. Your pa let the fire go out and we have to use the tinder box to get one going. It's mighty hot and the fire will just about suffocate us, but supper needs to be cooked."

P.K. hurried out to the back yard to avoid more talk on the subject and wrestling some wood from the woodpile began to split it into small pieces. Fortunately, it had already been cut to length so the task took only a few moments. The discovery of the wildcat den receded from his thoughts. He carried the wood into the house just as his father came in with the buckets of water. He made a hasty retreat outside as his father called to his mother, "Ann, it sure smells like cat in here. You know I don't like cats. They make me sneeze."

Farming Is Work

The corn grew high in the fields called the bottom land. It received its nourishment from up-stream of the Shenandoah from past floods. It didn't take much for the river to rise above its banks but most of the bottom land would only receive a true flooding every decade or so. P.K. had been taught how to thin the corn using a hoe to chop out some of the extra corn stalks. Since no one except God knew which of the seeds would germinate, two or three would be planted in each hill. The extra ones that grew would be thinned out once the stalks started their progress toward maturity.

P.K. enjoyed farming. It seemed to him a wonder that seeds that were placed in the ground could bring to life these giant stalks which in time would grow ears of corn of their own. Then the entire process would be repeated. His father, Peter, worked with him and taught him the ways of farming. When the heat of the day demanded a rest, a nearby shade tree and a jar of water would be most welcome. It was at these times Peter would talk of the past and one story would always be repeated. "Did you know that the rows of the ears of corn always grow in even numbers?"

P.K. would nod, having heard the story many times but when repeated it gave him extra time to sit under the shade tree.

Peter would tell of his friend, Jo Anderson, who won his freedom from slavery by altering an ear of corn as it was growing and making his master believe he had found an ear of corn with an uneven number of rows.

P.K. knew Jo Anderson as he was the ferryboat man for a long time. There was another story about Jo Anderson that was never told as he could see his mother seem to tighten up when he was talked about.

His father was a great story teller, but it was difficult to get him to talk of his life before he came to the Shenandoah Valley. There seemed to be something there that was a part of his past that shut out those stories. P.K. knew he had been named after a great-grandfather on his grandmother's side. That was about all that Peter would talk about. Just as P.K. was drifting off his father would jostle him with, "It is time to get back at that thinning. You don't think some groundhog is going to come along and dig them out for you."

Back they would go and pick up where they left off. *One of these days someone is going to figure out a way to know which seeds are going to grow,* P.K. thought. *Then this job is going to be a whole lot easier.*

Summer continued on and the work continued. The weeds would fight for their right to be a part of the crop and a single shovel plow behind the rear end of a horse occupied his days as he kept the corn rows as free of weeds as was possible. There was a continuing fight against morning glories as they would become entwined around the stalks and choke them. Then there were the corn worms that would get into the ears and eat the sweet kernels before they matured. Many farmers would also fight the crow that came to feast in the corn field. There were many attempts to get rid of these pests but Peter always cautioned against killing the crow. He told P.K., "I have seen a lot of crows and a lot of corn worms. One thing I have noticed, the more crows the fewer corn worms. I think the crow eats more corn worms than he eats corn."

Weather played the most important role in the success of the corn crop once the thinning was done. Late afternoon thundershowers would be a blessing or a bane depending on past rains and the severity of the storm. Sometimes the rain would come and stay. The fields would become sodden and the water would run off into the creek or into the river, hopefully not meeting water from the river on its way up. Other times the rains didn't come and each thunder storm would be watched in the hope that it would bring water to keep the corn from dying of thirst. Crops lived or died from the generosity of the weather.

No matter how generous the weather was, in due time the crops were harvested. Corn was attacked with corn knives that were much like machetes. The corn stalks would be stacked in rows. Later in the season, it would be shucking time and the ears of corn would be pulled from the stalk and its husk and in time the ears would be hauled to the barn or silo.

Wheat and barley would be stroked with the scythe. One learned to keep the cut wheat in the crook of his arm and when it was filled, the arm load would become a part of a shock that would be left free standing in the field until it could be hauled to the barn.

Soap Making

"P.K. don't plan any work for the next day or so. I need you to make soap."

"Ma, that's not one of my favorite jobs. Why can't we afford to buy soap? They carry it at the store now," P.K. replied to his mother's command.

"And it cost precious dollars," his mother replied. "Besides we need to get rid of the ashes and bacon grease."

"Bacon grease? Why not use lard? It works a lot easier and doesn't smell as bad," he countered.

"It's bacon grease because we have a lot of it and it's not lard because we have hardly enough to last until butchering time."

P.K. knew that further arguments were futile, so he went outside to begin the full day process of making soap. The ashes from the fireplace had been carefully saved and kept away from rain water. Now he got out the large kettle and hung it over a fire pit. He started a fire under the kettle and filled it about half full with water from Prospect Creek that ran nearby. As the water began to boil he shoveled in the ashes until the pot was almost filled. The lighter debris in the ashes floated to the top and he skimmed that off as the concoction began to boil. Continual stirring was necessary to insure that all the potash was exposed to the heat and the water. The entire process of leaching the potash out of the ashes took some six hours. It reminded P.K. of making apple butter where stirring was a real necessity to keep the apple butter from burning. As he stirred, he would stop occasionally and skim off more material that kept floating to the top. The heavier ashes tended to settle to the bottom.

By the time this process was completed it was almost dinner time and the chore of dipping out the solution was done before dinner. As it was dipped out, it was poured through an old sheet to strain out the fine ash particles. Some ten gallons of liquid was the result. The kettle was removed from the fire and taken to the creek to be cleaned. The residue of ashes would be dumped in the fields to help the soil.

During dinner, his mother asked of the progress. "I am ready to start the soap process as soon as dinner is over. I have all the potash ready."

"Do you want me to taste it to check the 'bite' of the lye?" Ann questioned, knowing that was one thing that P.K. didn't like to do.

"No, I will save a bit of the potash solution as we make the soap so that I can add it at the end if the soap isn't just right. You can taste it then."

The next bit of the process was a bit chancy. The bacon grease needed to be mixed with the potash solution in the kettle and heated. If the grease was put in first and heated, there was danger of the potash splattering as it was poured in. P.K. found that if he put in a reasonably small amount of potash solution first and then scooped in some of the grease, there was less danger of spattering.

He began the process by restarting the fire and putting the kettle over it. He then poured in some potash solution and as it started to bubble, he ladled out some of the grease. He stirred it a bit and then repeated the process until the kettle was nearly filled.

Now came the hard part. The solution needed to be continually stirred. He used an old stick from a sassafras tree, as it was mountain lore that the soap wouldn't set if any other type of stirrer was used. Also a part of the lore was that the stirring had to be counter-clockwise, but P.K. would only let the lore control him so far. Besides, it was tiresome to only stir in one direction.

It was well into evening before the solution took on the semblance of soap. What started out as a thin solution was now a thick brown mess that almost defied stirring. P.K. took the stick out of the kettle and let a small amount dribble onto a plate nearby. He called his mother to come out and make the taste test. If the small dab that was put on the tongue burned the tongue, then there was too much potash in the mixture. If it didn't tingle at all there was too much grease. P.K. had done this so many times that he was pretty sure he had it right but it needed his mother's approval.

Ann came out and made the perfunctory test and pronounced it soap. P.K. lifted the kettle off the fire and began to ladle the soap into molds that were about a foot square in size. They would set overnight and could be used on the morrow. P.K. took a small twig and carved his initials in the corner of each mold. Another job well done.

1834 The Baltimore & Ohio Railroad comes to Harpers Ferry & Charles Town

P.K. had recently turned eighteen and his mother, in cohorts with P.K.'s brother Uriah, planned a surprise. They were to meet Uriah in Charles Town some fifteen miles away for the ostensive purpose of hauling some fertilizer home. P.K. wondered why both his mother and father wanted to go along when it was a one man job. *Did they think he was not capable of handling a four horse team?*

As they arrived in Charles Town he could see a large expanse of smoke that had to be indicative of a fire somewhere. His mother, Ann, motioned to P.K., "Shall we drive over and see what the smoke is from?"

As they neared the source, it was obvious it was manmade and that it was coming from some sort of a machine mounted on rails.

Uriah was there to meet them. "P.K. what do you think of this contraption? It's a train and the rails have been finished from Harpers Ferry to Charles Town on their way to Winchester. You can ride all the way to Harpers Ferry and back in a few hours. The train is called the 'Tennessee.' What say we go aboard and make the trip to Harpers Ferry? This is your birthday present."

P.K. almost said he wanted nothing to do with such a monster, but his mother seemed not to be afraid and he followed her and his father as Brother Uriah led the way.

"We have been hauling some of our freight from Charles Town rather than Harpers Ferry because of this train. Makes the trip a lot easier," Uriah admitted. "This will be my first trip also as a passenger."

The locomotive gave a snort and slowly the pistons started to move. The wheels slid a bit on the rails but soon picked up traction. It wasn't long before the train which consisted of the locomotive, two passenger cars and three freight cars was moving rapidly toward Harpers Ferry. P.K. had trouble keeping from being dizzy as the countryside spun by. The conductor came by and noting the green color of P.K, advised him to look out a distance so that the motion did not affect him.

P.K. did and soon he began to enjoy this ride at a breakneck pace. He looked over at his father, wondering what he was thinking.

"How do you like the train?" he called out to his father, Peter. Peter looked back and said above the noise. "I remember another trip to Harpers Ferry when I was only a few years older than you. It was on horseback and it took a lot longer. I'll wager we won't meet the famous person I did on that trip," referring to Meriwether Lewis.

It seemed like only a few minutes before they arrived at Harpers Ferry. Uriah suggested that his mother do a bit of shopping or maybe order some dry goods that he could haul later. His mother gave a snort and jumped off the train. "That monstrosity is as close to the devil as I ever hope to be," she complained.

Uriah laughed, "There are a lot of folks who will have nothing to do with the train because they fear it is really the work of the devil. There is some talk of using the train to carry the mail but a lot of folks don't want their mail carried by the devil."

While Ann and Peter were shopping, Uriah showed P.K. the Great Falls and the United States Arsenal that was powered from the water that poured over the falls. The roar was so much that P.K. covered his ears.

Moving away, Uriah said to P.K., "To my way of thinking, Harpers Ferry will be a hub of the future. It will be the supply depot for the Shenandoah Valley to the South and the gateway for the settlements in the west."

P.K. nodded. He had never seen such display of raw power. This and the train were almost more than he could comprehend. "It only makes me want to be back in the mountains, my big brother," he commented.

P.K. Becomes a
Sharecropper

The day P.K. turned twenty one he noted quite a back up at Berry's Ferry. The year was 1841 and there was still some use of Ashby's Gap as the route west. March was a bit early for heavy traffic and curiosity brought him to the Ferry. He recognized one of the persons waiting to cross and rode up to him. "Mr. Sowers, what seems to be the backup on the ferry today?"

John Sowers said, "There's no real reason. One of the travelers had a balky horse and every time they tried to cast off, the horse would go wild. Actually it's quite enjoyable to see all the consternation. Nothing much else seems to happen around here."

He continued, "See that fellow over there? He's heading for Washington for the inauguration address of William Henry Harrison tomorrow. I hear Harrison is going to stand out in his shirt sleeves to show how tough he is. He may be a great Indian fighter, but to stand outside in this weather in your shirt sleeves is downright idiotic. I hope his speech is short, or he'll catch his death of a cold."

P.K. took the opportunity to bring up a subject that had been on his mind for a while. "Mr. Sowers," he began. "I know you own Lakeville farm but you don't live on it. Are you farming it now?"

"Not really, there is enough farming to be done on my own farm next to it. Don't know why I bought it. Guess the bargain was too good to pass up."

P.K. smiled and said, "I have just turned twenty one and it's time for me to leave the nest. Could we make a deal where I could tenant farm some of Lakeville and maybe sleep in one of the out buildings? I'm a single man you know."

Sowers smiled and agreed. "There is no reason why we can't make a deal. Maybe we could use sharecropping as a method of paying."

P.K. came to an agreement with John Sowers, wondering all the time where he was going to get the farming equipment. He would need at least two horses, a plow and a harrow. Maybe he could talk his pa out of some of the where-with-all. After all he had a month or so to work out the details.

That evening P.K. discussed it with his father. Peter seemed to be more than anxious to see P.K. off on his own. He leaned back and looked skyward. "I am just turning sixty-five and there are only Sarah and Anna Maria at home. It looks like they will be marrying next year and if you leave, that will end my job of being responsible for children. I want to turn the farm over to Mathew."

P.K. paused. "I will be needing some equipment to start farming. Do you suppose.... .?" he trailed off.

Peter picked up on the unasked question, "Certainly we will have plows, harrows and horses that you can use. Are you going after wheat, barley or corn?"

"Corn is my specialty," P.K. answered "and I can plant with a minimum of energy. Depending on the harvest, I can probably do it alone or I may have to ask for your help."

The spring wore on as P.K. prepared for the move to Lakeville farm. In April a traveler rode by and told the news that the new president did indeed prove the stupidity of giving a long speech in cold weather. William Henry Harrison caught a cold for his efforts and died after only a month in office. "Old Tippecanoe was dead. Now we have Tyler too," was the way he put it. P.K. mused on these happenings and realized that they didn't affect him one way or another. He still had a lot of plowing to do if he was going to get a crop of corn come fall.

1844 The Magnetic Telegraph Invented

By 1844 P.K. had three crops harvested. It was hard work but rewarding. God smiled on him those first years and sharecropping was good for both him and the landowner. On a trip to Millwood he stopped in to see brother Uriah. Uriah was always proud of his knowledge of current events that he learned from his freight business and all Uriah could talk about that day was something called the magnetic telegraph. "Would you believe that they can send a message over a wire that tells them things that are happening in Baltimore right now? They can tell you when the trains leave. They can tell you about the weather. They can tell you what's being shipped. In time I won't have to go and wait at the train station to see if a shipment is on a particular train. They can tell me by telegraph if it is on the train and if the train left on time."

This completely mystified P.K. "How in the world can they do that?" he wanted to know.

"I am not sure how it works but they make little clicks that can be heard many miles away. Depending on the number of clicks and how they are separated, a person can tell you what words they are saying.

They are naming it the Morse Code after the feller who says he invented it."

P.K. scratched his head, "I can see what use the freight people have for it and maybe knowing who is on the train. Otherwise I can't see what people in places like Washington would want to know what people in Baltimore are doing."

With that he gave the reins of the horse a chuck and headed them back towards Lakeville.

A few weeks later, Uriah again saw P.K. and brought him up-to-date on the progress of the telegraph. "Seems like there is a fellow named John Butterfield who is really taken to the telegraph. He is building lines in New York and is talking of connecting them to Canada."

P.K. snorted, "Next you will be telling me that there will be lines all over the nation and that it will take over writing letters."

Uriah grinned that mischievous grin, "You never know. If you can send all you want to say in less than an hour all the way across country, why would anyone want to write a letter that takes two weeks to deliver?"

P.K. left with the admonition, "Don't try and send me any stuff that is telegraphed, I want to see it in writing."

"So I will brother, so I will. I doubt that the mountains would have any need for the telegraph anyway."

P.K. Meets Mary Ann
Summer-1845

It was one of those oppressive hot days that can come to the Valley. While P.K. delighted in being a farmer there were some days when the river beckoned and he knew just the spot. Above the ferry, one could let the horses wade into the river and there was just enough brush to insure privacy. Letting the horses drink and slobber in the water, P.K. went up stream just a bit and took off all his clothes. He slipped into the water and cavorted around like a twelve year old would.

Looking up toward the sun at its zenith, he shaded his eyes and calculated the time. *Just about dinner time*, he thought. His mind began to think back to the many years he had been coming to this spot. Home had been just across the river up near the turnoff to Wildcat Hollow. Maybe he would waste the whole day and stop in and see his mother. His father, Peter, would most likely be working the bottom land or if not working, would be seeking the solace of his favorite spot at the Spout Spring.

Leaving the water and drying out, he donned his clothes and made his way down stream to the ferry. The ferryman, Jo Anderson, was stretched out under a sycamore tree hoping that no one wanted a trip across the Shenandoah. P.K. walked up to him and kicked his shoe to awake him. "How about a trip across?" P.K. inquired

"Mister P.K.? What are you doing making me work in the middle of the day?" Jo Anderson said, his black skin glistening with the sweat of one just waking from a noon day nap.

P.K. laughed. Jo Anderson was just about the smartest man he had ever seen and one who was always inventing things. He had been a slave but had talked his master into freeing him. Right now he was doing what he liked to do, running a ferry boat across the Shenandoah River for "Old Man" Berry.

"Whatcha need to do across the River?" Jo inquired, "I thought you had turned into a 'Valley' man."

"Once you have lived in the Blue Ridge, you are always a mountain man just waiting to return home," P.K. answered. "But at this moment, I can almost smell Ma's hot pork and gravy that she always has simmering on the back of the stove no matter how hot it gets."

"I agree," Jo said. "I think my ma learned that recipe from your ma. Maybe, I will hitch a ride on one of your horses once we are across and I will get some dinner from my ma." Jo Anderson's mother lived in a small cabin a few hundred yards from the Peter Royston house. She was a favorite of P.K. as she had midwifed his birth and there always had been a closeness between them.

They slipped up on the backs of the draft horses and rode bareback toward the mountain. The trip was well less than a half mile and as they approached the cabin of Jo's mother, Arissa, P.K. suggested that Jo keep one of the horses and ride him back to the ferry after his dinner. P.K. continued on to the Royston home and looked for his mother as she sat in a rocker in the shade of the front porch.

Recognition came to her as her favorite son came closer. She bounded out of the rocker and ran to embrace him. "Why don't you ever come to see me?" she wanted to know. "It's not like you are married and have a passel of youngens."

"Ma, I make so little money farming, I can't afford the ferry fare," he joked. "I came this time to get some of that pork and gravy I know you have cooking. It is too hot to work anyway."

Ann Royston sized up her twenty-six year old son. He was the largest of the sons, just about the size of her husband Peter. He had a twinkle in his eye that always made him appear to be joking. He had been able to avoid many a childhood punishment when he flashed that smile and let the eyes do his talking. She wondered about who he might marry. He seemed in no hurry to find a bride.

He doesn't seem too interested in the world beyond the local area, she thought. *And that is a good thing.* According to her son Uriah who hauls freight from Harpers Ferry there are a lot of arms being shipped out of the Federal arsenal. No one knows exactly where they are going, but they are the most modern percussion cap type. Some thought they may be headed for Texas. There were rumors of a possible war with Mexico. She was just as glad her son wasn't interested in fighting in some war at places that you couldn't even pronounce.

"Where is Pa?" P.K. interrupted her thoughts.

"He was working the bottom land and came home to get some dinner. It was too hot in the house, so he took his plate over to the spring to eat." Ann said. She gave no other reason for her husband being at the spring.

"What are you doing the rest of the day?" Ann wanted to know.

"Nothing special" P.K. answered. "I have just finished cultivating the corn near the lake, so I won't start the other field until tomorrow morning."

"Then I have just the chore for you," Ann said. "Son Joseph is fixing some shoes for me over at the shop in Paris. I need someone to pick them up."

"Glad to do it," P.K. agreed. "However I might have to borrow Pa's horse, since my work horse might take all day to make those two miles. I haven't seen Brother Joe in a coon's age anyway."

Joseph Asbury Royston looked up from his "last" as Doctor Payne walked in. "Got those boots done for me?" the doctor wanted to know.

"I told you 'next week'. Are you running out of footwear, making all those rounds?" Joe rejoined, with the assurance of a cobbler who makes quality a part of his life.

"Not really. I was just going past the shop on my way home from a stop down past 'Bleak House' and I just needed to visit. I also wanted to tell you that you had better get ready for a visit from that brother of yours as I saw him making his way past Ashby's Gap. No way you can mistake that fellow from his size and the way he rides that horse. Even though the horse looks like one of your father's." Doc Payne prided himself in his eyesight and his ability to recognize persons and animals from a distance.

I wonder what P.K. wants, Joe thought, as the description given by Doc Payne could only fit one person.

"That brother of mine needs to find a woman and marry her," Joe told the doctor. "He is twenty-six now and shows no sign of looking for a bride.

Doc Payne rubbed his chin and said, "I have just the answer for that lad's problem. If you don't mind, I will send him on an errand once he gets here. Seems that I have some medicine I need delivered down at the Adams' place. Just came from there and promised that I would send some over. Ask your brother to stop by my office once he is through here."

P.K. stooped to get through the door to Joseph Asbury's shop. "Little Brother," Joe exclaimed. "What brings you over the mountain?"

"Ma's shoes. She says you should have them done. It was so hot working the cultivator that I went for a swim in the river. One thing led to another, including the thought of Ma's simmering pork and gravy and here I am. How do you stand to be cooped up in this hot shop when you could be out working the land?" P.K. knew the answer but it was great to tease his older brother.

"The shoes are right here, but I have only one pair finished. Ma insists I use the new 'right and left foot' lasts so she doesn't have to break them in again."

"Guess I will have to take the finished pair home and she can send someone else to pick up the second pair," P.K. concluded.

"Don't run off too fast. Doc Payne saw you coming down from the Gap and said he wanted you to run an errand for him before you went back across the ridge."

"Don't know why Doc would want to see me. I know less about medicine than I do shoe making and you know my talents for that. Besides, he has that young helper he is training to be a doctor."

"You are talking of young Tommy Settle. Yes, the lad wants to be a doctor but he's hardly old enough to be entrusted with the delivery of medicines. I think he can't be more than eleven. In any case the doc was pretty insistent. So throw these shoes in your saddle bags and stop in to see the Doctor."

Doc Payne's office was in his house. P.K. rode past the main gate and stopped at a side entrance. He dismounted and strode toward a small door at the side of the house. He knocked and then opened the door trying to get his eyes accustomed to the lack of lighting in the office. Doc Payne was hunched over his desk looking through some papers. He pushed his chair back and greeted P.K. "What brings you to the Doctor's Office?" he asked officiously.

"What do you mean, 'What brings me?'" P.K. thundered, wondering if he had heard his brother right.

Doc Payne laughed, "Oh yes, I told Joe I had a chore for you. Since you are already saddled up, and it is way too hot for a man in his right mind to have to saddle a horse, I would like for you to take some medicine to a lady just down the road toward Crooked Creek. Won't take over an hour or two."

P.K. knew it was hopeless to argue with the doctor, so he watched the doctor break out a mortar and pestle and grind up some medicines that he removed from the glass cabinet behind him. He wrote some instructions on an official looking pad and handed them to P.K.

"The family you are looking for is the Adams Family. Go past the Bleak house and take the next road that turns toward the mountains. The area is called 'Pleasant Vale.' About a mile in, you can look over and see a house just as you cross a creek. The creek runs right by the house but the brush is pretty dense there, so go a bit further and you will see a road that takes you to the front of the house. Tell the lady of the house that I sent you and give her the medicine."

P.K. retraced his ride back through Paris and at the end of the street, turned his horse toward Piedmont. The land was filled with grazing cattle that seemed to have an endless supply of forage. He saw the entrance to the Bleak House and passed it by. Shortly he reined his horse into a small but well used road that had been described by Doc Payne. It was close to three o'clock when he came to the creek. He glanced up and saw a house about three hundred yards away whose back porch overlooked a large garden. He could see where the creek meandered past the house on its route to where he was. Some few hundred yards ahead he could see where a lane turned off to go to the front of the house. Looking up the creek, it appeared that once you got past the brush right along the road, you could ride right up the creek to the house.

"Why should I use up an extra fifteen minutes on this task?" he muttered aloud, kneeing his horse into the brush. He cleared the brush and could see that the creek took a number of turns as it tumbled down from along side of the house. He began following the creek and just before rounding one of the bends he heard laughter drifting toward him. He eased his horse to the turn where he saw two girls enjoying the creek. They were laughing and throwing water at each other. Their dresses were pulled above their knees in an attempt to keep them dry and he could see the pale white bareness of their legs. It appeared he had intruded on a very private moment. Embarrassed he quietly backed his horse and returned through the brush to the road.

He had lost more than fifteen minutes as he went to the lane that took him to the front of the house. As he went towards the front door, he could hear the giggles and laughter of the girls returning to the back of the house. He knocked on the front door very loudly as if to give a warning to anyone inside that a stranger was intruding. After an indeterminable period, the door was opened and there stood a young lady who couldn't be more than sixteen years old. Her black hair was shining from the water and the tresses were turning into ringlets. She was the most beautiful person P.K. had ever seen.

"My name is Peter Kemp Royston but most people call me 'P.K.'" he stammered.

"My name is Mary Ann Adams, but my friends don't call me "MA,'" she giggled, adding. "That's what they call my Ma."

It's your Ma that I came to see," P.K. said, wishing he could say something that would keep her at the door.

"Ma, there's a man here to see you," she called and with that she disappeared into the recesses of the house.

Presently a lady appeared who seemed to be in her mid-fifties. There was a sadness in her eyes that P.K. knew was a story that he needed to hear. P.K. explained who he was and why he was sent there. She seemed surprised to get medicine from Doc Payne but accepted it without comment. Not being able to think of a reason why he should be standing there any longer, he said his good-byes and rode back towards Paris.

As he passed through Paris, he saluted his brother, Joseph Asbury. Joe appeared confused that P.K. was still in the area and called out to him. "I thought you would be across the mountain by now, little brother. Did you get lost?"

"You know I didn't get lost," P.K. muttered. "I did a chore for Doc Payne, although the lady seemed surprised that someone showed up. I will be back to pick up Ma's shoes next week."

"Why you and not Pa," Joe pondered. "I thought you were a busy man."

"I am but Pa is getting a bit old to be riding this far," P.K. blushed when he said it.

Joe turned back into his shop wondering about the change in his brother that seemed to make a trip to Paris a bit more agreeable to him.

Doc Payne was standing at his front gate. He said nothing but touched his fingers to his hat as P.K. passed.

P.K. urged the horse up the steep road that was called the Ashby Gap Toll Road. A few pennies were collected by an operator of the toll gate that was at the top of the mountain called Ashby's Gap. He stopped and let the horse rest before starting down the western slope. Before him was the northern end of the Shenandoah Valley. A slight haze hung over the valley but he could make out many of the farms and plantations that were sprinkled through the valley. It had only been seven or eight years since the area had broken away from Frederick County. He remembered signing his name on two petitions that were submitted to Richmond asking that a new county be formed. It took a couple of tries to get the job done but a new county they had, He laughed as he wondered if those who checked the signatures knew he was only 13 years old when he signed that first one.

As he crossed Portage Creek, he took a left turn and worked his way toward the Wild Cat Den. It was just about dark now and as he approached the area he could see some movements of the animals as they started to scurry for cover. As they did, he could see one sniffing the air and turning around started to run towards him. *How well they remember*, he marveled. There had been a number of families born since he first made friend with the wild cats. They accepted him and he had never given up the secret of the location of their lair.

The horse snorted as he reached down and picked up a younger cat. The cat began purring and snuggled into the crook of P.K.'s arm. "Where have you been?" it seemed to say.

P.K. found himself talking out loud to the wild cats and telling them of the day's happenings. "Would you believe I met the most beautiful girl in the world? I'll bet she would think you were the cutest animals she has ever seen." He rambled on as he dismounted and checked the den to see if he could still fit into it. With the practiced ease of many entrances, he squeezed his body past the opening and enjoyed the utter darkness and the silence that was only broken by the purring of the cats. Reluctantly he squeezed back through the opening and mounted the horse. It knew the way home and P.K. gave it its lead.

Arriving at the house where he had grown up, he was met by both his father and mother. "P.K., where you been? I could have walked to Paris back and forth twice in this time. Where are my shoes?"

"Slow down, Ma. Only one pair was done I will have to go back next week to get the other ones for you."

"You don't have to do that, son. I can get somebody going in that direction to do my 'picking up.'"

"No trouble at all, Ma. I just realized how much I miss seeing Brother Joe." He blushed a bit as he said it. "Guess I had better unsaddle Pa's bay and turn it out for the night. Maybe you might have some of that simmering pork left and some biscuits. Might even have to sleep here on the porch as the ferry will be closed down."

"The porch might be a good place to sleep as the night is going to be a hot one. It will be better than that hut you are living in while you share crop those fields at Lakeville. Besides you smell like cats like you used to years ago. Don't know what you young ones are coming to." Mothers have a way of getting to the nub of things.

The Courtship Begins

The next week P.K. showed up at the Royston house ready to go and pick up his mother's second pair of shoes. This time he was riding his own horse and he showed signs of a recent haircut, questionable though as to who used the scissors. Assured that the shoes still needed to be picked up, he made his way over Ashby's Gap and down into Paris. Joe brought the shoes to P.K., indicating that he thought P.K. had other reasons for being in Paris.

"Tell me about the Adams family," P.K. asked.

"Well, there's not much that I know. They have been in this area for three or four generations, came from Charles County, Maryland. The ones I think you are interested in is a family of five daughters. Their father died some thirteen-fourteen years ago just before the youngest daughter was born. The first four girls were two sets of twins. The oldest ones married sometime ago and one of the second sets of twins married last spring. She was just fifteen. The last two are at home and I would expect the mother would be very happy to see them married also."

"Being a widow explains why the mother has such sad eyes. Raising that many girls must be a difficult job. How does she run the farm?" P.K. wondered.

"All I know is that she has some slaves, although I believe they are owned by the estate of her dead husband, Thomas Adams, which has yet to be probated. The mother just has a dower's interest in the estate. That has to add to her sadness, also. I am sure all of the responsibility and none of the rewards don't help either."

"Maybe I should check with Doc Payne and see if he has any more medicine that needs delivering down that way. I would like to get to know them better. Maybe I could help them run that farm. All I am doing now is share cropping over at Lakeville."

"I am sure that Doc Payne knows you are on this side of the mountain. There isn't much that gets by him. Stop in and see." Joe suggested.

A few minutes later found P.K. knocking at the office door of the doctor.

"Come on in, unless you are too sick to open the door," boomed Doc's voice from within.

"Hello Doc, I was just over at the cobbler shop and I ..." P.K. started.

"Yes, you are right. I need to have a prescription delivered over to the Adam's place. Seems that lady is always in need of some medicine," Doc Payne interrupted. "Think you have the time to do that chore for me?"

It wasn't long before P.K. was knocking on the door of Mrs. Fanny Adams. This time the door was opened by a younger girl who appeared to be about fourteen. "Did you come to see Mary Ann?" she wanted to know.

"Why no," P.K. stammered. "I came to deliver some medicine from Doc Settle for Mrs. Adams."

"That's too bad," said the young girl. "Mary Ann was sure you would come back to see her. I will have to tell her she was wrong."

"No, wait," P.K. almost shouted. "Don't tell her that. I did come to see her, but I needed an excuse so I brought some medicine to her mother." P.K. realized that he wasn't making any sense, but he couldn't let the younger daughter mess up his chance to visit with Mary Ann.

At this time Mrs. Adams appeared behind her daughter. "Has Susan been teasing you, Mr. Royston?" she wanted to know.

"Why no. Well, maybe yes," P.K. stammered. "I brought you some medicine from Doc Payne. And I did want to talk to you about farming your place and also it would be nice to visit with Mary Ann." He got it all out in one breath.

"Why come on in. Mary Ann is out in the back yard. I think she knows you are here but she didn't want to appear forward. And I would like to talk to you about the farm. Maybe you would like a cool drink of last year's apple cider. We need to drink it before it turns hard," she offered as an excuse.

Mary Ann came in and sat quietly as Mrs. Adams related the condition of the family; how her husband was a part of the John Adams family that had emigrated from England in the early 1700's and settled in Charles County, Maryland. The family had lived on this property near Paris since about 1750 when he acquired about 3500 acres. Her husband, Thomas Marshall Adams had inherited a portion of it, but he died an untimely death in 1831. Mrs. Adams had raised the five girls, the last of whom was born after her husband's death. "It hasn't been easy," she said, wiping a tear from her eye. "My two oldest daughters, they were twins, you know, were married in '41 and '43. Mary Ann's twin Joanna was married last April to Robert Long. Did you know Robert Long? Joanna was only 15 when she married, but she got a good man who loves her truly. Now only Mary Ann and Susan are left to help me."

"I am share cropping over at Lakeville in the Valley," P.K. offered. "My family has some mountain land and they farm the bottom land near the ferry. I farm mostly corn. It's easier to predict the outcome. If you could use someone who would help with the crops on your farm, I am offering myself as your answer. I wouldn't be available until after the crops are in this fall, other than to come over and do planning."

"Mary Ann, we forgot completely about you. Here you are sitting here and not being recognized at all," Mrs. Adams apologized. "Come here and get to know P.K. I don't know what P.K. stands for but maybe he will tell us."

Mary Ann slipped into a chair near them and answered, "He doesn't have to tell me what P.K. stands for, I already know," she blushed. "But it would be nice to get to know him better."

Mrs. Adams pronounced, "Mary Ann will be seventeen, come May nineteenth. How old are you, P.K.?" she asked boldly.

"I will be twenty seven next March, so I am a bit older than your Mary Ann." He found it easier to talk to Mrs. Adams rather than directly to Mary Ann.

Mary Ann smiled a coquettish smile that seemed to indicate she might be the older of the two. "Ten years is just something that only is evident when it is written on a piece of paper. It has no meaning in real life."

P.K.'s heart leapt. *It sounds like she thinks I am all right*, he thought. "When would be a good time to come and plan? The weekend would be best for me." he directed the question to Mrs. Adams.

"We are here most of the time. Come next weekend on Saturday afternoon. We can plan further visits at that time. Alfred will be here whenever I say," said Mrs. Adams.

"Alfred?" P.K. questioned.

"He and Lucinda and their six children are our slaves," Mrs. Adams explained.

"Slaves? I have no experience working with slaves," P.K. offered.

"They are more like family." Mrs. Adams said. "The only difference is they have to do what we say."

"I will work with him as long as I can treat him as a man. My closest association with persons who were slaves are Jo Anderson and his mother, Arissa. And they are friends and a whole lot smarter than I am." P.K. was definitely not at ease with slaves.

The weekends at the Adams farm began. P.K. was introduced to the slaves and liked them immediately. They seemed like hired hands but without a say in how anything was done. P.K. asked Alfred what he thought about a farming method and after a bit of hesitation, he received a very intelligent answer, one that would benefit the farm. P.K. wondered how many more good ideas were in Alfred's mind.

Somehow it fell to Mary Ann to show him the farm and how things were done. She had a natural ease about her that made her easy to be around. He was definitely falling in love with this beautiful young girl.

P.K. Proposes

Christmas time came and P.K. made his usual visit home. There seemed to be an inordinate amount of noise as the grandchildren of Peter and Ann looked for presents. P.K. snorted. *It wasn't that way when I was little. Sometimes we hardly knew Christmas was here. The Christmas tree that was placed in the parlor and left untrimmed until Christmas Eve was the real Christmas tradition. Santa Claus trimmed the tree after we children went to bed,* he mused silently.

He glanced up on the mantle of the fireplace and saw the familiar sight of a carved horse and buggy that had been his Christmas present so many years ago. It was a Santa Claus present when he was only a few years old. Now a germ of an idea came into his mind. He had been wanting to ask Mary Ann Adams to marry him, but he had little in material possessions to offer her. No ring, no broach-maybe a few ears of corn and with that a chuckle escaped his lips. His mother glanced at him wondering what her mischievous son was up to.

After an early supper, P.K. excused himself and told his mother that he had better run over to the Adams' place and wish them a merry Christmas. As he left he went by the fireplace and took the horse and buggy carving along with him. He saddled up his horse and carefully put the carving into the largest saddle bag he had.

It was near four when he reined up in front of the Adam's house. Mary Ann met him at the door as if she had been waiting. He spent a few minutes saying hello to the others and then asked Mary Ann if she would like to go for a walk with him. As he passed by his horse, he reached in the saddle bag and carefully took out the carved horse and buggy. They walked toward the lee side of the barn where there was a bit of sunshine still present.

As they walked, P.K. stammered a bit then came out with the real reason for his visit.

"Mary Ann," he began, "you know how much I care for you. I have little to offer but my love. If you would have me, I would like for you to be my wife."

"Why P.K.," she teased, "I had no idea. But the answer is yes, yes, yes. And you speak of having nothing, what's that in your other hand?"

"It's the only thing I have that's of value to me. It is a carving that was under the Christmas tree for me many years ago. If you would have it, I would offer it as proof of my love."

"I would gladly take it but somehow I think it also has the heart of another. Could it also be your mother's prize possession?"

"She does keep it on the mantle over the fireplace, but it is rightly mine."

"Let's return it to its home over the mantle and we will work on accumulating our own prized possessions. You talk of having nothing. I have no male in the family who can post bond for our marriage. I don't know how I am going to get around that."

P.K., glad to be able to offer something said, "I will post bond for you." As he said it he wondered how much and where he would get the money.

They began making plans. She had not met his family. Where would they get married? How to tell her family? He would stop in Paris and talk to his brother Joseph about the posting of the bond. It was agreed that since he would be moving near the Adams to run the farm, it would be proper to schedule the wedding as soon as possible. They hatched a plan where the family would come to the opening of annual services at Mt. Carmel Church and Mary Ann could meet his family at that time. It seemed possible that March would be the earliest time for the wedding.

They went back to the house and as they entered there was an air of expectancy. Mary Ann's mother made a few comments about P.K. coming to work soon, but she seemed to be waiting for words from the couple.

Finally, P.K. spoke and said, "I have asked Mary Ann to marry me and she has said yes. I hope we have your blessings."

Mrs. Adams hesitated and said, "In earlier times it would have been proper for you to ask the hand of our daughter from the father, but since he no longer lives, and I know of your good intentions, I will gladly give my blessing."

Mary Ann ran and hugged her mother and her sister. There was a bit of girlish screaming that made P.K. feel uncomfortable.

As soon as practical he made his excuses and left hoping to find his brother Joseph at home. It was getting cold enough that he would like to have the comfort of a fire as a backdrop when he talked to Joseph about the bond that was necessary.

Sometime later, he was knocking on the door of his brother's house. The smoke coming from the chimney was a welcome sight and the opening of the door was a more welcoming one. He explained to Joseph that he had proposed marriage to Mary Ann Adams and she had accepted. There were some legal hitches that he knew had to be overcome, like the posting of a bond.

Joseph nodded in agreement and said, "The wife's family normally does this."

"I know that but she has no male in the family who would do it and I said I would do it. I knew I had an older brother who knows all about these things."

"And you are lucky I do," Joseph teased. "I know it's a lot easier if you are a resident of the county. I think if I post the bond I wouldn't have to put up any actual money. Just my written bond. Since I know the family well, I have no concern as to actually needing any money."

As P.K. prepared to leave, Joseph added, "We just left Ma and Pa's a short while ago. Ma practically searched the children looking for your old horse and buggy carving. I hope you know where it is. Otherwise we will never be welcome there again."

P.K. blushed and said, "I'll try and help her find it. I'm sure it's there someplace."

As he mounted and started up the toll road he began to whistle a tune of happiness. He saw Doc Payne leaning on the gate and gave him a hearty salute. Doc Payne himself had a self satisfied smile that couldn't be contained as he turned and went back into his house.

P.K. eased his way through the toll gate at the top of the mountain knowing that the operator wouldn't be around on Christmas Day. As he headed down the mountain, he contemplated going by the wildcat den to tell his furry friends of his good luck. The darkness was such that he had trouble staying on the toll road so he bypassed the den and worked his way down Fox Trap Hill. Going into his mother's house he pulled out the wood carving and restored it to its proper place on the mantle. Ann looked at him quizzically and he explained that he had taken it to show to Mary Ann. She started to ask him something but thought better of it.

As P.K. spent more time east of the Blue Ridge he became closer to his brother Joe. Joe tried to mix cobbling and politics and it was unusual to enter his shop and not find a handwritten sign promoting one candidate or another. One of his particular favorites was Henry Clay. Clay filled the era of the early 1800's with his wisdom and his ability to bring disagreeing parties into agreement. P.K. loved to listen to Joe expound on the virtues of Clay. "If it wasn't for Henry Clay, this country would have been fighting amongst themselves way back in the twenties," Joe would say referring to Clay's efforts that brought about the Missouri Compromise. "He's been speaker of the House so many times they automatically pass the gavel to him as he walks by." Joe liked to remember that he saw Henry Clay pass through Berryville in '34 and that Clay could have easily been killed when his stagecoach overturned as it crossed Opequon Creek on the way to Winchester. "He keeps trying to save the country from itself." Joe said. "One of these days he is going to be President and it would be a blessing."

P.K. and Mary Ann
Are Married

P.K. and Ann were married in Warrenton and returned to the Adam's house. P.K. settled into running the farm with the aid of the slave, Alfred. Little could be done to improve the farm as Mrs. Adams had only a dower's interest in the farm and the true owners would be the five daughters. The condition in which P.K. found himself was untenable. This concerned P.K. deeply as he would have to find another farm. The thought of returning to sharecrop at Lakeville was on his mind but the small shack he had lived in was not suitable for a family. Finally it dawned on him. Lakeville had a manor house in which no one lived. It had the reputation of being haunted and only a few had dared to make it a home.

As the sale of the Adams farm became a reality, P.K. talked to Mary Ann about living in the manor house. He was sure it was available and the only question was whether Mary Ann would want to live in a haunted house. She laughed it off and said "The only ghosts are in peoples' minds. No one can bother us as long as we love each other. If the ghost shows up we will invite him to dinner."

P.K. explained that the ghost was a woman who had committed suicide in the lake after her brother had killed her lover. The brother then too was killed as he fled west ahead of an avenging family. P.K. rode across the river and found the owner of Lakeville. After a bit of dickering P.K. had an agreement not only to farm the entire farm but to live in the old manor house.

The property was put up for sale by the five daughters. It was decided that the personal property and the slaves would stay with P.K. and Mary Ann when they moved and they would be sold at a separate offering. Alfred didn't seem to understand why he would be sold. "Haven't I served the family well? Why do I have to leave you to go somewhere that I may not be treated well?"

P.K. found it hard to explain to Alfred that he was actually owned by more than one person, and that no one had the money necessary to buy him and his family outright. *Now I know how Solomon felt when he was called on to find the true mother of the child. If we could just divide him up.* Aloud he said, "You will be able to stay with us when we move. Who knows what tomorrow will bring?"

Alfred appeared a bit mollified but answered, "Here we were subject only to you and the Adams. We will live with the fear of being sold."

P.K. had no answer for that logic and could only nod silently.

Most of the furniture in the house was divided into wagon loads and P.K. drove the wagon for the first of many trips across the mountain and the river. Alfred drove and his family rode in the second wagon. The wagons had to be loaded judiciously as the horses had to be able to pull the load up the mountain and also to hold it back as it descended. Most of the families living near the toll road were out to wave at P.K. as he worked his way up and down the mountain. Both his mother and father were at the doorway to their old house as he passed by. He looked at his father and wondered at how he had aged since the house across the road had burned and killed brother Mathew's little daughter, Louisa. There was no question she had been the favorite of his father and it seemed that he didn't want to get close enough to the others to be hurt by any problems that befell them.

P.K.'s four year old son Toad waved at his grandparents and snuggled close to his mother as they started the slight rise from the entrance to Wildcat Hollow toward the River.

Mary Ann asked the question that had been bothering her since they left the Paris area, "How much longer to Lakeville?"

"Well, it's about fifteen minutes to the ferry and about an hour across the ferry if Jo Anderson is busy. Then about a half hour to Lakeville."

As Toad and Mary Ann looked to the future, the wagon passed by Arissa who was standing at the door of her cabin. She had been there when Toad was born and didn't like playing second fiddle to the doctor from across the mountain that did the actual birthing.

P.K. waved to Arissa and in a few minutes was loading the wagon onto the ferry boat. Jo Anderson was curious as to why P.K. would leave a good farm in the Piedmont section to fight the limestone outcroppings in the Valley. P.K. said that he couldn't spend much time visiting, but that before the many wagon loads were finished, he was sure that Jo would know the whole story.

Mary Ann rode with the first load and kept young Toad there to keep her company as she and Alfred's wife moved the furniture into the house and selected the right spot for it. She was heavy with her second child and P.K. cautioned her not to lift anything that could harm her. They had started the day early and before dark most of the house furnishings were transported to Lakeville. The farm equipment would wait until the morrow.

At the end of a long day they feasted on the food that had been prepared before the journey. The tiredness overcame them and they went to bed in a quickly made bed. All the family slept in the same room as Mary Ann was sure she could take care of any ghosts but she was unsure of Toad's reaction to strange noises.

Lakeville was a large farm and took all the energies of P.K. and Alfred to plant the entire acreage. P.K. defaulted to corn crops wherever possible as he was more confident in the results. Alfred had more experience with wheat and barley but soon became proficient at the vagaries of harvesting corn.

"Maybe if we had one of Jo Anderson's reapers, we could plant more wheat and barley. As it is now we can't get sufficient help with the harvesting."

The Ghost of Lakeville

The family settled in and fought with the ghost for the right to be there. The story of the ghost went back a number of decades when the manor house was first built. The owner thought a certain married man, a Major Endicott, was showing too much attention to his young sister. The owner rounded up some friends and waylaid the Major up near the Farnley Farm and killed him by beating him to death. The owner then took off for the west with the Major's sons in hot pursuit. The young sister was mortified and in her despair she went down to the nearby lake and drowned herself. For many years the house sat empty. Later, many persons passing by in the wee hours of the morning swore they heard the ghost of the young girl as she sang her mournful dirge. The story of the ghost was a natural outgrowth of the drowning and had no credence. Or did it?

It was shortly after P.K and Mary Ann moved in that their next child was born. They named him Charles Littleton Royston but nicknamed him "Dink" as he was such a small child. Maybe it was the presence of a new life that stirred the spirit of the ghost to action.

It was late fall and the fire was a welcome sight in the fireplace. Mary Ann had spent some time with young Toad telling him stories about her family. He nodded and snuggled in her arms anxious for some of the attention that was now being given to the new born.

Just as she gathered both in her arms to put them to bed, there was a loud crash out in the kitchen. P.K. had just gone to bed and the noise brought him bolting down the stairs.

"P.K.," Mary Ann yelled, "You left the hound dogs in the house and they have knocked over the kitchen cabinet and probably wrecked everything."

P.K. shook his head. "I'm sure the dogs are outside. Let's go and see what damage has been done and who did it." He looked for the shotgun that was always close by and picking it up they made their way into the kitchen.

The kitchen was spotless. Not a thing was out of place. The plates were on the table waiting the cooking of the breakfast meal. As usual there was the tradition of the extra plate that was set just in case a visitor happened by. "Are you sure we heard it right? Could the noise come from any other part of the house?" P.K. queried.

"We can look, but I am sure it was in the kitchen," Mary Ann said nervously.

A search was made and nothing amiss was found throughout the house.

They returned to the kitchen and stared at each other. What could have caused the noise? P.K. said to no one in particular.

Toad was now nearing four and a half and talking well. He tugged at Mary Ann's apron and said, "Maybe the lady did it."

"What lady?" P.K. and Mary Ann said in unison.

"The lady who was standing in the kitchen doorway when we came in the first time. She's gone now. I bet she did it."

"You saw a lady?" Mary Ann asked incredulously.

"Oh yes, she comes and talks to me and Dink lots of times. She said she almost lived here a long time ago."

Mary Ann stared at P.K. and said, "And we thought the story of ghosts was somebody's imagination. You don't suppose it really could have been the lady who drowned?"

P.K. was not a believer in the supernatural but now his faith was shaken. "Why not go back into the living room and stoke up the fire?" he suggested. "Somehow I feel a chill in the house."

They went back into the living room and talked of the events of the evening. "What bothers me is that we both heard it and Toad says he saw her and that he has seen her a number of times," P.K. said quietly.

Mary Ann took a deep breath and said, "I do believe in ghosts, but this one shows no signs of hurting us. Maybe she is just lonely. If she has talked to Toad a number of times, that means she has been around and in the house without advertising her presence."

"Other than talking to Toad," P.K. added. "Maybe the noise making was a sign that she is trying to tell us something."

"I wonder what that could be," Mary Ann said with a sigh. "Let's go to bed and see if we hear any other noises. We will ask Toad to tell us if she comes to talk to him again."

With that decision made they went upstairs to bed. The next morning both Mary Ann and P.K. ventured downstairs together. Everything appeared to be in order. But there was one thing. The extra plate setting was missing. Mary Ann went to the cupboard and counted the dishes. The extra plate was stacked neatly with the spare plates. Mary Ann shivered as she turned to P.K. "You don't suppose she is trying to tell us that she has left the house for good."

The spirit lady was never heard from again and after a while Toad couldn't even remember any conversations with a lady who only talked to him and Dink.

The Property Is Divided

Days turned into weeks, into months, into years. Crops were good but it took all the efforts of P.K., Alfred, and his two young sons to keep the acreage planted and harvested. By October of 1856 there were two more children, Fannie and Augie, in the family.

P.K. was just coming in from the fields when he saw a group of ladies riding in a carriage toward the house. *They appear to be Mary Ann's sisters,* he thought. *I wonder why they have come all the way from Paris to visit.*

P.K. came in just as the sisters started their visit. They appeared to be all business. "It has been some years since Ma died," one said. "It is time to clear up all of her details and close out the property. Mr. David McGuire has made us a good offer for all the personal property including Alfred and his family. We need P.K. to do the signing of the deeds."

P.K. shivered. *Not only would he be responsible for the legality of the process, he would have to be the one to tell Alfred and his wife, Lucinda, that what they had been fearing was coming to pass. Also much of his farming equipment was left over from the Adam's family.* These thoughts raced through P.K.'s mind as he listened to the sisters rattle off the details of their visit. Mr. McGuire was from Clarke County, so all the legal details would take place in Berryville, the county seat.

The sisters wanted much of the assets now held by P.K. as they pointed out that it was through the efforts of the slaves that they were amassed. He had some wheat and barley planted on Mr. Bell's property as well as some on his brother's land.

"We think it is only fair that we split it with you, as P.K. was the one who was responsible for the success of the crops and the farm equipment that was purchased," another ventured.

P.K. chuckled as he thought, *Actually it should be given to Alfred as he was the one doing the work.* He said nothing aloud awaiting Mary Ann's agreement.

Mary Ann nodded, "It seems that we have little choice. We will need time to finish harvesting and sell the crops. Getting all the farm equipment together and sorting out what will go will also take time. It will also give us time to figure out our future."

After the sisters left, Mary Ann and P.K. sat for a while and mused over what to do next. "There will be enough farm equipment for you to do planting and harvesting," Mary Ann put her thoughts into words.

"Yes, but I cannot farm the entire Lakeville by myself. Toad is getting big enough to be a real help, but I would need to hire hands," P.K. responded. He then added, "I have been thinking about moving back across the river. Brother Mathew is at an age where he wants to let someone else farm his land. I already have about thirty acres in barley up near Mt. Carmel. As soon as I finish getting the crops in and Alfred is no longer with us I will pay him a visit."

It came time for Alfred, Lucinda and the children to be taken to the McGuire place, and it was only now that P.K. realized how much he would miss Alfred and his family. The David McGuire house was located some six to seven miles away on a knoll overlooking the southeast corner of Berryville. It was a part of a large farm that was mostly farmed in wheat and barley. The house was new and was all brick.

Unusual in the construction was that all interior walls were of single row brick. The barns and out buildings were to the southeast and the slave quarters some 100 yards from the manor house to the southwest. Two entrances to the farm were used, one off of Springsbury Road in the North and one through the Edward McCormick farm going past a colored cemetery.

P.K. tried to convince Alfred that he was moving up in the world.

Alfred replied with tears in his eyes, "Mr. P.K., it's hard to move up when you are still a slave."

P.K. nodded. "Mr. McGuire and his wife Elizabeth are known to be fair persons. But if you are ever mistreated, get the word back to me and I will go pay him a visit. And no matter what happens in the future you are always welcome at my house."

The wagons were loaded and the livestock were tied to the rear of the wagons. Alfred's family found room toward the rear of one of the wagons. Alfred picked up the reins of the two horse team and fell in behind the last wagon. As the wagons worked their way down toward the lake, one of Alfred's boys in a very quiet gesture, blew a kiss toward P.K., Mary Ann and the rest of the Royston family, who had assembled to watch the proceedings.

P.K. turned away abruptly and pulling out a colored handkerchief from his pocket, blew his nose and said, "Why are you all standing around? We have a lot of chores to finish. Let's get at them."

Peter Royston Dies

December is always a bad month, P.K. thought. *The crops are all in and if you don't have cattle to feed, it's a temptation to just sit around and do nothing but the daily chores.* Four children were now a part of his and Mary Ann's lives. Thomas Adams (Toad) had been born in 1849, Charles Littleton (Dink) in 1851, Frances (Fanny) in 1853 and John Franklin (Augie) last February. Now it was December of 1856 and while farming in the valley was more profitable than the mountains, he still only felt at home on the east side of the Shenandoah.

The morning was a miserable one with the rain coming down in oblique sheets as if God was insuring that every spot on earth got a good soaking. He was sitting just inside the front door of the manor house at Lakeville when he heard the rattling of hooves as a rider dismounted and made a dash for the porch. P.K. reached to open the door as it was opened from the outside by his oldest brother, Uriah.

"What brings you out here on such a day?" P.K. wanted to know. "No man in his right mind would even think of riding in this weather."

Uriah retorted, "And you are not a Teamster. This is mild weather for a man who hauls freight." He shrugged off his MacIntosh coat and moved toward the fire.

Keeping his eyes diverted from P.K. he blurted out, "Pa's dead. Mathew found him over at the Spout Spring this morning sitting near those white oaks just like he was alive. Now he sent me after you and your family to try and get us all across the river before the ferry quits running. It looks like flood time."

"How could Pa be dead? He sure seemed well just a few weeks ago when we saw him last."

"You know he hasn't been the same since little Louisa died in the fire. Somehow he always blamed himself for letting her play with those new fangled matches. He also spent so much time at the Spring that the weather probably played a part in hastening his death."

Mary Ann had heard the conversation and rather than getting into it, she set about getting the bare necessities to take the four children to Peter and Ann's house at Wildcat Hollow. It was less than a mile to the ferry and about the same to the family's house. In a short while the family and Uriah rode toward the ferry. Jo Anderson awaited them and found enough space on the ferry boat for their wagon and Uriah's horse.

"I wouldn't be doing this 'cepting for your Pa," he groused. "I am going to leave the boat on the mountain side and sit out this storm staying at Ma's cabin. Your family," he said, nodding at Uriah, "has already made the crossing, so this is the last of the ones who needs to cross during this storm."

The ferry boat touched shore and both P.K. and Uriah helped Jo add extra lengths of tethering ropes to the boat's mooring lines so that it wouldn't be pulled under as the flood waters rose.

Jo jumped up behind Uriah's saddle and hitched a ride to Arissa's cabin which stood only a short distance from Wildcat Hollow's entrance. As he slid off the horse, Arissa opened the door and waved at the group. Tears were in her eyes as she too, though of a different color and culture, had been profoundly affected by the life of Peter Royston.

Ann opened the door as they arrived in front of the old house. P.K. always enjoyed this moment as it took him back to his childhood.

Never had the thought of being here because of the death of his father entered his mind. Somehow he thought the old man would live forever. He glanced at the fireplace which was the center of his early memories. He had been only a few years old but he could remember snuggling with Arissa as she lay on a pallet in front of the fire when her cabin was threatened by the flood waters. He looked at the mantle and saw the carved horse and buggy that was a Santa Claus present when he was three or four. He knew now that this Santa was really his brother Uriah and that moment washed over him and he wanted to hug not only his mother but Uriah.

His mind was jostled back to the present as his mother's voice penetrated his thoughts. "P.K., dry out as much as possible as I want you to ride over the mountain to Paris and get Joseph Asbury. Since you came by wagon, take Pa's bay."

P.K. shrugged. *So much for memories. That rain out there is real. Don't know why I should dry out first. I'll be just as wet before I make it up Fox Trap Hill.*

Uriah, reading his thoughts added, "Take my Mac coat with you. It does a pretty good job of keeping your shoulders dry while running all the water down your boots."

It wasn't long until all the family had assembled and plans for the funeral were made. The rain continued unabated. It was agreed that Peter would be buried up on the knoll across the creek and next to his granddaughter, Louisa. At the moment his body had been left near where he died at the Spout Spring. Friends volunteered to keep watch until it was time to bring his body across the creek and be placed in a simple wooden coffin.

The question on everybody's mind finally surfaced. "Why did Pa spend so much time over at the Spout Spring? It seemed like he was actually talking to someone while he sat near those old white oaks and watched the water as it filled and spilled over the top of the buckets."

P.K. listened for the answer that never came from his mother's lips. The most she would say was, "Your Pa first saw the spring when he came across the mountain on New Year's Day in 1800. From that time on the only place where he wanted to live was near the spring. I think he actually heard voices there-maybe-maybe not."

After the burial, the families scattered back to their own homes. The Shenandoah finally cooperated and the ferry boat ran once more. As P.K. was getting ready to leave, he approached his brother Mathew. "Since Alfred and his family have been sold, farming the entire Lakeville farm is just too much. I am thinking about moving to the mountains. Is there anyway we could make a deal on some of your land?"

Mathew thought for a while. "I am just able to farm the bottom land these days myself. The land up around Mount Carmel Church has been left to turn back into woods. You are already farming about thirty acres of it. Also both of our sisters are thinking of moving from the houses they built a few years ago. Going up to Warren County, I think. Maybe we can make a deal for the land and the houses."

ARISSA DIES

It seems so peaceful, P.K. thought as he worked his way along the newly rutted toll road toward the river. The only sounds were the birds as they competed for their position in the avian choir. P.K. thought of the recent preachings of Abolitionists from out in Kansas. There was concern of Negro uprisings and their burning of buildings. P.K. had little direct contact with the black people. He had worked with the slaves of Mary Ann's mother, and had found them easy to be around. They had been sold when the other heirs wanted their share of the estate. Now the only blacks he ever talked to were Jo Anderson and his mother Arissa and they were no longer slaves. Jo still ran the ferry across the Shenandoah but his heart didn't seem to be in it. Arissa had been the midwife for most of the children born in the mountains. After P.K. and Mary Ann moved across the river the only one not to be a part of "Arissa's Children" as she called them was their youngest, Walter Settle. Doc Settle, who was taught his doctoring under Doc Payne was now a full-fledged doctor. He had become a family friend of P.K. and Mary Ann and had crossed the ridge to bring the new one into the world. While Arissa was there to help, it was thought that Doc Settle was needed as it had been a long and difficult pregnancy. To commemorate the new arrival and the part Doc Settle played in it, the new one had been named "Walter Settle."

All these thoughts pressed in on P.K. as he passed by Arissa's cabin. As usual he could see her sitting in the rocking chair on the front porch. He reined in to say hello and when he didn't receive an answer, he dismounted and walked toward her expecting her to wake up as he did. Receiving no response to his voice, he reached over and shook her gently. Her head which had been resting on her chest dropped further and P.K. could see that she was dead. Memories of Arissa and her closeness to him from the time she attended his mother at his birth flowed over him. He wanted to yell; he wanted to run, he wanted someone to explain why people have to die.

After a while he realized that it was up to him to move her body to a more suitable place and to tell Jo that his mother was dead. He walked inside the cabin and found a blanket on the bed. Gathering it up, he returned to the porch and wrapped it around her body. He lifted the frail body as if it were a baby and carried it inside and laid it on the bed. After covering her, he checked to make sure the eyes were closed, and he left closing the door as he did. He mounted his horse and headed toward the ferry where it would be his duty to tell Jo.

He dismounted as he reached the east ferry landing and walked toward Jo. Jo turned and quizzically asked P.K. whether he was going to leave the horse on the east side while he crossed alone. P.K.'s voice stumbled as he told Jo of finding his mother.

Jo turned and leaned against an old sycamore tree and gave a short sob. He mumbled a few words and turned back to P.K. "Could you spread the word in the mountains and I will tell our people on the valley side. I don't know where to bury her as the only Negro graveyards are on the plantations or over near Berryville."

"Let me think on that a bit," P.K. said. "Let's get the people told and we can pass the word again when it's decided where to bury her."

P.K. turned back toward the entrance of Wildcat Hollow and told his mother, Ann, about Arissa. "Jo is not sure where he should bury her and he has left it up to us to tell the mountain folk," he said.

Ann gave that little snort that she made when there was a decision forthcoming. "She will be buried as a part of our family in the plot on the ridge. Your pa is buried there along with little Louisa. There is a lot of room. I will send the grandkids to tell everyone. Practically everyone in the mountain has been touched by Arissa and you know she was one of our family's people." Ann couldn't bring herself to talk further of the relationship Arissa had with the Anderson family, perhaps because it was only in whispers that the tales had been told.

It was one of the largest funerals ever seen in the mountain. The weather on this April day in 1859 cooperated fully and the pine casket was hoisted on the shoulders of six white men, representing the families along Ashby Gap Toll Road. Jo Anderson followed closely behind as the only black man in the procession. Behind him were all of the mountain children that Arissa had brought into the world. They ranged in age from just babies in their mothers' arms to bearded men in their thirties. There were some second generations in the group. Behind them trailed the rest of the families from the mountains. There was little formal talk as most were unsure of how these events were supposed to be handled. But talk they did in a continuing eulogy as each stepped forward to tell of how Arissa had been a part of his life. P.K. looked around and wondered how he was going to conclude the ceremony. He was running out of speakers and knew it would be up to him to say the last words.

As the mountain people's eulogies were waning, P.K heard the sound of singing that was in the distance toward the river. It became louder until all were aware of it. The mountain people looked out to see a large contingent of blacks coming from the ferry to the graveyard singing spirituals as they walked. The whites parted and let the Negroes surround the casket and continue their singing. Finally Jo gave a nod to P.K. indicating it was time for the white people to leave and let the blacks finish the ceremonies.

A few days later, Jo came and talked to P.K. "I am going to move west to Illinois. The McCormicks' have moved their reaper business there as the demand on the prairie for the reaper far exceeds the need here. Ever since old John Deere invented that plow that would shear the prairie sod, everyone out there is planting wheat. The reaper may have a McCormick name on it but it has a Jo Anderson heart and I expect they still need me."

P.K. nodded, understanding the need for Jo not to be a part of Virginia at this time. He knew that the state was becoming very divided and a black person, particularly a free one, was not going to be popular. "What do you think we should do with Arissa's cabin?" P.K. wanted to know.

Jo pondered as many thoughts ran through his mind. *There were no other blacks living on the mountain side of the river and there was little reason to think that any others would try and live there. It wasn't that the mountain people were anti-blacks, but, well, they were a very clannish bunch. And there was no way they would live in a house once occupied by a Negro.*

Jo turned to P.K. and said. "Since it is on Royston land no one else has any say, I would like to burn it down. That way it will always be Arissa's."

After talking it over with his brother Mathew and getting his agreement, the cabin was set on fire by Jo. As it was reduced to ashes, Jo stared at it and with moist eyes, he turned to P.K. and Mathew. "Your pa was the finest man I ever knew and his boys are not far behind. I will truly miss you." He mounted his horse and rode toward the river and onto the ferry boat where for once he was a rider and not a worker. As he cleared the other side, he turned and gave a salute to P.K and Mathew.

John Brown-Harpers Ferry

"Ma, Ma, a 'feller' by the name of John Brown done took over the arsenal at Harpers Ferry and the 'Niggers' are going to 'uprise' and burn all the crops," shouted Toad as he raced into the house.

Mary Ann looked at her oldest and with a quiet admonishment said, "They are not 'Niggers' but where did you hear all this?"

"Cousin Bob just came back from Harpers Ferry with a load of freight and he done told us all about it. I'm going to load the shotgun and be ready for them."

"Thomas, you are being pretty frisky for a ten year old. That shotgun would do you more harm than anybody in front of it. Now settle down and tell me everything you heard." She responded and as always called him by his given name and not the nickname given him by his grandfather when he was born. Thomas was only ten but large for his age and could actually handle the old shotgun almost as well as a man.

Toad related as much as he could comprehend in a ten year old mind and told of an abolitionist from Kansas who with a small group of followers had seized the arsenal at Harpers Ferry and called on slaves to rise up and follow his leadership and strike for freedom. Mary Ann sighed as a myriad of thoughts went through her head, *It's finally com-*

ing. Everybody who would rather fight than work will use this as an excuse to kill others. It's good we live in the mountains. The Valley folks, white or black, don't cotton much to take on us mountain people. Here I am with five children and the youngest only six months old.

Aloud she said, "Let's wait for further news. A lot will be decided by how the government handles this bit of anarchy. It's their arsenal, you know. Meanwhile go and find your father over near the McDonald tract and tell him what you heard. He should be shucking corn. Go easy on the names you use as you know how your father reacts to the use of demeaning names. Then get back here and get some wood cut. These October evenings are getting cold."

The Ferry area was the source of news. As passengers gathered on each side to await the crossing, they would learn of births, sicknesses and deaths. As the travelers alighted they would pass on happenings from the valley or mountain side. Right now all the news was about John Brown and his small band of followers. The word came quickly that he had been captured by a company of Marines led by Colonel Robert E. Lee. Soon the news was that John Brown would be tried in Charles Town some twenty five miles away. The judge would be a local Clarke County judge who lived down river near Castleman's Ferry.

"Ma, Ma, can I go watch the hanging?" young Toad implored. "I can hitch a ride with Doc Settle. He has something to do with the hanging and he could use someone to watch the horses."

"Why would you want to see someone hung?" Mary Ann inquired. "Seems to me there is enough hurting in the world without it being done on purpose."

"I wouldn't really get to see the hanging," Toad compromised as he was elated by the lack of a downright "no."

"Well, let's wait and see what your father says," Mary Ann said.

It was the first of December when Doc Settle drove by in his carriage. "I hear young Thomas has volunteered to go with me to Charles

Town. I am one of the official witnesses though it's not to my liking. I would rather be present at the birthing of babies. By the way, how is young Walter Settle doing?" he asked of the one named after him.

"Walter is doing fine," she said distractedly. "It's Thomas I am worried about. He's way too young to be going to a hanging."

"I will take care of him and he will keep me company as I know the trip back will be a long one."

Toad threw a small bag in the rear of the carriage and hopped up beside Doc Settle. As they drove off, Mary Ann averted her eyes so that the tears would not be evident to Toad as he turned to wave goodbye. Four other children needed her attention. Fortunately most of the corn crop was in so that P.K. could help with the chores normally done by Toad.

Three days later, Mary Ann was brought to the front porch by the sound of a carriage working its way up Fox Trap Hill. It was Doc Settle and Toad returning. Doc Settle stopped just long enough for Toad to get his small bag and hop off the carriage. With only a few words to Mary Ann he chucked at the horse and it began its trip up the rest of the mountain. Toad came into the house with a very somber face and said little.

Mary Ann was reluctant to ask penetrating questions but it was obvious that the event had affected Toad greatly.

Finally Toad burst out, "Ma, it was terrible. I never want to see that again. People were yelling and cheering like it was a carnival. Not only did they hang him, but they cut his throat just to make sure. Then, they gave him back to his wife to be buried. Doc Settle cried all the way back. He just couldn't keep the tears away. I don't think he said ten words to me all the way."

Mary Ann sighed. *I think I made a mistake when I let Thomas go along. Just because this is a historical moment doesn't make it any easier,* she thought.

The Signs of War

P.K. pulled his wagon into line on the west side of Berry's Ferry. It was a sunny May morning in 1860 and there seemed to be a lot of traffic waiting to cross the Shenandoah. The largest numbers of wagons were heading west and appeared to be loaded with personal belongings. As he watched, P.K. began to pick up on conversations that were mostly political. It was apparent that the nomination of Abraham Lincoln for the Republican Party was going to split the country. The Democrats had their convention in April in Charleston but were sharply divided to the extent that they adjourned their convention without nominating a candidate. Slavery was the issue and the party broke into two factions with neither side willing to give in.

Lincoln was nominated over Seward because Seward was identified as being a part of the radical wing of the Republican Party. "If Abe wins," said one of the travelers, "There's going to be a war and I want none of it. Never owned any slaves and I don't see losing my life to protect those who do. I'm heading west into the territories."

"It's not about slavery," another disagreed. "It's about states rights. Those Yankees have no right trying to tell us how to live our lives."

P.K. sighed, *I don't like the sounds of all this. If people are willing to pick up stakes and move to an unknown region just because someone was nominated to run for President, then there are going to be an awful lot of people willing to kill each other for the same reason.* He somehow blamed South Carolina for the turmoil. They seemed to be the ones who were all fired up to wage war.

Crossing the river, he snapped the reins of the horses and they made their way up Fox Trap Hill to the waiting Mary Ann.

He unhitched and unharnessed the horses and came into the house with a somber look. Mary Ann sensed a mood in her husband she hadn't seen for some time. "What bothers you, P.K.?" she wanted to know.

He recounted the conversations he had overheard at Berry's Ferry. "It looks like we may have a war on our hands and it is none of our making."

"None of our making?" she queried. "You and I have been against slavery for a long time, but are unwilling to speak out. Now we will probably pay for our not taking a stand."

"You know, if a war comes we will have to stand with Virginia. This has been our ancestral land for too long," P.K. warned.

Mary Ann sighed, *Men*, she thought. Aloud she spoke of the possibility of the Democratic Party winning and maybe staving off the possibility of a split nation.

"I don't think so," P.K. answered, "The Democrats are split into Northern and Southern groups. They are going to meet again in Baltimore in June, but it, too, will probably result in a stalemate. If the party splits along states lines, the Republicans will win sure. There's going to be a war, I can feel it," P.K. muttered.

November came and along with it the cold winds of the election results. The country split almost unanimously along states lines. The Southern Democrats carried the South and in the north the Northern Democrats fell to the Republicans. Douglas, under the banner of the Northern Democrats carried only one state, Missouri.

P.K. felt that the only chance Virginia had was that they didn't go for either. They and two other border states, Kentucky and Tennessee, went to the Union Party. Bell was their standard bearer, but P.K. would have felt better if the party wasn't made up of a coalition of the old Whigs and the "Know Nothing" groups.

Clarke and Frederick County went to Breckinridge and the Southern Democrats. *That could have been because of old John Brown and his raid on Harpers Ferry. That really put a scare into the county,* P.K. thought.

Lincoln would be the next president but Virginia was on the fence. Maybe they would vote to stay in the Union. With that possibility, he moved on to the routine work that was necessary to harvest the crops on the lands he had tilled.

Christmas 1860 was a cold day. It looked like snow but the leaden clouds held off for P.K. to make his trek to his brothers and sisters. He saddled up well before dawn and rode off with the admonition to Mary Ann, "I will be back before supper, but don't wait for me."

Mary Ann sighed, "How many times had she heard these words tossed over his shoulder as he rode off?" He was always back before dark it seemed, but why did he have to visit his family on Christmas Day.

P.K. urged his horse as it made the rounds, first to Paris to say hello to Brother Joseph, then back to Wildcat Hollow to see Mathew; over the River to Millwood to see Uriah, then to Front Royal to see his sisters. He turned back along the eastern side of the Shenandoah and came in to the house just before dark. He had missed some of the family but it was just too many to see in one day. Prayers were said and the family sat down to the dinner that had been prepared by Mary Ann. It was the quietest dinner P.K. could remember. Even the boys who took every opportunity to tease each other were somber. The threat of war was on their minds. South Carolina had met a few days before and seceded from the Union and because she did, a number of states would most likely follow. *What would the North do? Send in troops? Where would Virginia stand? What if the South left the Union but did not fire a shot? Would the North still come in with guns?*

All these questions went through the minds of the family. P.K. said to no one in particular. "This may be the last year that I am able to go visit my brothers and sisters. This may be the last year we have our own Christmas dinner in peace for a while. Let us enjoy what we can and not worry about tomorrow or next year."

The year 1861 began with the threat of war. P.K. used every excuse he could muster to try to visit populated areas to listen for news. His brother Joseph in Paris picked up all sorts of rumors from the Piedmont section as customers came in to pick up their repaired shoes. Joseph would report to P.K. the feelings of that section of the country.

Brother Uriah in Millwood was a good source as his freight business gave him reason to be in many areas of the Valley. The feeling was that Virginia would go with the southern states. With South Carolina already seceded, it took only the firing on Fort Sumter to complete the makeup of the South. Virginia was among the last to secede but joined Arkansas, Tennessee and North Carolina as they, too, took that fateful step. A convention was held in Alabama but Richmond ended up as the capitol of the Confederacy.

April 1861
The Beginning of the
Battles

It was just about the most beautiful spring day one could imagine. The call had gone out throughout the county. "The Recruiting Officer for the Second Virginia will be in Millwood on the 14th of April, 1861, asking all able bodied males from the age of eighteen to thirty to answer the call of the Confederacy. To those who want to be close to their friends, the Nelson Rifles will be a part of this recruitment."

There was joviality among those assembled as if they were awaiting the circus coming to town. They jostled each other and bragged that the Yankees would not venture into the State of Virginia once they saw the skill of those who had spent their lives on the trigger end of a rifle. Those who had horses brought them, some showed up on "shank's mare," some with their own weapons, some barefooted, some in boots, but most in the shoes of a farmer. The grandchildren of Peter Royston were there in force. When it came time to line up at the recruiter's table, the grandchildren seemed to assemble by seniority, that is, the age of their fathers and their mothers.

The recruiter looked up and growled, "Name, last first.

"Royston" came the prompt answer.

"First name."

"George Riddle," Uriah's oldest answered

"Next"

"Royston"

"First Name"

"Matthew Thomas"

Turning back to the next in line, "And you."

"Royston, Theodore"

"Next"

"Royston, Robert"

"And you"

"Grubbs."

"That's a funny first name, "Grubbs Royston?"

Not a Royston, I'm a Grubbs, but my mother was a Royston."

"First name"

"Frances."

"That's your name?

"No, that's my mother, my name is William."

"This is going to be a long day," the recruiter complained to the scribe next to him.

"And you?" he asked of the next in line.

"Nathanial L."

"Grubbs?"

"I'm surprised that you didn't say your name was Frances," the recruiter mumbled.

He looked up at the next in line, "First name?"

"Hannah"

"I don't mean your mother, I mean yours!"

A deep breath was taken, "Epaninondas."

"What kind of name is that? And how do you spell it? Maybe we should write down just 'Pam' and let it go at that."

"No sir, Epaninondas was a great Greek general and I want to be worthy of him. Besides, if I am killed in this war, I want everyone to know it was me."

The scribe sighed and asked him to step aside and spell out the name for him.

"Next."

"Grubbs"

"And what kind of first name do you have?"

"Phillip Lewis"

"Another Grubbs?"

"Yes, Matthew K."

"And you?"

"Grubbs, James Thomas."

"Next"

"Grubbs, William"

"Thought we already had a William Grubbs?" the recruiter turned to the scribe.

"You do, I am William B. He is William G. His mother is Frances, mine is Hannah."

The recruiter looked up at a lad whose size seemed sufficient to qualify but whose voice sounded a bit too young. "How old are you, William B.?" he inquired.

The recruit drew himself as tall as he could and said "Almost twelve."

"Get out of line and wait for the next war," the recruiter almost shouted.

The scribe tossed his pen into the air and muttered, "I hope we are through with the Roystons and the Grubbs."

The next in line said, "You are, even though you just threw out the best shot in all the Royston clan. There are at least four more Roystons, but they are joining up over in Fauquier County. My name is 'Doran'"

"And let me guess, your mother is a Royston."

"How did you know? Her name is Mary Catherine. My name is Matthew."

The Recruiter mumbled something to himself about the quality of recruits, and shouted next!"

"Doran, Joseph," came the response.

"Next."

"Royston, P.K."

"Wait a minute. I thought we were through with Roystons. Are there more of you?"

"Yeah, a lot more but either they are too young or not of a warlike disposition. I am a generation removed but am willing to fight."

The recruiter looked up and surveyed the massive frame of one who appeared to be a bit old for this war. "Why are you signing up, you look over forty."

"I am, but my children are too young to sign up so I thought I would represent them."

"I tell you what, old man, I'll take your name and register you but you are a part of the home protectors until we call you."

P. K. Royston moved out of line and took with him his very young son, Toad, who had snuck into the line a few recruits after him. "I hope the war doesn't last long enough for twelve year olds to become of fighting age."

The group of Peter Royston's grandsons and one son gathered near the old mill and talked more quietly than before. The die had been cast and now their lives would be controlled by others and this might be the last time they would gather as controllers of their own lives. While they would most likely be in the same Second Virginia, they would be scattered as they went through training.

While Fort Sumter was where the first shots were fired, it was on Virginia soil that the first blood was spilled. The North called it the Battle of Manassas and the South called it the Battle of Bull Run.

Word of the battle seeped back to the mountains along with the word of losses.

P.K. walked quietly into the house and Mary Ann was almost afraid to ask about his somber mood.

It came out in a blurt. "Pammie Grubbs was killed, killed in the first battle. Must have been a shell as he was a saddler and they are not normally in the front lines." P.K. knew he wasn't making much sense but neither did this war. "He must have had a premonition as I recall his insistence that his name be spelled correctly when he joined up."

Mary Ann sighed in that pragmatic way. "You men were so joyful to be signing up a couple of months ago. There is not much I can do except to name my next one after Pammie. And that will be in the fall. I got the feeling it's going to be twins. Surely one will be a boy."

To her word, on November first she gave birth to twins, both boys. One was named Epamnaydous by Mary Ann and the other Nimrod, by P.K. *At least one will live on in the spirit of our fallen soldier at Bull Run,* thought Mary Ann, wondering why P.K. would want to name a child with a name meaning a great hunter.

P.K. snorted as he felt her unsaid question. "I am naming him after my mother's brother who died back in '42. That was shortly before I met you."

THE DROWNINGS
1862

It was obviously his first command. He commanded a troop of Union cavalry made up of more than one origin if one judged by the disparity of their uniforms which turned the entire troop into a less than disciplined affair. Many of the soldiers had weapons that had been thrust on them by well-wishers and family. The captain was over dressed and appeared to have little experience. He led his command to the ferry area from the west side and demanded passage across the swollen but passable river. There were three ferry boats tied up on the west bank and the captain yelled at the ferrymen to grant them passage. The ferry leader asked for payment and the captain drew his saber and said "This is the payment you will receive if you do not take all of my troops across at once."

The ferryboat man looked at the large group and his three boats. "With this swift water it will take at least three crossings to accommodate the entire company."

With this saber and with my demand you will do it in one crossing," was the reply.

The ferryman shrugged his shoulders and said "I know my river and if you want to kill me, go ahead. It would be better than drowning with a bunch of Yankees."

"My orders are to cross this river and proceed to Paris. This I will do with or without you," the Captain shouted.

He drew back his sword and as he did a disheveled woman stepped between them. "So, it's crossing the river you want and needing a ferryboat driver it is. I can drive a ferryboat. Did so for many years at Castleman's Ferry."

"Aunt Tillie Beth," the ferryboat leader began.

"Get out of her way," the captain shouted. "She has more courage than any of you."

And a brain that is a bit addled, the ferryboat man muttered under his breath.

With a wild laugh, she encouraged the soldiers to help her lash all three boats together. When the chore was done she invited the troops aboard with all their horses and equipment. The ferryboats were almost awash as the current did its utmost to prove the ferryboat leader correct. There was some apprehension from the troop as they were laden with their own personal equipment and many were wondering at the sanity of the captain.

"Cast off," Aunt Tillie Beth shouted and as they did, she slacked off the drive line to allow the boats to be pushed toward Burwell's Island.

"She's trying to drown them all; I think she's doing it on purpose," one of the ferryboat men yelled.

"That may be true. Since they killed her boy at Bull Run she hasn't been quite right. I was wondering why she volunteered to help the Yankees when she hates them so much."

Just as the three boats approached the sinkholes around Burwell's Island, she began singing and rocking the boats. The water from the upstream side began to wash into the boats as the boats tilted further and further into the river. The troops began to panic and this contributed to the instability of the boats. Finally the first boat capsized and as it did the other two boats, following the leader, dumped all the soldiers, horses and equipment into the water.

Just as the boats made their final turn and they ended upside down, Aunt Tillie Beth gave out a Rebel yell and leaped for the point of Burwell's Island. The boats in their upside down position prevented the entangled soldiers from reaching any part of the island. Screams of the soldiers could be heard as their heavy equipment pulled them under the water. Aunt Tillie Beth could be heard laughing as she made her way down the length of the island and as she moved into the woods. She herself then disappeared forever.

The following day the river had quieted and the loose debris had floated north toward the Potomac, returning the soldiers' possessions toward the land of their ancestry. A few bodies floated onto Burwell's Island but most were under the boats.

The call went out to those living on both sides of the river to help with the recovery of the bodies. No matter what you thought of live Yankees, dead ones had to be recovered and buried. P.K. joined the volunteers and a plan was developed for the up-righting of the ferry boats and the recovery of the bodies. Most of the horses had escaped the fate of the soldiers, so it was only the soldiers' bodies and their personal equipment that needed to be found. One after another the bodies were brought to shore. Finally the job appeared to be completed and the bodies were put into wagons and taken to the closest Union detachment and the story told of their drowning.

P.K. Finds a Rifle

Weary to the bone and saddened by the sight of all the dead, P.K. sat on the west bank of the Shenandoah and watched everyone leave. He needed to get to the east bank but lacked the strength and the will to move. "So this is what war is all about," he said aloud. "I'll wager that when the cheering was going on at the time of their enlistment none of them thought they would end up this way. What a waste."

The sun was almost set when P.K. worked his way down river to a shallow area where he could ford the river to Burwell's Island. Once on the Island he could swim the short side to the bottom land on the east bank. As he started his swim across the narrow channel, his eyes were drawn to a bush whose branches reached out into the river. There was something there. He poked into the brush and the face of a body floated to the surface. The unseeing eyes seemed to be staring at him. P.K. reached down and closed the eyes as he had seen his brother do at the death of his daughter. The body itself seemed to be weighted down with the equipment of the soldier. P.K. pulled and tugged until he could begin to unstrap the equipment. The soldier seemed to have an unseemly large amount of equipment, but the heaviest of all was a rifle and a backpack of ammunition. P.K. carefully removed the rifle and bullet pouch and laid them on the bank. The body was that of a young soldier, perhaps eighteen or nineteen years old. *What to do now? Everyone was gone. All the other bodies were on their way to Millwood.* He was drawn to the fanciest of rifles which was a part of the dead soldier's equipment. As he pondered his next move, he examined the rifle. Most cavalrymen carried short carbines that could be put in a saddle scabbard. This rifle had fancy tooling and a barrel that was that of a sharp shooter. He looked at the markings through the twilight that was now fading. He could see the word "Colt" along with identifying serial numbers. Perhaps the rifle was given to the soldier by his father as he sent him off to war. P.K. wondered how much the weight of the rifle and its ammunition contributed to the soldier dying.

Finally he made a decision. The rifle could come in handy during the war in case he had to defend his house. He remembered the words of the recruiting sergeant when he tried to enlist. "P.K., you will do the effort good if you stay at home and defend the mountain people." Perhaps this was the way of letting him know how he was supposed to do it.

But what about the body, P.K. thought. *Maybe I should bury it myself. That way no one will know anything about me finding a body and the rifle.* The rifle now occupied a lot of his thinking.

Now the question of where to do the burying. *It would be a lot easier just to bury him here on the river bank. That didn't seem proper. Besides, the water might rise and uncover the body in flood times. Why not bury him in the Royston Graveyard near his father and little Louisa? There was plenty of room there. Maybe he could talk his brother Mathew into helping him.*

P.K. carefully tied the body to the bush where he had found him and then he lashed the rifle and ammunition to his saddle and rode toward the Royston house. Before getting there he temporarily hid the rifle near the cabin area where Arissa used to live. He continued on and found his brother, Mathew, resting on the porch. Mathew had been helping in the recovery of the bodies and was now showing the sign of his age. P.K. roused Mathew and told him of finding the body and the need to bury it. Mathew didn't question the burial location that was picked by P.K. and the two of them went back to the river and together they found strength to load the body onto a horse. They made their way up the hill to the cemetery and selecting a spot that seemed to be the softest, they dug a grave. The body was placed in the shallow hole. P.K. knelt and said a few words heard only by himself and then covering the face of the dead soldier with his handkerchief, began to shovel dirt into the hole. The job completed, they distributed some leaves over the newly turned soil so that a casual observer would not notice a new grave. *Tomorrow*, P.K. thought, *I will come back and put a small piece of slate so no one else will dig in that area.* He looked over at the grave sites of his father, little Louisa, and Arissa, who was once a slave and who had ties to the family beyond that of servant. And now a soldier with no name. The cemetery might be small but it represented all that was a part of his life. He wondered if he would be here when his time came.

The rains came again and P.K., not being able to plow or sow, used the time to examine his new rifle and the ammunition that came with it. Where to store the rifle was the first of his problems. At home it would be a source of speculation. Hidden outside, it could be discovered and perhaps traced back to him. He also had to check the ammunition and see if the rifle was properly sighted-in.

Finding a place to check the rifle was easy. Behind Slatey Ridge was a small valley where only the brave dared to venture. Most were afraid of the rattle snakes who asserted their right to be there by being on or under every rock, or so it seemed. P.K. didn't mind the rattlers and they seemed to tolerate him. *Much like my wildcats*, he thought. *That's it, the Wildcat Den. That will be the perfect place to hide my rifle.*

A trip to Slatey Ridge and he found that the ammunition that he had recovered was undamaged by the river water and after a few shots at a target, he pronounced the rifle as one of superior class. He made his way from Slatey Ridge and crossed the Ashby Gap Turnpike at the

Mount Carmel Lane area. He paused to make sure no one saw him cross. He made his way across the ridge and dropped down to the Wild Cat Den. He slipped under the leaves and into the small cave. The animals accepted him as always. He rubbed each and a soft purr told him he was a friend. There was a small ledge just long enough to hold the rifle and the ammunition. There he left it and made his way back home.

The War Comes Close to Home

Living on or near the Toll Road left families open to the whims of the troops that came by almost daily. Some were well supplied, some were foragers. Some were in blue and some were in gray. Most of the ones in gray were well mannered as their lives might depend on the local populace and their desire to help those of their own. The sound of horses and the metallic equipment that served as the means of war was always heard with apprehension. It was left to the children and the women to face this daily challenge as the men were either off to war or were working the fields as they attempted to keep a semblance of order to the food supply for the family and the stock.

The Royston clan had three homes that were on the toll road, starting with the old home place at the entrance to Wild Cat Hollow. Mathew Royston lived on the old home place, with P.K. and his sister living in the second and third one. Signals were worked out so that troop movements were picked up when they crossed the Shenandoah until they cleared the area at Mount Carmel Lane.

Since the route to Shepherd's Ford joined the toll road at Mount Carmel Lane, the families were only subjected to those troops crossing at Berry's Ferry. It was rare that the troops used the road up Wildcat

Hollow as a route to Ashby's Gap. This left P.K. with an open way to recover his rifle if it were needed. P.K. worked the upper fields and Mathew the bottom land. P.K. would leave the house before daylight taking a sack of food with him for his dinner. Supper was at home sometime after dark.

Mary Ann by now had seven children and it was obvious that the man of the house was not too far from home as the swelling of her stomach indicated another was on its way.

This particular morning was interrupted by the sounds of mounted cavalry outside the house. They had already been warned that troops had crossed the river and this same signal was heard by P.K. as he worked the field near the old slab mill.

The company of troops had assembled outside the house and were refreshing themselves from the spring that was between the house and the toll road.

"Hello the house," called out the captain. "Hello the house."

Mary Ann came to the door and stood in the shadow of the porch. "How can I be of help?" she wanted to know.

"Are there any men about?" asked the Captain. He stayed on his horse, making a striking figure as he had a colorful plume in his hat, well creased uniform and gloves reaching almost to his elbows.

"There are no men, only some children." she answered.

"I can see that there has been a man about," he said pointing to her stomach. Some of the soldiers snickered

"Sir, you are a cad and not a gentleman. My man is out working the fields and is not aware of your presence. It is good for you that this is true," Mary Ann retorted in an angry voice.

At once the captain's voice became mollified and he continued. "We need food and will take anything you have available."

At this time a dismounted trooper came out of the chicken house with a number of chickens in his hands. "We will take those chickens and any more we find."

"Certainly you can see that they are laying hens and not pullets. Is it your method to eat today and not plan for tomorrow?"

About three hundred yards away, P.K. watched the events transpire. While he could not make out the words he could see what was happening. He raised his rifle and drew a deliberate bead on the side of the head of the Captain. With his shooting skill there was no way he could miss. He could see the expression on the man's face as he started to pull the trigger. He sighed. He could not deliberately kill a man. He raised the sights to the top of the plumed cap and pulled the trigger.

The Captain watched as the trooper started to wring the first chicken's neck. Just as he did there was the crack of a sharp shooter's rifle, and his cap sailed lazily through the air and landed right side up near the porch. The troopers poured out of their saddles and looked for the source of the shot. There was no obvious location. Each was terrified, knowing they might be next.

Mary Ann stepped out from the shadows and picked up the plumed cap. Looking at the pale face of the captain, she said, "Your cap, Captain. Are you aware of how lucky you are? You were the target of the Mountain Sharp Shooter, whose accuracy is uncanny. If he had wanted you dead, you would be dead." This she made up on the spur of the moment, not knowing herself where the shot came from.

The captain donned his hat and called to his troops, "It is time we were in Paris. Mount up. We have no time to chase these mountain yokels."

That evening P.K. came in after dark and the children met him with a chorus, each trying to tell the story. "You should have been here, Pa. I have never seen such a passel of scared Yankees. They took cover so fast, you would have thought that Jeb Stuart was after them. Then they took out for the top of the mountain just as soon as their captain gave them an excuse. I wonder who could have been the shooter. Maybe one of the Carroll boys!"

Each had their own version while Mary Ann sat quietly, watching P.K.'s reaction to the stories. It seemed he was hearing the details for the first time.

P.K. said "There are a number of boys in the mountain who can shoot like that, but who has a rifle that is that good for that distance? Must have been a lucky shot."

"No-sir-re-bob," said young 'Toad.' "That was no lucky shot. That is just where it was aimed. I can't wait to get a shot at those Yankees myself."

Mary Anne winced, thinking of the cousins who were already dead from this crazy war. "By the time you are old enough to fight, the war will be over," she said in an unconvincing voice.

That night Mary Ann questioned P.K. "Where were you working today? Did you hear the shot? It wasn't you doing the shooting, was it?"

P.K. gave noncommittal answers to the barrage of questions, concluding by saying, "You know that I don't have a firearm of that quality and all I have are here at the house 'cepting that old sawed off shot gun I carry with me to use against rattlers or copperheads."

Within a few days the story was told and retold, not only in the mountains but on both sides of the warriors. Those on the side of the South were sure it was an accurate shot by an unknown mountain squirrel hunter. Those on the Union side thought it was very lucky that the shooter missed his target and maybe the next time they would not be so lucky. They knew it was fruitless to try and find the shooter and no one wanted to volunteer for the task. In the mountains each had his own choice for the identity of the shooter with most suggesting someone who was away at the war but who might have been home for a few days of leave.

And so the legend began.

Jessie Troops
May 1863

"Hallo the House!" By now it was a familiar ring. While there had been little contact with the Union Troops in recent months, the warm May weather seemed to bring out the rattling of traces and the snorting of horses as both sides passed by the house as they moved from the Valley to the Piedmont area and back again.

P.K. went to the door, glancing at the shotgun in the corner that was within reach as he slouched in the doorway. He always tried to make his bulk as small as possible as it seemed to bring out the hostilities in the other person. He looked at four soldiers in the gray uniform of the Confederacy and relaxed a bit. "What can I do for you?" P.K. asked.

"Good day, Sir," one greeted P.K. "Could we bother you for some water?"

P.K. nodded toward the spring. "Help yourself," he offered.

One of the soldiers moved toward the spring while the others waited. "Are there any other troops around?" one asked. "We have become separated from our company and need to make contact with other 'Rebs' in the area. That way we can do the most damage to those Blue Bellies."

P.K. assayed the group. They were well dressed for Confederate troops and the soft accent seemed to be a bit affected. Maybe they were from out of the region.

Then again, maybe they weren't who they said they were. *Better play it safe*, P.K. thought. He answered aloud, "We know of no troops in the area from either side. They pass through on their way to and from the Valley. We are generous with our water for both sides."

P.K. expected a bristling of the spine from Rebs who would think P.K. was helping the enemy but there was no perceptive change in their bearing.

"Maybe you know where some of Mosby's men are. They could surely direct us to find our company," they persisted.

Now P.K. was pretty sure these men were "Jessie Troops." He talked with them further but gave no information and they drank their fill of water and left towards Paris.

Going back into the house, he said to Mary Ann. "Those were 'Jessie Troops.'"

Mary Ann nodded. "They didn't seem to be regular Confederate troops."

Before she could continue, young "Dink" broke in, "What's a Jessie Troop?"

"A Jessie Troop is a Yankee dressed up in a Confederate uniform and snooping around to see what he can find out. If we told them anything they would pass it on to the Union side. Not only would some Confederates maybe lose their lives, but we could be identified as someone who can give them information."

"Why are they called 'Jessie troops?' That sounds like a girl's name," Dink wanted to know.

"It is a girl's name," P.K. informed Dink. "They were named after the wife of General Fremont. She was very active in Missouri politics before the war. Her father was a senator from Missouri before he became a turncoat to the will of Missourians and announced he was against slavery. That was enough to kill his chances to become reelected. General Fremont is well known for his discovery of routes to the west."

"I know him," Dink remembered. "Ma taught us about him. He was known as the 'Pathfinder.'"

"It still doesn't make any sense why the soldiers would be named after a woman," Dink muttered as his mind turned to other things.

"Just be sure you don't give out any information to anyone about anything," P.K admonished, as he, too, moved to the fields where spring planting was almost over.

SHELLING ACROSS THE RIVER

P.K. awoke to the unmistakable sounds of horses pulling artillery. He would have suspected it to be from the south side of the house as most traffic was along the Ashby Gap Toll Road. This appeared to be from the north side of the house and seemed to be heading to Mockingbird Hill. He pulled on some trousers and made his way to the back porch where he could see the shadows of troops and weapons as they passed above the pines that lined the side of the hill. Normally such action would have sent him to the Wildcat Den to find his rifle, but the troops were in the position he used to protect the house.

He watched as the troops moved the cannons to the crest of the ridge where they overlooked the valley. *What a natural spot to shell across the river*, he thought. He wasn't sure whether they were Union or Confederate troops but thought from the voices he heard that they were Rebs. There had been word of a Union encampment across the river which was reachable from this position. Not only that but the difference in elevation was sufficient that returning fire couldn't reach them.

The firing began. All night and all day the whistling of shells could be heard as the projectiles were fired across the Shenandoah. Mary Ann joined him on the porch. At least they appeared to be out of range of the batteries firing from the west side of the Shenandoah.

It was a time to remember. February of 1864 had brought a set of twins to her but only Marcus lived. Little Mary only survived for a month before succumbing to consumption. Mary Ann thought of the war and its toll. There were sixteen grandchildren of P.K.'s father who had signed up for the war. Pammie Grubbs had lasted only a few months and died in the first battle of the war at Bull Run. He had insisted that they spell his name correctly when he signed up just in case he didn't make it back. Mary Ann wondered if he had a premonition. Theodore had been killed just last July at Upperville. Thomas had lost an eye. William Grubbs had been killed at Spotsylvania. Things were getting so desperate that she was fearful that they would want P.K. to be an active part of the war. Son Toad was now fifteen and big for his age. He was anxious to be a part of the fighting as he wanted to avoid the stares of those who judged worthiness to be killed by size rather than age.

"I'm concerned about the shelling," he muttered. "It's way too close to Ma, Mathew and Minerva, down at the home place. What if the house gets hit?" he wondered aloud.

"It sounds like you won't be satisfied unless you are down there where you can get hit yourself," Mary Ann worried. "Why not head down Fox Trap Hill and see if they are in danger."

P.K. paused only to stop at the spring to get a drink of water and turned toward the west. Just as he did he could see an explosion down near the old house. "I think the house is hit," he yelled. "Stay here with the babies and if Toad comes by send him down. They will need everyone's help."

P.K. looked at the two horses that were still harnessed from the field work. "I'll take them with me just in case I need some real strength." With that he grabbed their reins and started to run down the hill.

As he neared the descent part of Fox Trap Hill he could see that the house had been hit. Minerva and Mathew were trying to get doors open so that everyone could get out. It appeared that a number were in the house as they used it for shelter from the shelling. P.K. could see the smoke rising from the east end of the house, but there was little evidence of fire.

"How many are in the house?" he yelled at his brother, Mathew.

"Eight," came back the reply. "Ma is over at the Spout Spring so don't worry about her. There are a number of travelers who were waiting to cross on the ferry and they had taken refuge in the house. Try and get them out and anybody else you find."

P.K. covered his face with a handkerchief and pushed his way into the house. Debris was everywhere. He helped guide five unfamiliar faces out. He then saw his son "Dink" carrying out a small body of a young girl.

He looked down at the floor and memories came flooding back. There on the floor were the demolished remains of the toy horse and wagon that had been given him so many years ago by his brother Uriah. It was past repairing. P.K. sighed and picked up some of the pieces. With a shrug he threw them into the fireplace. *Another causality of the war*, he thought. P.K. was his usual pragmatic self.

"Go into the sitting room," Dink yelled. "I think cousin Isabella is hurt real bad and this baby I believe is dead."

P.K. found Isabella lying on the sofa and he reached to lift her.

"Don't move me," Isabella begged. "I think my back is broken." Isabella was only twenty years old but knew that her injury was very serious. "Tell my pa to get a stretcher."

P.K. made his way back outside and found Mathew. "Your daughter Isabella is hurt real bad. She has to have a litter to move her."

Mathew rushed inside and finding Isabella, agreed that the best thing to do would be to move her to an undamaged part of the house. "There doesn't appear to be any danger from fire. Have "Dink" go over to the spring and bring back fresh water. He can tell Ma to come and help if she wants to give people drinks."

The shelling had stopped, as if it had realized the damage that it had done. Some Confederate soldiers ventured out of the hills and helped to straighten out as much of the wreckage as possible. One officer said, "We also have some wounded and it seems that your place is large enough to care for them. Could we use your house as a temporary hospital?"

Mathew looked at Minerva, who nodded yes.

The litters became a stream of wounded as the Rebs were brought in. Looking up, P.K. recognized Doc Settle who began to move among the wounded.

Mathew came inside and nodded to P.K. to come outside. He motioned toward the river ferry. There P.K. could see a soldier in the familiar blue of the Union Army carrying a white flag.

"It looks like you have the makings of a hospital here and we too can use such a facility. Could we declare a truce long enough for emergency services to be rendered?"

Mathew again looked at Minerva, who again nodded.

Thus the war came to a halt, if only for a short time as soldiers on both sides were tended to.

When it was over Doc Settle slumped down in a chair. "It looks like you are going to have some burying to do. The little girl is dead. I think she was from Ohio, but her folks are nowhere to be found. We have some body parts from amputations that could be a part of the burying. The Rebs will take care of their own as will the Union. I have taken care of Isabella as best I can. I have to rejoin my troops but I will come back to see Isabella as soon as possible. There are some other injuries but I think Minerva can take care of them."

Mathew suddenly felt very tired. "I may not be a soldier, but I feel like I have been a part of the war since it started. It had better get over soon or I may not outlast it."

P.K. looked at his brother. Mathew was just past fifty but looked seventy. *The war has had an effect on all of us,* he thought.

P.K. finally walked back home alone with "Dink." Dink was brooding and was very open in his criticism of the North.

"You are only a lad," P.K. offered.

Dink lashed out, "It's because of persons like you that the South is losing. If we all fought like the Mountain Sharpshooter, this war would be different."

P.K. gave a wan smile but said nothing. As he reached home, he related all that had happened to Mary Ann. "Tomorrow we will bury the little girl who was killed. I hope that her folks come back to be a part of the burying. I wish we knew where Toad was. We haven't seen him since they started fighting over around Cool Springs."

Just as he finishing talking there was a shadow at the door and Toad slid through as though he didn't want to be seen. His clothes were tatters and his hand was bandaged with a rag that was soaked with blood.

Mary Ann rushed to him and took her oldest son in her arms. "Where in Heaven's name have you been?" She wanted to know. "They shelled the old house and we could have used your help in tending to the wounded and dead." She was almost afraid to ask where he had been, as if she knew the answer.

"I've been fighting in the War," he said to no one in particular. "I didn't get to shoot at anyone but I did carry water to all the soldiers as they "hunkered" down behind the rocks. Got my little finger shot off for my troubles," as he lifted his bandaged hand.

Mary Ann gasped. *This war is getting way too close. When will it be over?* she thought. "Did anyone bandage your hand or did you just wrap a rag around it? If that wound gets infected.... ." she let the words trail off.

"A doctor washed it with spring water and some medicine, then put a hot iron to it" Toad said "but it hasn't stopped bleeding. Maybe you can look at it."

Mary Ann carefully unwrapped the bandage and could see where the iron had cauterized the stub of the finger but had missed one small point that was seeping blood. The bleeding looked worse than it really was. She reached for her sewing bag and pulled out the smallest needle she could find. Threading it with some silk thread, she sterilized it over a flame and warning Toad to grit his teeth, she pulled the needle through the bleeding part of the wound and sealed off the blood.

"I hope you have seen enough war to last you," Mary Ann admonished. "After all you are only 15 years old."

"I have seen men dying and have seen men dead, but I must be who I am and that is a Virginian who will fight any invaders of our soil. As soon as this wound heals, I plan on joining up." Toad spoke with finality and Mary Ann knew was useless to argue.

The battle was over and the troops on both sides of the river melted away. Dink pulled Toad aside and said, "I'll bet there is a lot of war stuff up on Mockingbird Hill. What do you say we go and see what we can find?"

Toad needed no urging. His hand still hurt where the finger was missing but the thought of war booty made the pain go away. They made their way up the hill and through what was once a field of corn. It was now a trampled mess. Out toward the point where the valley came in view there were the remnants of the soldiers bivouac. Harness chains, double trees, chocks for the wheels of the cannons were strewn about. Dink picked up some pieces that seemed to interest him, stuffing them in his pockets as he searched among the trash.

Toad let out a whistle, "Would you look at this? A couple of real live shells with canister shot and powder still in them. Let's take them home with us."

Dink looked at the projectiles and almost agreed. Then he rationalized, "Ma would whip us if we came home with those. Let's hide them where no one can find them. Then after the war is over, we can come back and dig them up."

Toad nodded, "I brought along a shovel. Let's take a line on that oak tree and the dogwood bush. We'll bury them half way between."

"My hand is hurting pretty bad," Toad admitted. "So you will have to do the digging."

Dink dug a shallow hole and the two shells were placed in it. He covered everything and tamped down the soil. "Lucky this area has some pretty good soil and not the shale that is every place else. Otherwise we would have to set off one of those shells to dig a hole," Toad laughed.

Their task completed they worked their way back down the hill and cut over to the toll road. They came sauntering into the house like they had just been out for a walk. Mary Ann looked up and acknowledged their presence by warning them that supper was just about to be served and dirty hands were not going to eat any of it. Toad and Dink scrambled for the wash basin and poured some water out of the ever-present bucket which sat on a nearby stand. They looked at each other and smiled knowing that they had a secret together.

THE BATTLE OF MOUNT CARMEL 1865

The War had taken on a sense of desperation. There seemed little that the South could do that would win the war. They only seemed to want to prolong it. The soldiers of the North were fighting for personal survival. What good would it do to win the war if they were among the casualties? The battles around the Roystons' houses were mostly skirmishes and had little impact on the outcome of the big picture. Gathering places such as ferry crossings were places to avoid. Berry's Ferry had seen a number of drownings and there were continued shellings across the river.

Mosby must be really irritating the North as there seems to be a lot more activity over around Paris and Upperville, P.K.thought. Just this morning a company of Bluecoats who apparently crossed the river at Shepherd's Ford came by Mount Carmel Church and headed across Ashby's Gap toward Paris. Mary Ann sensed danger and tried to keep the children close. By now she had given birth to ten children but only seven had survived. The oldest were healthy but those born during the war seemed to be just as much the victims as if they were soldiers.

Maybe it was because Doc Settle was off taking care of Southern soldiers and with Arissa dead, there was no outstanding midwife in the area. Toad was the oldest and seemed to want desperately to get into the war. His hand had healed to the point where he hardly favored it as he worked. Dink was only 14 and showed little interest in the fighting. The rest, Fanny, Augie, Walter, Pammie, and Jim were so young that the war didn't seem to be more than something that kept them from playing outside as much as they wanted.

Mary Ann listened to the sporadic firing up near the Green Place. It seemed to be getting nearer. By now she could tell the difference in the sounds of the weapons and as the sounds neared Mount Carmel Church she could differentiate between the pistol and the carbine fire. It sounded like troops on the run. She wondered where P.K. was as he seemed to disappear when there was fighting nearby and then re-appear when it passed. Somehow she sensed that he was there to protect them but wanted to be away from the house. He never had a weapon that she could see, but there were bruises on his shoulder that were there only after there were sounds of rifle fire nearby. She wondered about him being the Mountain Marksman that people kept talking about.

All of these thoughts kept passing through her mind as she herded the youngsters into the house. The firing became more intense and she could hear the screams of the wounded and the muffled sounds of the dying as the battle waged near the house and turned north toward Shepherd's Ford. As the sound of the battle died away, P.K. appeared and without a word picked up two buckets which he filled from the spring. He motioned to Toad to do the same and for Dink to bring as many rags as he could carry. Armed with the water and the rags, they went toward Mount Carmel Church. It was obvious they were going to care for those still alive.

Later P.K. reported on the battle. "The Yanks didn't have a chance. They were armed with carbines and Mosby's men with pistols. Mosby's Rangers could ride up behind them and fire their pistols. It was hard for the Yanks to try and turn around to fire their carbines. The best thing the Yanks could do was to beat a path for Shepherd's Ford as fast as they could. We found a lot of bodies in the brush and pulled them out to the road. There will be burial details coming by soon and I will help with that. I think that Toad and Dink got a bit more war than they wanted."

As spring wore on, desperate measures were begun by the North. General Sheridan was instructed to destroy the food making ability of the Shenandoah Valley. And he seemed intent to do just that. Many farms buildings and crops were burned. There were reports of savagery that were intended to undermine the will of the South to fight.

While there was little damage done to the interior of the mountains, the toll roads leading through the gaps were heavily damaged.

General Custer, tiring of his inability to stop the raids and attacks of Mosby's Rangers announced that he would hang any Ranger caught as they were not regular soldiers and were acting as guerillas only. This he did in Front Royal, a town about eight miles up the River. The reports spread like wildfire as the number reportedly hanged went from five to ten to upward of twenty. Mosby retaliated with hangings of his own and Custer realized the futility of his actions.

Mary Ann, on hearing the reports, shrank into the confines of the house. The fear of the unknown was real and she was afraid of what might happen next. Being alongside the toll road, they were too close to anyone who might venture by and who wished to retaliate.

The War Is Over

The words that Mary Ann was praying for finally came. A rider came down the toll road yelling "The war is over, the war is over. They signed the surrender at Appomattox Court House on Palm Sunday." Mary Ann and P.K. held each other closely and they cried as if they were babies. The fear that their oldest would become a part of the war was gone. Toad had signed up in March at Front Royal to be a part of the Quartermaster Corps but had not been assigned to a unit. He would not become a statistic of this war. No longer would they recoil when they heard the rattling of harness and trace. The Valley was a shambles with many barns and fields burned.

The mountains had not fared too badly. It was not a good agricultural area to begin with and the only ones to suffer during the war were those with houses near the roads frequented by the troop movements. Most of their losses were livestock and some damage to houses. The old homestead that had been shelled last summer had been patched and one had to look hard to find the physical scars on the house. Only one person who suffered injuries was still recovering. Isabella was permanently bent over from the damage to her back. Many young persons at the age of twenty two would be bitter having such a debilitating injury. Not Isabella. She was happy. One of the Reb soldiers that came to help straighten up the house from the shell's damage stayed to help Isabella in her early recovery days. Now it appeared that they would be married sometime in the fall.

"We will celebrate Easter Sunday in a new way. Maybe it is time to have another Sunrise service at Mount Carmel," Mary Ann offered.

"There's not much time to prepare but it sure would be appropriate. There hasn't been one since the war started."

The mountain communication system worked well. Easter Sunday found a large number of families at Mount Carmel awaiting the sunrise. It turned out to be a very somber morning. No smiles. Only a few acknowledged the presence of the other. They were all lost in their own thoughts. It was supposed to be a day of rejoicing-not only for the day itself-but for the freedom from war. No matter how one felt about the war, it was good that it was over.

But now another calamity was upon them. On Good Friday, the President was assassinated. The details were sketchy but the fear of the unknown was upon them. The air was rife with rumors. It was said that one of Colonel Mosby's Rangers was a part of the assassination plot. Since everyone in the mountains knew many of the Rangers, each one had a guess at who that man could be. It was rumored that the Union Army would occupy the county and make everyone pay for their possible part in the killing of Lincoln. While the large majority of mountain families stood for the South, they wanted to return to normalcy and continue with their lives.

P.K.'s thoughts went back over the years. He remembered the first Sunrise Service at Mount Carmel that was instigated by his father back in '32. What a festive day that was. He remembered the Easter dinner the family enjoyed afterwards with all his brothers and sisters present. There were no thoughts of war. If only we could go back and live our lives over. There would be three of my nephews still living, rather than being sacrificed for a lost cause. Even if the South won the war, they would still be dead. It's good that Pa didn't live to see the war. He loved the grandchildren so much and to see sixteen of them fighting in a war that raged over our own land would have overwhelmed him.

P.K. looked at the church members present and knew they were thinking the same thoughts. There was open weeping from the womenfolk and a lot of men suddenly seized with allergies as they reached for the handkerchiefs hanging out of their pockets. The preacher called for forgiveness by all and prayed that the Almighty would deal gently with those present as they sorted out their lives and went toward the future. As the service closed P.K., Mary Ann and the children walked the short distance to their house. There would be an Easter dinner but it would be a somber one.

After dinner P.K. built a small fire in the fireplace, needing a solace for his thoughts. There had been ten children born into their marriage. He thought back on the first one born who carried the two family names. Thomas had been the name selected by P.K.'s father and it represented some name from the past. Adams was from Mary Ann's side. While he had such normal names it was the nickname given him by his grandfather that would stick. Swearing that the lad when born looked like a toad, the name was his for life.

Others followed and before the war was over there were ten, though only seven had survived. Now Mary Ann had just told him she was pregnant with her eleventh. The house was stretched to its limits. It was time to think of another place.

Mary Ann, sensing his pensiveness, came and sat beside him. "What are your thoughts, P.K.? Are they something you want to share?"

The heat of the small fire and the tenderness of Mary Ann brought a warmth that he had not felt since the beginning of the war. No matter what turn life took, the two would stand together as they faced the future. He talked of the past, his parents, the Spout Spring; he even alluded to the wild cat den. The thoughts of his children growing up and the one who was to come, all these thoughts came tumbling out. Finally he said, "The house is too small. It is too near the toll road.

Now that the war is over you will see an exodus through the Gap that will turn its shale into a cloud of dust. It is time to move."

"And where did you have in mind?" Mary Ann queried.

"I was thinking of building a house out Mount Carmel Lane, high on the hill just past the bend in the road, near the old slab mill. There is a good spring there and we would be away from the crowds. We could build a house that could hold all our family. We have some money left over from your mother. Thank God it is Union currency. It will be enough to at least rough out the house. We will get by."

P.K. Builds His House

The stand of pines reached from Fox Trap Hill to Mount Carmel Church. It was the last of the magnificent pines that had provided logs for most of the buildings along Ashby Gap Toll Road. It was said that it supplied the logs for Mount Carmel Church that was built in the 1760's. The Blue Ridge Mountains had long given up on pines with the hard woods taking their place. But this one lone stand survived as if to say "I am needed for the mountain folks to survive." Once the sap receded in the fall, the trunks make for easy cutting. The tops reached stately to the sky as if to thank their Maker for their right to be of use. Many were sprigs that were living when the settlers first came to Jamestown.

P.K. walked among the pines and chose those that could be hauled the three-quarters of a mile to the top of the hill he had selected. Most could be snaked along the ground using horses to make the pull. Before it was through, a small two wheel caisson recovered from the war was stripped of its ammunition holder. The front end of the logs could be lifted onto its carriage and the horses found the pull much easier. They were collected and sized to fit the foundation that had been prepared. Cedars from the nearby "Green Place" provided the shingles and by the spring of '66, the house took on the semblance of a home.

"Just in time," P.K. exulted. The traffic on the Toll Road is coming unbearable. He directed his young sons as they worked to finish the house and to load the wagons with all the furnishings. Mary Ann had given birth to a girl in the fall of '65 and was still recovering from this birth. She had given the baby her namesake, "Mary Ann" and it was a healthy rollicking baby that needed full attention. She, too, was glad to get out of the small house on the Toll Road and into one where she could spread out.

The Shenandoah River was a natural divider which isolated the mountain people from the Valley folks. The county, as well as the rest of Virginia, was under martial law as the lawmakers struggled to write the new constitution that was required for the reentry of Virginia into the Union. Complicating the matter was the requirement that all officials not only sign an oath of allegiance to the Union, but had to stipulate they had never taken up arms against it. The first was easy to do, not so the second. Even if they were not in active combat, they were sensitive to their neighbors' thoughts that they might be a turncoat. Thus many offices went unfilled, even after a new constitution was submitted.

The mountain folks appreciated the division afforded by the Shenandoah. There was little of value in the mountains that attracted the vultures that swooped in to eat on the carrion that was left of the South. In addition, the mountain people let the legend of the "Mountain marksman" grow to where he would protect them from anyone dumb enough to venture across the river. The one shot that lifted a Northern Cavalryman officer's cap grew to one that took shots throughout the mountains at anyone who sought to use the mountains for the wrong purpose.

The Mountain Folks Survive

"Pigs!" An animal that was dirty, dumb, mean and untrainable. It saved the mountains! It would eat anything fed to it and in a rather efficient manner turn it into protein and fat. Turned loose in the woods it would root for acorns and any other edible shoots it could find. There was little other food available.

The winter and spring of 1866 seemed to join in an unending effort to punish those who were on the wrong side of the war. Persons froze, crops were ruined. The rains did not come and when they did, they were accompanied by winds of such ferocity that plants that had ventured above ground were destroyed.

The pigs turned their backs to the wind, huddled in the corners of their pens and ate whatever slop that was given to them. Last year's corn husks were a last resort but the pigs ate them as if they were a delicacy.

And how were these hogs rewarded for their efforts? They became the main entrée on the mountaineer's table. Some corn survived in protected areas and potatoes became a rare treat. The stoic mountaineer survived, but many perished from the harsh weather and the difficulty in obtaining nourishing food. Consumption was the defaulting reason for their deaths. In March of 1866, P.K.'s brother Mathew died, as well as his sister Anna Maria. Mary Ann's mother, who had been a part of their family since P.K. and Mary Ann married had been in frail health during the war and became one of those who died in 1866.

P.K.s mother, Ann, who had been living with Mathew, came to live with P.K. P.K. was her favorite son, but it meant that she could no longer visit the Spout Spring. It held an attraction to her that no one understood. While her husband Peter was alive she shunned the spring as much as P.K.'s father loved it. After his death, she practically lived there. The move of Ann coincided with the moving of P.K. into their new log house. As they loaded her meager belongings into the wagon for the pull up the hill, P.K. saw the first sign of his mother's failing memory. "Where's P.K.s' toy horse and wagon?" she wanted to know. "We can't leave without P.K.s' horse and wagon."

"Ma," P.K. pleaded, "You know the toy was destroyed when they shelled the house during the war. You do remember that, don't you?"

Ann looked with a far off stare, "I had forgotten for a moment," she dismissed it.

P.K. sighed. His father had been dead for around ten years. Somehow he thought his mother would live forever. She was now in her mid-eighties but seemed in good physical health.

While times were tough, the mountain people were good at procreating. Many of those born on the mountains opted for promises of better pastures across the river and toward the lands to the west. There seemed to be one in each family that stayed on the mountains and chose a life that while austere, had the pull of the evening sunset, the hum of the insects, and the beauty of a cloudless night with the stars so close one could almost touch them.

It was good that only a few stayed, as the mountains could not support a large number. Some left to work or farm in the Valley and to return sometimes as their own life became short. Others heard the call of the West and moved to the lands where "money could be picked from the trees."

The move to the new house was a welcome treat for all. No longer did pallets have to be laid each night for the children to sleep. There were bedrooms and beds sufficient for each gender to be separate and an extra bedroom for P.K.'s mother.

P.K. loved to come in from the fields and turn back toward the East, as if to feed on the view from the front porch. About 100 yards away and to his right was the spring, springhouse and pond. You could still see the outline of the old road that once was Mount Carmel Lane before it was shifted to the higher ground to avoid the marsh near the toll road. He wondered what the horses thought about this shift in the road as they were called on to pull their load up a steep hill past the church. Before, they simply followed the terrain across the marshy area to the meanderings of the creek that flowed from P.K.s' spring.

Satisfied with what he saw he went on into the house and washed up at the communal wash basin off the kitchen. The face towel was mounted on a roller so that it could be rotated, as sometimes it was difficult to find a dry spot on the towel.

He took time to consider how well the years had treated them. P.K. was now nearing fifty and Mary Ann was in her late thirties. Mary Ann had come from a family that produced twins and she followed that trait. The only complaint P.K. had ever heard about the number of children was a comment one time from Mary Ann, "It seems I have been pregnant all my life."

P.K. counseled his family to stay on the east side of the river as much as possible. The rest of the county seemed full of problems stemming from the reentry of Virginia into the Union. It was easy for the boys to get into a fight as they were outspoken in their love for Virginia and the lost cause.

Son Toad was going to marry the very young Lucy Ellen Lee and move sometime in the summer. Surprisingly enough he was going to start farming at Lakeville. P.K. chuckled as he thought about it. Lakeville seems to be the answer for all the Roystons' problems. *I won-*

der if that ghost will come and visit him as she did us, he thought. Toad said he didn't want any fancy church wedding but didn't tell of any other plans.

The county now had a regular weekly newspaper, the Clarke Courier, and P.K. made sure he obtained every issue. He would pore over it for every bit of news, and then pass it on to Mary Ann and the children for their perusal. He could read between the lines where the editor seemed to be holding back in his criticism of the South's treatment from the North. P.K. guessed the penalty for too much rhetoric might be the closing down of the newspaper by the Military General.

Slowly the county seemed to be recovering from the ravages of war. The physical scars seemed to heal faster than the mental ones. Most of the old plantations survived though it was now difficult to find replacements for those who in the past worked because of their servitude. Most of the slaves had headed for better promises, though some stayed on as employees. P.K. rejoiced at his decision to move back to the mountains when Alfred was sold to Mr. McGuire. He wondered how Alfred was enjoying his freedom. *Was it worth the unknown which he faced as a freed man?* Certainly in the long run it was good, but in the short term, there were many decisions a black man had to face.

KEROSENE, THE
MODERN LIGHTING

P.K. always debated the route back to the farm from Berryville. He had begun hauling the grain to the new mill in Berryville for grinding and for the sale of his surplus. While the Burwell Mill at Millwood seemed to have a better grind, Berryville was closer to the markets and if you had grain for sale you tried to fetch a higher price. While his grain was being milled, he drove back to the Main Street section of the town. He had spotted something that might catch the fancy of Mary Ann. There in the dry goods store was what he was seeking. He had heard of them but hadn't quite screwed up the courage to make the purchase. Going into the store he couldn't believe how well lit the area was. The clerk welcomed him and P.K. asked about the new lamps that were lighting the store. "Kerosine they call it although some spell it K-e-r-o-s-e-n-e. Others call it 'coal oil.' No matter how it's spelled or called it makes for a mighty fine light."

P.K. nodded, "And I hope the price on some of these lamps is something I can afford."

"Easiest purchase you will ever make. I can sell you the lamps but you have to go to Millwood to get the kerosene. Your brother Uriah hauled in a whole wagon full to the store there just last week. Guess because he lives there, Millwood got the first delivery."

P.K. grinned and armed with the money just received from the sale of his grain, he purchased three lamps. "Tell me how they work," P.K. asked.

The clerk went through the process of removing the glass globe from the lamp, unscrewing the wick mechanism from the base of the lamp, filling the lamp with a small amount of kerosene, replacing the wick holder. He then allowed a few minutes which he said was only needed when you put in a new wick. He then turned the screw on the side of the wick holder and advanced the wick up above its container. He struck a match and lit the wick. The flame flickered and the globe was replaced over the light. The wick holder had some holes around it that allowed air to be replenished as it burned the oil.

P.K. whistled, "What a fine replacement for our candles and Betty lamps. Mary Ann will be amazed. Now show me how to put it out."

The clerk turned down the wick until the light was dim. He put his hand behind the top of the glass and blew a sharp gust. The light went out. The clerk had P.K. try it and when it appeared he had mastered this new chore, the deal was completed. P.K. was instructed to stop in Millwood at Horner and Nelson's store and purchase some fuel for his new lights.

P.K. thought, *At least my choice on the route home has been chosen. Berry's Ferry is the way.*

It was near dark when P.K. turned from Mount Carmel Lane up towards his house. What a good time to arrive with the new lights, he thought. Rather than going to the back of the house as was his routine, he stopped at the front and unwrapped one of the lamps. Carefully he filled the lamp base partway with the funnel he had purchased. He then replaced the base and turned up the wick. He waited the prescribed time and scratched a match against the door frame. He carefully lit the wick and replaced the globe.

He opened the front door and into the increasing darkness he walked, carrying the lit lamp.

Mary Ann turned from cooking supper, startled by the light coming from the hall. "What on earth do you have, P.K.?" she asked.

One of those new fangled lights," he replied, "No more candles or Betty lamps."

"I've heard of them but never thought we would have one. Show me how it works, where shall we put it? How dangerous is it?" The questions came pouring out.

P.K. armed with his day old knowledge answered as best he could, telling Mary Ann he had purchased three lamps so they could be available in a number of rooms.

While all this was going on, P.K.s mother, Ann, walked into the conversation. She had a genuine fear of the new lamp, remembering the loss of her granddaughter, Louisa, many years ago when the strike anywhere match first was introduced. "Don't worry about one in my room," she said with a note of finality. "I have lived this long without them, I can die without them."

Two Faces from the Past

Without Toad to help farm, P.K. was left with young Dink. Only sixteen, he was called on to do a man's job. The next boy, Walter, was just past ten and he was the one to do the chores. Milking the cows and cutting the wood took a lot of his youthful energy. It was difficult to clear any more acres for planting without more help. Just a few days ago, someone had complained from Mount Carmel Church that some of his cows had broached the fence and were into the cemetery that was surrounded by P.K.'s land.

P.K. lifted his eyes to the heavens and implored his Maker to send him an answer.

And He did. Late one afternoon there was a gentle knock on the front door. This was a bit unusual as all mountain visitors came to the back door. Mary Ann yelled for P.K. to answer the door and as he did, he noted the shot gun as always was in the corner near the door.

Opening the door, he started to step back as a moment of fear came into him. There at the door were two of the largest young black men he had ever seen. Stories from the valley of damages done by freed blacks rushed over him as he started to back up.

"Mr. P.K., don't you recognize us? We are Jason and Joshua, sons of Alfred."

Relief washed over him as he did recognize the two boys that were a part of his life some twelve years ago. "Of course," he stammered. "Come on in. Would you like some spring water?"

"Why don't we visit out here on the porch for a bit? Joshua and I are thinking of moving to Baltimore. Everybody says, because of our size we would make good stevedores to unload the ships. He used the word 'stevedore' as if it was a brand new word."

"I can't argue with that," P.K. agreed. "You have grown up to be mighty fine looking boys. Come, sit on the porch steps and tell me what you have been doing. How are your father and mother?" .

Joshua and Jason took turns telling of the twelve years since they were sold to David McGuire. "Mr. McGuire treated us well. There was one year that our Ma was sick and Mrs. McGuire took care of her, rather than the other way around. It's been hard since we have been freed as many people don't know how to take us. Some think we want to hurt them and some think we are worthless. Our Pa still works for Mr. McGuire and lives in the old slave quarters. The other slaves have moved on."

"And what brought you to this side of the River?" P.K. wanted to know.

"Well, Mr. McGuire can't afford to pay us anything-just food and a place to stay. Joshua and I want to make something out of ourselves. To do that we figure we have to move to Baltimore. Our only problem is that we don't have the where-with-all to get there. We were hoping that maybe you might be needing some help and could pay us by getting us a stake to go to Baltimore."

Mary Ann, drawn by the conversations, had come and was standing in the door. She motioned to P.K. to come to her and they talked in muted tones for some time. P.K. could see the nervousness of Jason and Joshua as they wondered if they were doing a foolish thing.

Finally P.K. came back to the two young lads and proposed, "We, too, are a bit short of cash, but when the crops come in we should have extra, especially if we can use your help to open up some new fields. Not only that, Mrs. Royston suggests that she teach you your letters and reading skills so you can hold your own with anyone in Baltimore. Stay with us for a season and we will find you a place to sleep that is at least as comfortable as you were over in the valley."

Grins broke out on both of the dark faces. "To learn to read and to write. Now don't that beat all! We hope you are serious in your offer."

"We certainly are. Now come around to the kitchen and we will see if we can find you something to eat. You can tell us more about Alfred and Lucinda."

Mary Ann got out the griddle and stoked the fire in the stove. As it heated she sliced slabs of ham and slid them on the griddle. She then reached into a tin holding cornmeal and putting copious amounts in a bowl along with water and a small amount of wheat flour, she prepared griddle cakes. Apple butter came out next and she added a special thin gravy made of ham fat and spring water.

She motioned for the boys to sit and she dished out large quantities onto their plates. They lifted their eyes to the Heavens and said a prayer for this feast set before them. They dug in and consumed all Mary Ann had made.

"Shall I make another batch?" Mary Ann inquired.

"No Maam, I think we had better do some work before you think that all we do is eat. But we were hoping this would be the 'fixins' you made. It is what we remember best from the old days. Mrs. McGuire didn't cotton too much to the corn cakes."

As they talked, Jason told that Mr. McCormick in the land next to Mr. McGuire, was trying to divide up some of his property to sell to only black folks. They hoped that Alfred and Lucinda would be able to have a place of their own. The place would be called Josephine City and would be right alongside of Mr. McGuire's farm and surrounding a black cemetery called Milton Valley. "It sure would be nice for Pa and Ma to have a place of their own near where they work and where when the time comes they can be laid to rest."

Just then a toddler came running into the kitchen. Joshua looked at him and asked, "Is that your youngen? That's a mighty stupid question, Of course it is, who else would have babies here?"

Mary Ann nodded, "That is Robert Winter Royston and he is our youngest."

Robert was an outgoing child who appeared to be precocious. He pulled himself up on Jason's lap and asked "Why is your face so black?"

Mary Ann gave a small gasp but waited for the answer. Any word from her would not be a help.

Jason laughed and said "I wondered about that too. My Ma tells me that it is because our ancestors came from a place where the sun shines so hot we needed some help from God to keep from burning up. So he gave us dark skins."

That made perfectly good sense to Robert and he slid off Joshua's lap to search for other things to learn.

P.K.'s mother, Ann, came slowly by the kitchen and paused for just a moment. She moved on with a quizzical look on her face that seemed to reach back into her ninety years of life.

P.K. got up and followed his mother, wondering what she was thinking about.

"What are Arissa's kids doing here?" she wanted to know. "I thought they moved west."

P.K. was aware that his mother was rapidly losing her memory.

"They are not Arissa's kids and she only had one," P.K. corrected his mother.

"No, she had two. They were twins. Now I remember, the other died at birthing."

This information leapt out at P.K. *How would his mother know about Arissa's children unless she was there? Maybe the rumors of parentage were true*, he thought.

He forgot about his two guests and followed Ann into her room. It seemed like a good time to find out things. "How do you know that Arissa had twins?" P.K. queried.

"Cause my Ma was there at the birthing," Ann answered. "One was 'still born' and the other very healthy. Arissa had been the midwife for all the other babies, but she couldn't be one for her own," the words poured out of Ann's mouth. "My ma did the birthing and I helped. Pa took the baby that was 'still born' and buried it in the Anderson grave-yard. Not in the slave graveyard where it should have been buried. That's what started the rumors."

It seemed like Ann wanted to talk and he pursued other questions about his Pa and the love of the Spout Spring. "Why did Pa spend so much time at the spring?" he asked.

"That's because the spirit of the Lady lived in the Spring and she would talk to your pa," Ann talked with a finality that left no questions.

"A Lady in the Spring … that talked to Pa. How could that be? Did he tell you?"

"He never told me but he hinted. After Pa died I went over to the Spring and she talked to me. She told me things about Pa that I never knew, about how she told him he would meet me and marry me." She chuckled, "I guess I never had a chance against both your Pa and the Lady."

Ann continued, "Promise me that you will keep the Spring up after people quit using it. There's talk of these new fangled water pumps that bring the water right up to the house … maybe in it."

"It will be a long time before people quit using the spring," P.K. assured his mother, "But right now I have to get back and visit with Jason and Joshua. They are the kids of Alfred who used to be the slave family owned by the Adams," he told his mother so that she would be comfortable with new persons around. "They are going to work for us for a year or so. Then they are going to Baltimore to work."

"It won't be long before I'll be out of here myself. I get the hankering to be with your pa awful bad," Ann murmured, as if she was talking of maybe going on a trip to Berryville.

P.K. thought on that a bit and decided not to question her thinking on that subject. He moved back to the kitchen and began talking to the two brothers about what he would expect and how much he could pay. They seemed ready to go to work at once.

"You will probably have to go back to your pa's and get your clothes before you can start work," P.K. suggested.

Jason looked at Joshua and then volunteered, "Mr. P.K., we don't want to wade that river another time. We were hoping so bad that we could work here that we have a sack of clothes down by the rail fence. It will only take a minute to get it."

"Wade the river?" P.K. questioned. "November is no time to be wading the river, why not take the ferry?"

Jason hung his head, "Mr. P.K., the government says we are free and the master told us we could go, but white folk still look at us like we are in the wrong place. We try and stay away from places where we might offend someone. It's going to be a long time until we are really free."

P.K. had no answer for that.

Joshua went out to get their belongings while P.K. and Jason went out toward the barn to figure where they could sleep.

As Joshua returned, Mary Ann came out to be with them and suggested a corner of the barn that could be enclosed and turned into a bedroom for the two boys. She said, "I remember when you left us, one of you blew a kiss towards us. Do you remember that?"

The two boys bowed their head embarrassed and Jason said, "We both did. Only I hid my kiss behind my hand. So it was Joshua that you saw."

"We truly missed you and wanted to watch you grow up. It is good that you thought enough of us to want to work for us." With that she moved back toward the kitchen to begin peeling potatoes for the supper meal.

After supper P.K. and Mary Ann sat alone in the living room. "It's been quite a day," P.K. suggested. "We prayed for a solution to our 'help' problem and who would have guessed it would be Jason and Joshua who would solve it."

"Not only that but I am going to need help in the garden come spring," Mary Ann teased.

This was a signal that P.K. knew well. "Don't tell me we are going to have another baby."

"We are. I have missed my period and I have had enough children to know what that means."

"When do you think the time will be?" P.K. wanted to know.

"I figure around June some time," Mary Ann calculated.

While it seemed their off-springs were going to be more plentiful than the biblical Abraham, P.K. always looked toward another being born. "I will have to start thinking of a name if it's a boy," P.K. offered.

"Don't worry about it," Mary Ann cautioned. "Somehow I feel it's going to be a girl and your ma and I have already thought of the name. She will be Sarah Kirsten."

"Sarah Kirsten?" he questioned. "Those don't sound like family names."

"Well, the first name I picked out because I am just the opposite of Sarah in the Bible who had trouble conceiving and the second is because I told your Ma and she wanted a name of a long dead ancestor. So 'Sarah Kirsten' it will be."

"Don't know how you can tell it's going to be a girl," P.K. groused.

ANN ANDERSON ROYSTON DIES

Christmas came and went and the year 1870 dawned like a new star in the sky. The word was that Virginia would soon be back in the Union and martial law would be gone. Tensions would be eased and products would flow more easily to the North. P.K. was hoping for a good year to help him make good on his promises to Jason and Joshua.

The only dark cloud on the horizon was the failing health of his mother, Ann. She rarely moved from her bed and now she needed help being fed. P.K. could feel the final hours coming as she called him in and made sure she would be buried alongside her husband, Peter, on the knoll above the old house.

P.K. assure her it would happen and said, "We will miss you, Ma, but when it's time to go, there are others calling louder than we can."

"I will be gone in a few days so you may as well look for a warm day and get that grave dug. Maybe Peter's spirit is still at the Spring, so I might get to join him there before we make the trip to the great beyond."

P.K.'s eyes moistened as he thought of losing this monument in his life. "We will keep close to the Spring," he promised.

That night P.K. talked to Mary Ann about his mother. "She has already suggested we start digging the grave."

"She was always a practical woman. Maybe we should go down to the graveyard and pick a spot. I know where all the old graves are including little Louisa and the young girl that was killed in the shellings."

P.K. responded, "There were other parts that came from that that shelling and there is one other you don't know about, so we will have to be careful and not disturb any other graves.

"What do you mean, 'A grave I don't know about?' I know where everyone is buried."

"Not everyone," P.K. assured her. "There is one that Mathew and I buried back in '62; a Union soldier that drowned along with a lot of others trying to cross the Shenandoah."

The words came tumbling out as P.K. described the drowning and the finding of the rifle. He told of hiding it in the Wildcat Den and then he confessed he was the Mountain Marksman."

"I thought so," Mary Ann said. "You always seemed to disappear at the beginning of a set-to. And that explains the smell of cat that was on you when you came back. What other secrets are you keeping from me?"

P.K. assured her that was the only secret he had ever kept and he explained it was to keep the word from slipping out. They agreed and promised to keep this a secret of their own to their dying days.

It was on January 19, 1870 that Ann died and was laid to rest alongside her husband Peter. The body was placed in a plain pine box and carried on the back of a farm wagon. As the procession left P.K.'s farm, the mountain families seem to appear along the way growing to a mighty swell as they turned at Ashby Gap Toll Road and descended Fox Trap Hill. The two blacks followed behind and as the crowd grew they dropped back to the rear as if they might be considered interlopers.

P.K. looked back and thought of his father's burial. *It was Jo Anderson who was the black representative at that funeral.* P.K. thought of the many events that had occurred since his father died. *A war had been fought. Three of the family had lost their lives in that war. Others were scarred for life. Now an entire nation was being rebuilt with people of every culture trying to find their way in these modern but changed times. They had even built a railroad all the way to the Pacific Ocean. What a trip that would be-certainly not like that ride on the 'Tennessee' he was given when he was eighteen.*

There were a lot of words said by the minister from Mount Carmel, who was only a little bit miffed by P.K. not having the funeral at Mount Carmel. P.K. mollified him by saying this would most likely be the last buried in the family graveyard and he would see plenty of Roystons buried at Mount Carmel in the future. He took time to tell the minister that he had some help now and the fence around the graveyard would be repaired so that P.K.'s cattle would not be intruding into that sacred ground.

The weather turned nasty as if to tell the world that Ann Anderson Royston was missed. It rained for days and the Shenandoah River overflowed its banks and ruined the prospect of any farming being done that year on the bottom lands. Stories were told of the buildings floating down the river including one with a man sitting on top of it singing spirituals as it floated by. Flour mills were destroyed and the flood seemed to sound the death knell for any plans to use the river as a competitor for hauling grain instead of the railroads.

Jason and Joshua were a welcome addition to the family. Until now only the sons were available to help on the farm. Jason and Joshua would set off in the early morning and alternate between clearing new ground and plowing that which was available for planting. P.K. could always tell where they were as they sang their way through the day.

In the evenings Mary Ann would insist that they use the slate she gave them and trace their letters. She taught them how to write their names.

As they became proficient at the penmanship, the words 'Jason' and 'Joshua' became as easy to write as it was to hitch up a pair of horses. Joshua looked up from his writing chore and wondered aloud, "Are we ever going to have two names? All white folks have two names. When we get to Baltimore what will we tell them when they ask for our second name?"

Mary Ann thought for a while. Finally she answered, "You two are lucky. Most of us are stuck with the name of our parents. You get to choose any name you want. A lot of black folks take the name of their owner before they were freed. Some are taking the name of a president like Washington or Lincoln. Others take the name of their plantation."

The two young blacks looked at each other. "Why can't we do both? Our first master was an Adams and wasn't there a president named Adams. Why not take the last name of 'Adams'? 'Joshua Adams,' that sounds mighty good."

"Then 'Adams' it is. As soon as I get this new baby born we will take a trip to Berryville and you can stand up before the Clerk and get your new name legal," Mary Ann decreed.

June came and Mary Ann gave birth to a lovely baby girl. She was born with a full head of blond hair that signified the ancestry of P.K.'s mother. "Your Ma would be proud of this one. It looks like her and she helped with the naming," Mary Ann told P.K.

It was a good year for crops. After the flood, it seemed the Maker wanted to make up for the devastation brought by the earlier storms.

P.K. thought of the help given him by Joshua and Jason and wondered what he would do when they left. The agreement was that they would stay through harvesting and then move to Baltimore. The logistics of their move bothered him. *How would they get to Baltimore? Walk? Maybe a ride over to Martinsburg or Charles Town on one of the freight wagons. And then take the train to Harpers Ferry, then on to Baltimore.*

The Way to Baltimore

As he thought of the lads' problems of getting to Baltimore he watched the twin colts of the bay mare gallop around the area in front of the house. *Why, they are as frisky as Joshua and Jason,* he thought. A germ of an idea came to him. *These colts are about ready to be broken. They are from riding horse breeding and we have plenty of riding horses.*

After talking it over with Mary Ann that evening he waited until the two blacks came in from the fields. As the two washed up before supper, he asked a question in general. "I wonder if you two will have time to break those two colts from the bay mare along with your other chores."

Jason looked at Joshua and slowly acknowledged that it was possible, thinking all the while that it would cut into their book learning time. They were both beginning to look forward to that part of the day. "If you think so, Mr. P.K., we should be able to get it done."

P.K. nodded, "Good, I have some plans for those colts. They are going to be big and strong. Enough to hold any rider."

Jason looked up, "Are you thinking about racing those colts? They may be good but I don't know how fast they are."

P.K. replied, "Don't you worry about how fast they are or what I am going to do with them. You just take care of the breaking."

Every evening from then on during the next two months, both Jason and Joshua took turns working with the colts. They had experience from the McGuire Farm and it became obvious that they were skilled at the chore. The colts responded to their gentle persuasion and only once did one try to throw Joshua as he first slipped onto his back.

Well before harvest time the breaking was complete and the colts could now be considered horses and ready to be ridden at will.

It was in mid-October that P.K. assembled the family on Sunday for their weekly trip to Mount Carmel Church. It was a routine that was not to be missed. The girls went with the idea of seeing other girls and the boys went with the same idea. The church had two entrances, one for each gender. The women sat on the left and the men on the right. There was a divider down the center of the pews that separated the men from the women. Just inside the left entrance was a set of stairs leading up to the loft above the main seating area. It was open toward the altar so that those on the second tier could see and hear the sermon. This area was reserved for slaves in the earlier years though it was used rarely. Back when Arissa and her son Jo Anderson would come to church, they would sit in this area, even though they were freed. It was to this area that Joshua and Jason went as they felt more comfortable being together.

After the church meeting, P.K. and his family returned home. P.K. called them all together and began to reminisce. The children fidgeted as he went on telling of meeting Joshua and Jason's parents for the first time. He then recalled having to lose them in a slave sale. "That hurt a lot, but it is not near the hurt that I feel today as it is time to own up to my obligation and allow Jason and Joshua to take that next step in their life."

He turned to Joshua and Jason. "Now Joshua and Jason, it is time for you to leave. I have in an envelope the papers that certify that your name is Adams and there are some other papers you might find to be needing," P.K. added.

P.K.'s son Dink thought, *Pa sounds awfully officious. I wonder what is next.*

P.K. continued, "I know you have planned on leaving today and I want to make sure your feet don't get wet crossing the river this time."

Jason looked at Joshua wondering what P.K. was getting at.

P.K. looked over at Dink and in a gesture toward the barn, "You have a couple of chores to do. Now is probably the best time."

Dink disappeared and was gone about fifteen minutes. During this time, P.K. filled the time void with stories he had heard his brother Uriah tell of hauling freight to Baltimore before there was a train to Harpers Ferry.

Finally Dink came around the corner leading the two horses that were broken by Jason and Joshua. P.K. cleared his throat and said to both Jason and Joshua, "You did such a good job breaking those colts that they might as well be yours, along with the McClellan saddles."

Jason was the first to speak. "Mr. P.K., do you mean we can ride them to Baltimore? How could we get them back to you when we get there?"

P.K. responded with that twinkle in his eye, "Now that does present a problem. Maybe you should just keep them forever. They are yours. The ownership papers are in the envelope."

The two looked at him incredulously. "We don't believe it. What about the saddles? They are awfully expensive."

P.K. nodded, "They are yours, too. Actually they are McClellan saddles that were taken from the horses that were lost at the Battle over near Mount Carmel. They were fighting for your freedom as much as their riders were. My only problem is that I don't know how I can replace you."

Jason looked at Joshua and then volunteered, "Mr. P.K., we have another brother, as well you know. He might be interested in working for you. The only problem is he has taken a 'missus' and we are sure they would want to stay together."

"You must be talking about Jacob," P.K. remembered. "It's hard to realize you boys old enough to be married."

"Jacob, it is," Joshua agreed "and his missus is Ella. If you are interested we are sure you can find him over at Berryville near the McGuire place."

It was early the next morning when Jason and Joshua saddled their horses, packed their belongings, accepted the cash from P.K., made sure they had their envelope that showed ownership of the horses, and started to make their way down the hill to Mount Carmel Lane that fronted the property. As they neared the bottom, they looked to the left and the right, then turned left on a route that would take them to Shepherd's Ford. As they did, in unison both turned and blew a kiss to the family that was assembled to see them go.

P.K. snorted, pulled out his colored handkerchief, blew his nose and announced, "Doesn't anyone have anything to do around here? Winter is coming and there are chores to do."

Jacob and Ellie Come to Live

Later that evening P.K. talked it over with Mary Ann and found her more than lukewarm about having a helper in the house. "With Toad gone and Dink about ready to go, we have room for them to stay in the house. Years ago that wouldn't have been allowable, but now it should not be a problem."

"The only problem would have to come from outside our family and I think we can handle that," P.K. said in a somewhat stern voice. "I will go to Berryville in a week or so and see if I can find Jacob."

Early in the morning about ten days later, P.K. saddled the bay and rode toward the river. The weather was mild and Shepherd's Ford seemed to be the easiest way to cross. *In a few months this crossing would be by ferry,* P.K. thought as the fall rains and cold weather would make it nigh impossible to ford the river.

He turned the horse toward Berryville following the Springsbury Lane. As he did he thought of his father taking this same road as he headed to Anderson's Crossing to court P.K.s mother. He would be about the same age as Toad, maybe a few years older.

Coming into Berryville from the east end he began to inquire about Jacob. Berryville was not a large town but finding someone who was recently a slave and who may not have a permanent residence might be a bit difficult.

"Why don't you go out to a new colored town on the edge of Berryville?" someone suggested. "They may know where to find him. I remember the family that belonged to the McGuires."

P.K. turned south at the road leading toward Millwood and found his way to a lane that had a small sign saying welcome to Josephine City. While he had spent considerable time around Berryville, he was unaware that a new community was truly in existence. He turned the horse toward the east along the lane that advertised Josephine City but as he remembered was also the back way into the McGuire place. He wondered why it was called "Josephine City."

As he rode he began to see smatterings of houses that were built or being built. *This must be the place where McCormick is trying to divide up for the colored,* he thought. Just before he reached the Milton Valley Cemetery area there was an open field and he could see some men harvesting potatoes. It appeared to be a communal garden and he reined in his horse and watched them as they worked.

Finally one looked up and seeing P.K. nudged another and in a few moments all looked at him with some bewilderment. "It is unusual to see a white man here if he is not going between the town and Mr. McGuire's," one ventured.

"I am here looking for a particular colored man," P.K. answered.

"And why would you be looking for a black man?" questioned one in a defensive tone.

"No reason other than to offer him a job, if I can find him," P.K. responded. "I knew him before he was at the McGuire place."

"There were a number of black men at the McGuire place. Did he have a name? I hope it isn't Alfred 'cause we just buried him and his missus a short time ago. They caught the consumption. They are over there in the southwest corner of Milton Valley."

P.K. felt a wave of nostalgia sweep over him as he remembered Alfred and Lucinda. *Why didn't he come and find them after the war?* he thought.

Aloud he answered, "It isn't Alfred I am looking for, but his son Jacob."

"Jacob is pretty easy to find. He is doing day-by-day work mostly over at the McGuire's. He and his missus are staying at the corner house just where the road ends at the McGuire farm. The missus should be there now. Maybe Jacob will be coming home for dinner in a little while.

P.K. thanked them and headed further down the lane, finally reaching the last house. It was a small house with a clothes line full of washing blowing in the fall breeze. A colored woman was unpinning clothes from the line as he rode up. Hearing him, she stopped her work and turned toward P.K. as he sat on his horse, "Could I be of some help to you?" she asked.

"Might your name be Ellie?" P.K. wanted to know.

"Yes, it is but I don't know who you are," she said in a questioning voice.

"I am P.K. Royston and I knew your husband Jacob before he was at the McGuire place."

"Mr. P.K., Jacob has talked of you often. I know who you are. Joshua and Jason were by here last week as they headed for Baltimore. They were just in time to help bury their mother and father. They said you might be coming by."

"I would like to talk to you and Jacob about a permanent job over in the mountains at my farm. I need a hand to help with the farming and my wife Mary Ann could use full time help around the house and in the garden. We have small children as well as some who have already left home."

"Jacob will be home for dinner shortly. I saw his eyes light up when his brothers mentioned you might have a job. Real jobs are hard to come by, you know."

"The problem is that money is hard to come by since the war." P.K. explained. "About the only people who will loan you anything are the fertilizer people and they want a pretty good interest for their loan. A lot of small farmers have lost their lands when the crops weren't good enough to pay off the fertilizer lien. It won't be long before the Patapsco Guano Company will be the biggest landowner in the county." P.K. wasn't sure why he was talking economics with a person he had just met, but she seemed to understand the situation.

"I will wait until Jacob comes for dinner and the three of us can discuss what I have to offer. Meanwhile I will open the McGuire gate and let the bay forage a bit until Jacob gets here."

It wasn't long before a young black man came walking towards him from the McGuire barn. P.K. introduced himself and once he started talking to Jacob, he remembered him as a boy some thirteen years before. Jacob's wife Ellie came out of the house and P.K. told them both of his needs. "I can't pay a lot, but I will be as fair as I can and I will guarantee work for a year. We then will continue on if you are willing and if the farm produces enough to support us all."

They agreed on an amount and P.K set a time to bring an empty wagon to pick up their belongings. It appeared they could be put into one wagon.

"By the way," P.K. asked, "Do you know where the name Josephine City comes from?"

"Why, it comes from the first black lady who bought two lots just over there on the other side of the lane. Her name is Josephine Williams. She used to be a slave like us. Mrs. Ellen McCormick sold her the lots."

As they concluded their talk, P.K. said "I will cut across the lower end of the McGuire farm past the sinkhole to catch the Springsbury Lane. That way I don't have to go back into Berryville. I will get back to the farm before dark and Mary Ann can get news that you will be coming."

P.K. forded the river at Shepherd's Ford and made his way up the steep hill that headed past the Lloyd farm. He was thinking that the wagon trip would be easier coming across Berry's Ferry. The pull up Fox Trap Hill was steep but not nearly as steep as the one that would have to be negotiated if he came across at Castleman's Ferry. He turned into the lane running up to his house just before dark and was welcomed by Mary Ann. "They will be coming to work for us," he told her.

'That is good, because I am going to need some extra help in the garden come summer," she confided.

"Help in the garden!" P.K. exclaimed. "Does that mean what I think it means?"

"That's the only thing it can mean. I am pregnant again and there will be another mouth to feed. This makes thirteen."

There was a fall chill in the air and the crops were all harvested and either sold or in the barn. Butchering time was coming up and P.K., as always, enlisted the neighbors to help with this two or three day chore. He, in turn, paid them back when it came time on the neighbors' farm. P.K. looked down toward Mount Carmel Lane and saw the unmistakable bulk of his son Toad riding toward him. Normally Toad sat very erect as he rode but this time he was hunched in the saddle like he was protecting something. As he neared the house, P.K. could hear the unmistakable murmuring of a baby. Toad had a baby with him!

He called Mary Ann and bounded off the steps to get a good look at this new addition to the family. Toad proudly showed off his new son. "His name is Luther Lee and he is going to be a big one. He was born on the 16th of this month," Toad bragged.

"What a Thanksgiving present! I knew Ellen was with child but didn't know it was coming so soon," Mary Ann said "And here I am with a babe in arms myself."

"Ma," Toad said, "You make such beautiful babies, I hope you never stop."

"Aw go on, son," you're saying that just to make me blush," Mary Ann responded happily.

JASON AND JOSHUA ARE HEROES

It was not unusual to have company on Sundays. Some of the children would make a day of going to Mount Carmel Church by combining it with a visit to see P.K. and Mary Ann. It was, however, unusual to have visitors during the week. P.K. had just finished cleaning up in preparation for dinner when he heard a familiar voice. Son Dink came into the back door of the house but he didn't seem to be his usual affable person.

"Pa," he said, "I brought you yesterday's edition of the Baltimore Sun. I picked it up over at Charles Town this morning."

"And why should I be interested in the Baltimore Sun?" P.K. inquired.

Dink tossed it over with the front page up and the headline glared at him, "Two longshoremen killed trying to save another."

The fact that Dink had rode all the way from Berryville with a newspaper told him what he feared. The two who were killed were Jason and Joshua.

P.K. sat down and deliberately began to read the newspaper report. The report was methodical. The crew was loading a ship with grain. They were using a new gantry crane that had been untested. The load became unbalanced and the sacks of grain began to spill. There was a new Irish longshoreman under the crane. Both Joshua and Jason acted as one and ran under the crane throwing the Irishman to safety. The rest of the load collapsed on them and they were both killed. The article went on to say that they would be buried in Clarke County, Virginia with the coffins being brought by train to Charles Town three days from the date of the newspaper.

It seemed to be the heaviest burden ever placed on P.K. He had lost children of his own. He had watched his relatives die. He had seen the futility of war. Nothing prepared him for this.

Finally he stood up and announced to no one in particular. "I will meet the train and escort it to where they will be buried. I will help bury them."

Mary Ann turned to P.K. and said, "First you have to tell Jacob and Ellie. They think so much of those two brothers and will mourn them so."

P.K. called out to Jacob who was in the back yard, "Uncle Jacob, come here we need to talk to you."

Jacob came into the kitchen with a quizzical look on his face. "Why are you calling me in such a serious tone? Have I done something wrong?"

"No," P.K. replied, "Look at this newspaper."

"Mr. P.K., you know I can read some but there's a whole lot of writing there that is beyond me. Could you read it to me?"

P.K. hesitated and picked up the newspaper article and slowly read it to Jacob stopping a number of times to clear his throat. As he finished he could see the tears flowing from Jacob's eyes and those of Ellie who had come into the kitchen and stood behind Jacob.

"It ain't right, Mr. P.K. It just ain't right. No one should have to die like that."

Jacob then braced his shoulders and said, "Could Ellie and me borrow a rig to drive to Josephine City? We will want to be with our family at this time."

P.K. answered, "Mary Ann and I are going to the funeral and be available to help. If you need to go early there is the one horse carriage. If you want to ride with us we will take the two horse one. We will be there in plenty of time as we expect to meet the train in Charles Town."

Jacob thought for a moment and decided that all could go together in the two horse carriage.

Two days later, P.K. and Mary Ann hitched up the carriage.

"If we take the carriage, we won't be able to help carry the bodies from the train station to Milton Valley cemetery," P.K. said.

"That is true, but I believe you will find a lot of people wanting to be the ones to help carry them."

"You are right," P.K. agreed. He hitched the horses to the carriage. *It wouldn't be fair to have Mary Ann ride all the way to Charles Town in a freight wagon with no springs, anyway,* he thought.

Jacob and Ellie came out and started to sit in the forward seat and as they did, Jacob reached for the reins. P.K. pulled them from his hands and said, "Today you and Aunt Ellie ride in the back seat. I will do the driving."

Jacob protested, "It ain't proper for a white man to be driving a colored man. What will the other white folks think?"

P.K. shrugged, "By now you should know how I feel about the thoughts of others, especially when they don't understand the situation. It will be my honor to be your driver as we go to say goodbye to your brothers."

Jacob continued to protest, "You could get some black folks in a whole lot of trouble. There are many who blame us for everything they lost in the war."

"Let me take care of that," P.K. insisted. We mountain folks are used to being looked down on also. It takes a small man who needs to look down on people, but a giant is one who looks up to others."

Jacob and Ellie moved to the rear seat. "I sure hope you know what you are doing. I guess it helps that you are as big as you are."

Some six hours later the carriage pulled into Charles Town, just ahead of the train coming from Harpers Ferry. As the train snorted to a halt, P.K. could see a lot of commotion in and around the train. On an unenclosed car he could see the pine boxes of the two. Out of the passenger compartment came six of the most muscular persons P.K. had ever seen. On cue a black man drove a wagon alongside and the six men lifted the pine boxes from the freight car onto the wagon.

At the same time the next car was opened and two horses were led out and tied behind the wagon serving as a caisson. P.K. lowered his head to hide his feelings. The two horses were the ones he had given Jason and Joshua when they left the farm on the way to Baltimore.

The wagon turned and started toward Berryville. A second carriage sufficiently large to hold the six white persons who had unloaded the coffins from the train reined directly behind the coffins. P.K., Mary Ann, Jacob and Ellie were next in line with perhaps another ten carriages behind them.

As they drove, P.K. conjectured as to the identity of the six persons who seemed to be acting as pallbearers. Mary Ann said, "It is obvious. They are longshoremen and they are taking care of their own."

As they passed farms and homes near the highway, people came to stand and watch. Many had tears flowing down their cheeks. Two persons they had never heard of a few days before now became very important to their lives.

It was almost dark when the procession reached Berryville. It passed across the main section and went to Josephine Lane. There it turned left and in a short time stopped at the entrance to Milton Valley Cemetery.

A large contingent of local blacks and some whites greeted the group and escorted them toward two freshly dug graves. The stevedores jumped out of the carriage and lifted the two coffins, setting them near the graves. Torches were lit and an unusual nighttime burial service began. No one seemed to want it to end. Finally each of the stevedores took turns in describing the abilities of these two men who were taken from them so quickly. Each told of the pride that Joshua and Jason had in being the best stevedores who ever lived.

One said between sobs, "I would give my life if I could bring them back."

Finally it was over. Son Dink proposed that P.K. and Mary Ann spend the night with him as the ferry would be stopped by the time they would get there. "Uncle Jacob and Aunt Ellie will get a chance to visit with their family before you go back across the river."

P.K. agreed. The river was running a bit high and it would not be safe to ford it, especially at night. *It is good that son Walter decided to stay home. At least the cows are getting milked,* he thought. The stevedores were taken back to Charles Town where they spent the night awaiting the next train that would take them to Harpers Ferry, then on to Baltimore.

The next morning, P.K. and Mary Ann were just getting into their carriage to start their trip back across the river by way of Berry's Ferry. Two black persons rode up with the two horses that had belonged to Joshua and Jason. "We understand that these horses were given to Jason and Joshua by you. It is only right that you have them back."

P.K. looked at Mary Ann who shook her head. P.K. went to her and after a few words, he came back and said, "These horses belong to Josephine City. Why not have them available for anyone who needs a horse to ride on a chore. They can bring them back and the next one can use them. Of course someone will have to take care of them, but they are yours."

The two nodded in agreement. "Lots of times someone needs a horse if the distance is too far to walk. This will really help out." With that they wheeled the horses around and headed back to Josephine City.

P.K., Mary Ann, Jacob and Ellie made their way back to Berry's Ferry, stopping in Millwood to get some kerosene for the lights. By now kerosene lamps were considered a necessity and it was very unusual to see any candles lit. After crossing the river, they made a visit at the cemetery near the old home. P.K. seemed pensive as he saw the ease in which life could be taken from someone. After a visit at all the graves, Jacob picked up the reins and P.K. and Mary Ann returned to their usual seat in the carriage. He gave a chuck to the reins and the horses began their assent up Fox Trap Hill and out Mount Carmel Lane. It seemed like they had been gone forever.

THE CENTENNIAL YEAR
AND WITH IT MEMORIES

P.K. looked forward to the weekly Clarke Courier. The year was 1876. It was now a hundred years since the United States declared their independence from England. P.K. did some math. He had been alive for more than half of the country's life. The Clarke Courier was writing about a gift from France that would be called "The Statue of Liberty." It would be installed on a small island at the entrance to the New York Harbor. *Why New York?* he wondered. *Why not in the Potomac near Washington?* More reading and the reason for the selection of New York harbor became evident. It was to be a welcome for the immigrants arriving by boat and most of them came through New York Harbor. Another article noted that Colorado wanted statehood in 1876 so that it could be called the "Centennial State." P.K. sighed. He was now fifty seven. His chances for adventure were over. At times he had wondered about his life if he had traveled to the West when he was young. He saw many crossing the Shenandoah at the ferry who were headed west. At times he hankered to be with them. Of course that was before he met Mary Ann and the wanderlust subsided. He chuckled, *adventure*, he had plenty of it when the sound of saber rattling and caissons being pulled up Fox Trap Hill were a daily fare. Maybe a trip to the wildcat den was what he needed to help him recall his life when fear was a daily factor.

P.K. went out on the front porch and called back to Mary Ann, "I'll be back in an hour or so. I need to do a little visiting." A call of acknowledgement came from Mary Ann and he swung down off the porch and headed toward the pond and then along the familiar route toward the wildcat den.

He paused as he crossed the Ashby Gap Toll Road and looked east toward the top of the mountain, then turning toward the west he surveyed the beauty of the Shenandoah Valley. *What more could a man want?* he thought. He continued South over the hill to Prospect Creek and made his way to the outcropping of rocks only he knew was the location of the wildcat den. He dropped down through the mass of leaves and found the hidden entrance. He snaked his way inside and lit a small torch he had brought with him. The mustiness and smell of cat was evident though there was no sign of any recent wildcat activity. It was obvious that the cats had retreated to a more secluded area. He reached for the rifle still on the rock shelf above the entrance. He caressed the stock and sighted along the barrel. A wave of nostalgia came over him and he was embarrassed. *How could anyone be nostalgic about a time when lives were in daily peril?* he thought.

Laying the rifle back along the stone shelf, he worked his way out of the cave and rearranged the pile of leaves so as to disguise any activity there. He thought for a moment and instead of heading directly home, he began walking down the road toward the Spout Spring and the old home place. The spring was easy to get to as his daughter, Fanny, and her husband, Hubert, used it daily as their source of water. He went and stood near the white oaks that were the resting spot for his father when he made his visits to the spring some thirty years ago. He wondered if it was true that the spirits of his father, mother and niece were still around the spring. *And what about the lady whose spirit was supposed to live in the spring?* He said aloud, "Pa, Ma, are you still about? Can you hear me? I long to hear your voices." He stopped and listened.

All of a sudden he was startled by a man's voice. "P.K., are you talking to yourself? I don't see anyone else around."

He turned around and recognized his son-in-law, Hubert. Blushing, P.K. answered, "I was talking to myself."

"The spring area looks good," he said changing the subject, "Pa and Ma would be proud of it. I was just out for a walk. Thought I would visit the graveyard. Stopped to get a cold drink of water on the way," he said by way of explanation.

He waited while Hubert filled the buckets and helped carry one back to the house where he grew up. After a few minutes visit he crossed the creek again and made his way up to the graveyard. He looked for the small slate stones signifying the locations of the graves. His niece, Louisa, his father and mother and the union soldier were now marked. There were two other slate stones where the remains of the parts of soldiers and the unidentified young girl were buried after the house was shelled during the war. He remained a short while and then turned toward home using a log road that ran from the toll road to a field near his house.

He entered the house and Mary Ann greeted him with a hug and a remark about the smell of cats. He admitted to his visit down memory lane, all brought on by the reading of the Clarke Courier.

A rider picked his way up the hill after leaving Mt. Carmel Lane. P.K. walked out on the porch and awaited his arrival as it was apparent it was the first trip for the rider. "You are P.K. Royston?" he queried.

"I am," said P.K. "And how may I serve you?"

"I was asked to ride over and tell you that your brother Joseph has died. He will be buried at Thumb Run Baptist Church in Fauquier County."

"I guess the consumption finally got him. I kept telling him to get out of that cobbler's shop in Paris and use up some of that God given air doing some farming."

P.K. let his mind wander back to the days of his youth when Joseph and Dr. Payne collaborated to introduce him to Mary Ann. He turned toward the house and called for Mary Ann. As she came through the door he told her of his brother's death and left it to her to get the details. He went back into the house and sat at the kitchen table. His thoughts rolled back over the past. Joseph lived a good part of the nineteenth century and saw all of the Civil War that seemed to concentrate its being in the Paris area. He had mourned the loss of his son Lewis who had followed him into the shoemaking trade only to die as a private in the Confederacy from pneumonia in 1862. He had been only twenty two.

P.K.'s Son Buck Marries

P.K.'s son, Walter had picked up the nickname "Buckaroo" when he was young. Someone had given him a rocking horse and it was his constant companion. The name "Buckaroo" was a natural. As he grew older it became shortened to "Buck" and that would last him a lifetime. By 1885 he was courting Virginia Smallwood whose family lived just up the toll road. He came in to talk to P.K. and Mary Ann and it was obvious that he wanted to marry but didn't want to stray far from home. P.K. was now going on sixty six years old and the thought of losing Buck wasn't to his liking. After some consulting with Mary Ann, P.K. proposed that Buck marry his choice of bride and come to live on the home place.

"None of the other children are interested in living here so why not come and farm here. When Mary Ann and I are gone, the place will be yours."

While the idea appealed to Buck, he thought it best to talk it over with his bride-to-be before accepting the offer.

He saddled his horse and rode up toward the Smallwood farm. He turned left as he reached the toll road and rode past a giant outcropping of rock that had determined the route of the toll road for many years. The first road on the left was into the Smallwood farm. He crossed Passage Branch and worked his way to the house that sat some three hundred yards off the toll road. Just as he reached the gate going into the yard, Virginia's brother came out and opened the gate so that he could ride in.

"How are you today, Will?" he asked the brother who was just a few years younger than he.

Will Smallwood looked at him and answered, "I'm fine. I am just home for a short visit while my wife Mary visits her folks out at Morgan's Mill. Married life is great. Why don't you give it a try?" he teased.

Buck replied, "I'm trying. If you'll get out of the way, I might make more progress."

Will Smallwood reached up and held the reins while Buck dismounted from the horse. "Go on in and see Virginia. I'll see to your horse."

Buck walked to the back door and knocked. "Come on in, Will," said a voice from within. "Why are you knocking?"

"Because I am not Will; I am Buck Royston."

The voice let out a shriek and the slamming of a bedroom door could be heard. Virginia's mother came out and with an accusing tone said, "Why did you try and walk into the house when Virginia was in the living room half-naked.?"

The thought of his bride-to-be not fully dressed stirred the blood, but he stammered, "I did knock. She must have thought I was her brother Will."

"You younger generation. You have no morals at all. You need a Baptist's faith. You Methodists are way too liberal."

"Sarah Margaret," came the sound of Virginia's father. "Leave the boy alone. I'm sure he meant no harm."

In a few minutes Virginia came into the living room still wearing a blush from her mistaking Buck for her brother.

"I am sorry that I frightened you," Buck apologized. "Maybe I should have called out."

"No, it was my fault. I just wasn't expecting you."

"I came to talk to you about where we can live after we are married. My father says he would like to have us live at his place and we can have it after they are gone."

Virginia shook her head, "I'm not so sure that is a good idea. Two women in the same house can make for a lot of problems."

"I think we can make it work," Buck assured her. "Ma is easy to get along with."

"You may be right. I just don't know her too well."

"You would know her better if she were a Baptist," called Virginia's mother from the kitchen. "Your brother, Will, went out and found a good Baptist girl to marry."

"Ma, don't be such an old fence post. The Methodist church is only a short distance away. We have to ride all day to get to the Baptist church past Frogtown. Maybe we should give the Methodists a try."

"You be what you want to be," said her mother. "I know which is the right one for me and my family."

Virginia turned to Buck and said softly, "That settles it. Your Ma can't be any harder to live with than mine is. Tell them we accept."

"Maybe we should set a date to get married right now," Buck implored.

"I think sometime in February would be fine. Now we will let the folks decide which church will be the one that will do the marrying."

Buck headed back home and reported to P.K. and Mary Ann the gist of his conversations with Virginia.

P.K. thought for a while and finally said, "It seems to me that Mount Carmel would be the logical place for the wedding. It is a lot closer than the Mountain Baptist Church. The marriage is between two people not two churches. I will go up and talk to Virginia's father and see if we can make a decision. There are no church meetings in the winter time at Carmel because it is hard to heat, but I'm sure we can figure out a way to have a wedding there. Maybe if there is no heat, the preacher won't talk too long. Likely we can get the Baptist minister to come and preside at the wedding. That might make Virginia's mother happier."

And so it was on February 20, 1885, Buck and Virginia were married. P.K. and Mary Ann gave up the large bedroom and moved to one as far from that one as possible. They figured the newlyweds would need as much privacy as possible. Virginia had a persistent cough that told of her where-abouts in the house. She was a gentle person and Mary Ann found it easy to allow her to play the leading role in the house. Mary Ann still had children of her own who lived in the house and who needed to grow to adults. Discipline was a problem at times but all seemed to get along.

Ellie and Jacob, the black couple, who lived in the house for so many years, had one child of their own and they named him Peter, adding his last name as Royston. He had grown up helping around the farm and finally moved to Berryville, renting a home in Josephine City. As P.K.'s house started to fill with the next generation it was apparent that Aunt Ellie and Uncle Jake, as they were known to the kids, were showing signs of anxiety and wanted to move back across the river. Their son offered them a place to stay and the move was made.

As they prepared to leave, memories broke over the children. They had used Aunt Eillie as a shield when the threat of a whipping came. They would hide in her skirts and refuse to come out. The sight of only the eyes looking out from the folds of the skirt were enough to soften the threats that came from the parents.

It was on April 21 that the word came that P.K.'s brother Uriah had died. He was buried at Cunningham Chapel near Briggs Station. P.K. thought of his oldest brother and the impact he had on the community around Millwood. He and his son were both freight haulers and during the Civil War provided contact with the railroad. They crossed the enemy lines so many times some wondered if they were Yanks or Rebs.

Once in a while someone would venture to ask if they took the loyalty oath which was a normal part of an easy passage between the two lines. Uriah would grin that mischievous grin and reply. "I am a freight hauler. If it takes a loyalty oath to the devil himself to get my freight through, then it's to the devil I'm loyal. Meanwhile enjoy your salt and sugar. Otherwise it will be a long war without the essentials."

Buck and Virginia's first children were twins born on November 25, 1885. Only the girl survived. They named the boy "Marcus D." and buried him at Mount Carmel Church. The cough that had become a part of Virginia seemed to increase with the birth of her first born.

A Rider Out of the
Past

It was in the spring of 1889 when P.K. looked out to see a rider canter along Mount Carmel Lane. He stopped at the entrance to P.K.'s farm and appeared to be hesitant in his next move. Finally he rode the horse alongside the gate latch and lifting it, opened the gate enough to ride through. He rode erect as would a cavalryman and made a striking figure as he came to the house.

As he neared the front porch, he reined in and P.K. greeted him. "You appear to be a stranger in these parts. Is there something we can do for you?"

The rider stayed on his horse as if unsure of his next move. Finally he sat up even more erect and said, "I am looking for the man who was known as the Mountain Marksman back during the rebellion."

The accent and the use of the word "rebellion" told P.K that this man was from a part of the country well north of the Mason Dixon Line. "What makes you think we would know about that person? He could have been anyone of a hundred or so men who are a part of these mountains. And why are you looking for him?"

"Sir, I am James Upton and I came to thank him for my life," was the reply.

"You are such a young fellow and there is no way you could have been around during the War of Secession. How could he possibly be responsible for you being alive?"

"Sir, since I have studied the identity of the Mountain Marksman very carefully and since they tell me you are P.K. Royston, I am sure you are the Mountain Marksman."

P.K. hadn't thought of his role for quite a time and thoughts of the past went through his head. "If you are so sure of who I am, so be it, but that still doesn't tell me who you are and how this could possibly affect your life."

"I am the son of Captain Thomas Upton, late of the Army of the United States. It was he whose cap was shot off by the Mountain Marksman back during the Rebellion. He has told me the story so many times I can repeat it verbatim."

"I still don't understand how that event could be responsible for your life," P.K snorted.

"My father said you could have easily killed him but you spared his life. Had you not, I would not have been born. Therefore I owe you my life."

P.K. warmed to this very direct person who was still seated in his saddle. "Why don't you get down off that horse and rest a while? Seems like we have some 'getting to know each other' to do."

Upton dismounted and as he did, P.K. glanced back through the front door and saw the shadows of Mary Ann and his daughter Sarah near the door hearing every word.

"Ma and Sarah," he called out, "Step outside and meet this young Yankee who has come to visit."

Both ventured out onto the porch and Mary Ann stepped forward. She held out her hand to be shaken. Making conversation, she said, "I do remember your pa. And we did meet during some trying times. Since it is obvious he survived the war, is his health good?"

"It is not so good. Some of the travails of the war have caused him to suffer from bouts of influenza and consumption. It is because of his health that I am here as he was unable to come and thank you himself."

The young Upton continued, "My father said he grew up a whole lot that day when his cap was shot off. To that point the war had seemed more of a game than a place where men could get killed. I don't think he enjoyed his life in the cavalry much after that."

At that moment P.K remembered his manners and introduced Upton to Sarah. Sarah was a beautiful young lady. Her blond hair was a throwback to her Grandmother's ancestry. Immediately there was a spark in both of their eyes that said the conversation of a war long past was of little consequence. Sarah curtsied and said, "I am pleasured to make your acquaintance, sir." She then moved back and let the parents visit with this young person who had intruded into their life.

The conversation of the past continued and finally Mary Ann excused herself and said, "I must get supper. I am sure you will stay and eat with us."

"If you will have me. I have not eaten from a table in many a day and it is very thoughtful of you," James Upton replied.

At supper all the family was introduced to the man from the North. Whether by design or accident, he ended up sitting by Sarah. She blushed easily as he held the chair out for her. P.K. noticed and thought, *that's probably the first time that has happened to her.*

The brothers and sisters noticed and their table manners visibly improved.

After supper as darkness drew on, Upton asked, "I will be heading back north soon but could I camp down near your spring for the night? I have a tent that I can pitch to take away the chill and the nearby water will allow me to do some cooking."

"You are certainly welcome to do as you asked, but we will insist that you come and eat with us. You can stay as long as you like."

The one night turned into another and then another. The Northern visitor and Sarah would meet on the front porch and the laughter coming from Sarah told everyone she fully enjoyed the moment.

SARAH AND THE YANKEE
ELOPE

The days stretched into a week and then into two. Finally one morning P.K. walked out onto the front porch and the tent was gone. The ground around it was cleaned up and it looked as if no one had ever been there. P.K. remembered the conversation of last evening and as he thought of it now it sounded like James Upton was getting ready to say goodbye.

He turned back into the house and called to Mary Ann, "It appears that our visitor is gone, I'll wager that Sarah will be sorry."

Mary Ann said "I just came from Sarah's room and she is not there. There is an envelope and a note. I am afraid to open it."

P.K. took the envelope from her and slowly opened it as if he knew what he would find.

It read,

Dear Ma and Pa. I know you will be surprised when you find this. I had no other way of telling you. James and I are going to be married. I was afraid you would try and talk me out of it but it would be of no use. I love him dearly. We will be married in Hagerstown before the day is out and I will go and live with him out West. We are going to the Oklahoma Terri-

tory. I hope I haven't made you too angry. I love you both, Sarah Kirsten Royston. P.S. I will write.

"Those Yankees," Mary Ann cried. "They are not satisfied taking our land and our goods, now they are taking my daughter and she is so young."

P.K. answered in a measured tone. "Don't let our loss take away from their happiness. I guess we should have seen it coming. They didn't exactly avoid each other. And about 'sixteen,' I remember another lady who was married about that age and her marriage seemed to last."

Mary Ann blushed, "But we were different. I was much older at that age."

"Maybe so but we can only hope they are truly in love. If that is true, age makes no difference," P.K. reminded her.

They turned to go back into the house. It was time for breakfast and there were others who needed to hear this story.

Mary Ann waited for a letter to come. Every time P.K. went near Berry's Ferry, Mary Ann's first question upon his return was, "Is there any mail?"

Finally in late May, P.K. handed over an envelope that looked like it had traveled a long distance. Mary Ann's heart jumped when she saw the familiar handwriting of her daughter. She had waited for what had seemed an eternity but now she seemed reticent to open it. *What would it say? Was she all right?* The thoughts ran through her head.

P.K. finally pulled the letter from her grasp and carefully unsealed it. He pulled out two pages of small handwriting. "Do you want me to read it to you? Are you afraid of what it might say?" P.K. questioned.

Mary Ann nodded but answered, "Yes I am afraid but give it to me and I will go and read it in the bedroom where I can react in private."

After a while P.K. could stand it no longer. He went in the bedroom and sat beside Mary Ann on the bed. "Well?" he said.

"They are all right. Here, read it for yourself."

P.K. slowly read the letter:

Dear Ma and Pa

It seems so long since I left but it has been less than three months. So much has happened. We were married in Hagerstown and took the first train west toward Ohio. As we neared Arkansas, there were a lot of people aboard who were doing just what we were doing, looking for free land. The government set it up where all of the people in Oklahoma Territory were supposed to leave the land before the appointed hour. Then at a set signal everyone could rush in and claim whatever land they wanted. The railroad already crosses Oklahoma Territory as it goes all the way to Texas. We ended up in Arkansas City, Kansas and waited for the time they let us go look for land. James has some friends that he wanted to partner with and all of us waited until the bugle blew and for the train to start toward a place called Guthrie. They had spent some time in the territory beforehand and knew where they wanted to put down stakes. They made a lot of plans as who would file the claims and who would stay behind to protect the stakes they put down.

Ma, Pa, you have never seen so many people in your life crowded into that train. There were only a few seats and those were taken before you could say 'jack rabbit.' One of James' friends made a deal with the railroad man to stop the train at an appointed place and we got off before the rest of them. Some joined us as they thought we were near the place called Guthrie. They tried to get back on when they discovered we were no where near where they wanted to be. Why anyone would come all this way and end up in another city beats me. But they did. Somebody said there must have been 10,000 people who ended up in Guthrie in one day. We got this word from people who were unhappy with their decision to go west and they turned around and went back east.

We were lucky. There were a lot of people who had hidden in the hills before they were supposed to and never left. They got there sooner than anyone else and that is the name they are being called. If somebody has a good piece of property they are asked if they are 'sooners.'

We set up tents on our property and James went over to the land office to make it legal. He stood in line for what he said was forever, but he finally got it all legal. We have one section of land but there is nothing on it except a few wind blown trees. We will be digging a well as soon as we can get a dowser to bring his divining rod. We sure don't want to have to dig twice. The dowser charges a lot but everyone swears by him. Meanwhile we are getting our water from a small stream a few hundred yards away. It's awful muddy but if you let it settle for a few hours, it is all right. What I wouldn't give for our spring and pond.

All in all, I am happy and James is such a fine man. We have an address you can use to write to me if you want to. Make sure you prepay the stamps as they won't deliver it otherwise, Love, Sarah Kirsten Upton, she signed her full name.

The Cost of Giving Birth

Buck and Virginia were looking to the fall and the birth of their next baby. One after another followed until by fall 1895, they had seven children with six surviving birth. After every birth Virginia became weaker and weaker. The cough that started out as gentle was now deep and brought her to a halt as it became more uncontrollable. She stayed mostly in bed and Mary Ann took care of the raising of the children.

The doctor came for his last visit. He talked to the family and gave his diagnosis, "tuberculosis." It's very advanced and there is little that medicine will do.

After the doctor left, Mary Ann went into the bedroom to visit with Virginia. "What did the doctor say?" Virginia asked between coughs.

Mary Ann looked at this daughter-in-law and tried to choose the right words.

Before she could get them out, Virginia said, "It is not good, is it. Am I dying?"

Mary Ann nodded. How can you tell one who is only twenty eight that she has only a short time to live?

Virginia seemed to accept the inevitable. "My only fear is the raising of the children. I know that Buck will not be able to do it alone."

Mary Ann tried to assure her, "As long as I live, I will take care of them. You don't have to worry about that. I've raised a few of my own," she continued.

Virginia mustered a smile. "I guess seventeen would constitute a 'few'."

By late July the heat and oppressive humidity took their toll and Virginia died on the twentieth of July. She was laid to rest near her first born at Mount Carmel Cemetery.

At the end of the ceremony, one of Buck's brothers, Winter Royston, slipped along side of Buck and began talking in earnest. After an animated conversation, Buck came over to Mary Ann and said "Ma, Winter would like to take the two oldest kids to live with him for a while. That will make it easier on you."

"What ever you say is what will be done," she replied in a hurt voice. "I did promise Virginia that I would take care of all of them. And besides, the two oldest are old enough to help around the house."

Buck nodded but said, "Both will be able to go to school. Winter is real educated himself and he can make sure they get an education. Maybe they can come back when we get a school here in the mountains."

Public Schools Come
to the Mountains

P.K. leaned against the front porch post and watched the movement out at the slab pile. It had been a while since the sawmill had moved away and left its sawdust pile and slab pile. As time went on locals found it easier to come and cut their wood from the slab pile than to cut fresh trees. Mary Ann came by and asked P.K., "How many 'residents' of Slabtown do you see today?"

P.K. answered, "Only three or four. There is not much wood left in the slab pile. It won't be long until Slabtown will be in name only."

Mary Ann pondered, "I wonder how long it's been called Slabtown?"

"It all started when someone started calling the persons who scavenged the wood 'residents' as they spent so much time picking out the slab wood that had been left. It was natural to figure that if there were residents, there had to be a town where they resided."

P.K. continued, "Most of it now is gone and the time is right for change. We have a letter from the County School Board wanting the property to be used as a school. Guess this is a good location since they are building a two room school out at Providence Chapel. Schools are supposed to be three miles apart and this location just about fits that bill."

Mary Ann, smiled, "The world is changing. Before this, the only schooling the common kid got was what the parent could teach him. Now they will have a real teacher and can get at least some formal education here in the mountains."

"They still won't be able to go on to an advanced school like the one they built in Berryville. Maybe they will build one in Boyce or Millwood. That is almost within riding distance. Some kids will go and stay with relatives all week long, but most will be needed to help work the farm and do the chores."

The years were beginning to show on P.K. and Mary Ann. Raising a second set of children seemed much more difficult than it was when she was in her twenties. P.K. pretty well limited his activities to planting dynamite charges to help dig post holes or to remove stumps. The battle between the plowed land and the forest was ongoing and the "grubbing" axe was in continual use. By spring of 1898 P.K. could still move steadily with a lope that belied his age. February was an unusual month where the thunder and lightening came but brought no rain. It gave all the appearances of the heat lightning that one saw on hot summer days. There came a day that P.K. said to Buck, "Think I'll take a little walk down toward the toll road. Might get all the way to Wildcat Hollow."

He stopped at the shed and armed himself with a stick of dynamite and some cord. He then began to make his way to a place that he hadn't visited in years.

Returning some time later he and Mary Ann sat on the front porch and went through a ritual of remembering the children and watching the sun set in the reflection of the pond. When it was over Mary Ann went about getting supper ready and when she returned to rouse P.K. she found his sleep to be an eternal one. His chore of closing up the Wildcat den was the last of his duties on earth.

After the funeral Mary Ann returned to her task of raising the children. The new school at the northern end of their property was almost finished. It was only one room but it was a school. Buck took the opportunity to have his two oldest return to live with them, telling his brother Winter that a school was now available for them to attend.

Buck Finds a Second Bride

&

Mary Ann Adams Royston Returns to Lakeville

"Ma, I just came by the house where we lived before you built this place. The Sipe family has bought the place and moved in. They have a daughter.

Mary Ann nodded acknowledgement thinking that it was unusual for Buck to be so concerned about who lived where. It was now a year since P.K. died and three years since Buck's wife Virginia died. Buck had shown little interest in looking for another wife and Mary Ann had settled into bring up the family.

Buck continued, "I am thinking of asking the daughter over for dinner to meet the family."

Mary Ann tensed. *This is one thing she hadn't given much thought to and it disturbed her.* She had become used to being the mistress of the house and she wasn't sure she wanted to relinquish that title. She was raising the children the way she wanted them to be raised. A new mistress might change all that.

Aloud she said, "Tell me about the daughter, her name and age?"

She is Sarah Elizabeth and I think she is around twenty years old."

"Huh," Mary Ann pouted, "that would make her only six years older than your oldest. They would be more like sisters."

"Ma, it's not a sure thing yet but she is a fine woman and I think that she could handle that problem," Buck answered realizing that this might not be as easy as he thought.

The courtship of Buck and Sarah commenced in earnest and Mary Ann took little care to conceal her displeasure. They were married on December 29, 1899 and Buck brought his new bride home to hostile ground. As far as Mary Ann was concerned she could do no right. Finally it became more than Buck could stand. He called a family council of his brothers and sisters and when it was over, Mary Ann was asked to leave. Toad was the one who suggested that she come and live with his family. He said that his wife Lucy Ellen would be glad to have the extra help. Besides they were going to move from the Ferry Farm just across the river to Lakeville Farm. Since that was the first place that Mary Ann and P.K. had lived when they moved across the mountains, he was sure she would feel at home.

As Mary Ann prepared to leave, she couldn't resist a parting shot. "P.K. never did sign the farm over to you and since I still have a dower's interest in it, I guess you will have to wait until I'm dead to get your own title to it somehow."

Toad's son, Luther, was assigned the chore of transporting his grandma from Buck's place to Lakeville. The wagon was loaded and Mary Ann lifted herself up on the seat with a minimum amount of help from Luther. The horses were headed toward Mount Carmel

Church to connect with the toll road. It was then down familiar territory past the old Royston house and the family cemetery. The wait at Berry's Ferry all seemed a routine part of the trip. She took time to look at the structure of a bridge that was being built to cross the Shenandoah. The days of the ferry were about over. Luther followed her eyes and gave his own thoughts. "Wait until a good flood comes along. It's a lot easier to fix a ferry than a washed out bridge." They turned south along the river and then right into Lakeville Farm.

A flood of emotion came over Mary Ann as the horses worked their wagon up the hill past the lake. She was so young when she first came to Lakeville. Alfred and the family of slaves that were such an integral part of their lives crowded into her memory. And the ghost—. *I wonder if the ghost really left the place*, she thought. Maybe we should set an extra plate for her tonight.

The manor house looked as if it had not been lived in for many years. The story of the ghost was enough to chase many away. The drapes that were so fresh when she first saw them were covered with a sheen that came from mold. There's a lot of work to be done to get the house livable. This was the second time that Toad and his family had lived at Lakeville, the first being in the late 1870's. Toad's wife, Lucy, remembered their ghost episode which mirrored the one of P.K. and Mary Ann. Apparently the ghost was an inquisitive one who liked to come and visit any new family when they moved in. Their son Luther, who was now in his twenties, remembered the incident very well and was glad that Toad didn't insist he spend the night.

The nights were uneventful and the family settled in to do the farming on a rental basis. It was very common for mountain families to rent these river front farms as many of the landlords were absent from the farms. Toad and Lucy Ellen had ten children and most of them were grown and moved away from the family when Mary Ann came to live with them. Grandchildren were routine visitors.

Mary Ann found herself spending more time out on the front porch where she could see the river and the lake. She thought of the lady who had drowned in the lake and at the sadness she must have known. She was now living in a new century but her mind was on the one past. She thought, *The only thing I will accomplish in this century will be to die. It sure would be good to do it back across the river.*

Mary Ann Makes Her Last Return to the Mountains

That evening she expressed that desire to Toad and Lucy. Toad nodded and said, "The home place is available. Maybe it is time for all of us to move."

In a short time the move was made. It seemed that the mountain people were waiting for her return. First one, than another, came by to ask her advice and sometimes for her help. There were few doctors available and she was called on to help diagnose the ailments that were common to the day. She seemed to come alive again and welcomed being needed.

Only one thing seemed to nag at her. The relationship with her son Buck and his new wife was not resolved. There were new grandchildren being born and she was not there to hold them. Finally she said to Toad, "I need to have you hitch up the wagon and take me to see Buck and Sarah."

Toad made no comment but did as she asked. It was only a mile or so up Fox Trap Hill and out Mount Carmel Lane. The trip seemed to be over in a few moments. As they turned in to Buck's farm, Mary Ann seemed to be a bit nervous as she faced the unexpected.

Toad pulled the wagon up to the front porch and looked at Mary Ann. "You can leave the wagon here, but only strangers go in the front door; I will go around back," Mary Ann said.

She stepped down from the wagon and made her way to the rear of the house. Toad sat and waited for what seemed like an eternity. Finally Buck came to the door and called out, "Why are you sitting out there all alone? Come on in and have some sassafras tea."

Toad hoisted his enormous body out of the wagon and made his way into the house. Mary Ann and Buck's wife, Sarah, were laughing and talking as if there had never been any animosity. Buck smiled and gave Toad a hug. "I think she is thinking about leaving our earthly presence and it's mighty nice that she came by to tell us. Everything is all right in the family again."

Sarah left the room and came back with her oldest. "This is Pa's name sake," she said. "His name is Peter Kemp but we call him 'Bosie.' He's now five years old. And this one is Lucy. She is just two."

Mary Ann reached out and took the baby in her arms. The tears were streaming down her cheeks. "What fools we old people can be. I've wasted all this time when I could have been loving my grandchildren."

"Ma," answered Buck, "you did what you thought was right. You made a promise to Virginia and we didn't let you keep it. I guess we all need to ask forgiveness."

The visit over, Buck helped Mary Ann back onto the wagon. Toad gave a pull on the reins and said to Buck, "Well, guess I'll see you in church."

Once peace had been made, Mary Ann seemed to look forward to dying. The end came in January, 1906. She was buried along side P.K. at Mount Carmel Cemetery.

In time a memoriam signed only "a friend" appeared in the local newspaper.

It read:

"Mrs. Mary Ann Royston, widow of the late P.K. Royston, died January 6, 1906. She was born May 13, 1829 and was a true American woman; strong in character, mind and good neighbor; an affectionate and loving mother. After the death of her loving husband she remained true to his memory, sincerely mourning his loss until the Angel of death called her to that haven of rest, to dwell hereafter in the presence of Him who doeth all things well for those who seek and find Him. Mrs. Royston was the mother of seventeen children, many of whom are now living in Clarke County. They are generous and good men, willing at all times to assist their neighbors, and most of them are farmers. The daughters generally married farmers, and have made excellent wives. Mrs. Royston was well known for her many acts of charity, and not only did she raise her own large family, but assisted in the rearing of three other families, all of whom grew up to call her a blessed grandmother. This pure, good, kind mother needs no eulogy at our hands. We can best point to her and her life. May her example lead others to that Haven of Rest where only the good and pure can enter.

Lord, I have walked your mountains
I have visited your valley
I have tilled your soil
I have harvested your crops
I have served you as best I knew how
May my resting place on earth be
Only of short duration
And that soon I shall see you in a place
I can only dream of.

APPENDICES

Two Obituaries of Interest

December, 1909

Minerva Calmes Royston McDonald

A notable woman was taken by death yesterday evening when Mrs. Minerva Calmes Royston McDonald, the widow of the late Wm. McDonald, succumbed to the infirmities of age at her home on South Washington Street this city (Winchester, Virginia) in her 89th year of age. Mrs. McDonald has been in failing health for some time past.

Mrs. McDonald was descended from an old and historic family being the descendant on her mother's side of General Marquis Calmes who fought throughout the Revolutionary War with marked gallantry and distinction and who was the intimate friend of Gen. LaFayette.

At the battle of Yorktown, Gen. Calmes captured three prisoners single handed and took them to Gen. Washington's headquarters. He was a man of great public service.

Mrs. McDonald was a first cousin of Commander Perry the noted Naval officer whose expedition to Japan in the fifties opened the door to American trade in the Orient.

Mrs. McDonald was twice married, her first husband having been the late Mathew Whiting Royston of Clarke County. Her first husband having died some years ago in this city. With her first husband, Mrs. McDonald was a staunch Southerner and during the War Between the States she displayed her heroism for which her ancestors were noted.

In the thick of the Battle at Ashby's Gap a cannon ball from the enemy's guns crashed into "Roystonville," their beautiful home and completely demolished one room, killed one child, wounded several others and a servant. The heroic woman turned her home into a hospital where men of both armies were tenderly cared for. Mrs. McDonald, with her own hands, bound up the wounds and with the battle still raging she make several trips to the spring to procure cold water.

She was noted for her kindness and sympathy and ever ready to respond to the call of charity. Until a few years ago, Mrs. McDonald was a faithful member of the Methodist Church and until her health failed she took an active part in church work. She was a loving mother and a faithful friend and a woman of exalted character. Three children survive her. They are: Robert Royston of West Virginia, Mrs. L.K. Bennett of Baltimore, Maryland, and her youngest Miss May Royston who lived with her mother and nursed her for years. One sister, Mrs. L.D. Ryan of Loudoun County also survives her.

Funeral services will be held at her late home on Washington Street Tuesday afternoon and the burial will be made at Mt. Hebron Cemetery and Rev. J.M. Duffy Pastor of Braddock Street M.E. Church will conduct the services.

Nov. 16, 1930

Obituary

Thomas Adams (Toad) Royston

LIFE LONG CITIZEN PASSES ON

T,A. Royston Dies at Son's Home after Several Months Illness-Buried Tuesday. Citizens of Clarke and vicinity were deeply saddened to learn of the death of Mr. Thomas Adams Royston, who went to his reward last Sunday at the home of his son, near Berry's Ferry.

Although his death had been expected for the past few weeks, the end came as a shock and cast a pall of gloom over the entire community. He had been in impaired health for some time and had been confined to his bed for several weeks. A son of the late Kemper and Mary Royston, he was a life long citizen of Clarke County, having been born here May 13, 1849. Mr. Royston's life's profession was in agriculture and he was a prominent and successful farmer. He was kind and generous to all, always ready to lend a helping hand to those in need, and enjoyed the esteem and admiration of many people throughout the county and beyond its borders. He saw service in the War Between the States and was one of the few remaining county veterans of the Lost Cause. Mr. Royston is survived by four sons: Messrs. Luther Royston of Berry's Ferry, Charles Royston of Boyce, James Royston of Boyce, Benjamin Royston of Uniontown. Pa., four daughters: Mrs. John Yowell, Mrs. Alvin Dove, Mrs. John Reid, all of Boyce, and Mrs. Robert Vorous of Berryville, four brothers: Messrs. Augie Royston of Berryville, Edward Royston of Rippon, W.Va., Pam Royston and Walter Royston of Berry's Ferry; and two sisters, Mrs. Charles Smallwood of Berryville, and Mrs. Hubert Trussell of Round Hill. He also leaves forty-seven grandchildren and twenty one great-grandchildren. The funeral was held at Mount Carmel Methodist Church, of which he was a devoted member, at eleven o'clock Tuesday Morning with the Rev. B.L. Moore conducting the service. It was largely attended by life long friends, relatives and acquaintances from far and near. Interment was made at Green Hill Cemetery at Berryville. Those who served as pallbearers were Messrs. John Royston, John Yowell, Jr., Richard Royston, Floyd Reid, Henry Royston, and Robert Vorous.

This story is fiction and illusionary, but it could have happened this way.

If the readers are interested in more factual data about the family and others in the area of Clarke County, Virginia, they are referred to the following books compiled by Cousin Donald Robert Royston:

Two Good Trees, Their Nine Branches and Scattered Leaves

Cemeteries of Clarke County, Virginia

Green Hill Cemetery, Tombstones and Burials, Berryville, Clarke County, Virginia

All are available through New Papyrus Publishing Company, Athens, GA

Mary Thomason Morris, Archivist for the Clarke County Historical Society is a treasure trove of information on the history of Clarke County and its peoples. Her book, *Connections and Partings*, is a compilation of marriages, divorces, deaths and legal notices appearing in local newspapers from 1857 through 1884.

Too Poor to Paint
Too Proud to
Whitewash

The Navy Years

PREFACE

The book, Too Poor to Paint, Too Proud to Whitewash was a non-published book of the author's life, written in the 1970's.

Too Poor to Paint ..., The Early Years, which covered his youth through high school and until his entry into the Navy was included in his first published book, *The Spout Spring.*

There have been a few who requested that the details of the Navy Years of the *Too Poor....* be also published. To those few who have asked, here it is.

(The songs are included as a part of the environment and are, of course, the copyright of their authors.)

ANCHORS AWEIGH

Stand Navy out to sea,
Fight our battle cry,
We'll never change our course, so
Vicious foe steer shy -y -y -y,
Roll out the T.N.T.
Anchors Aweigh-
Sail on to victory
and sink the bones to Davy Jones, hooray

Anchors aweigh, my boys,
Anchors aweigh.
Farewell to college joys,
We sail at break of day -ay -ay -ay,
Through our last night on shore
Drink to the foam.
Until we meet again,
Here's wishing you a happy voyage home.

Anchors Aweigh

On a Saturday in late January 1948, I went to Winchester and as usual went to the movies. I don't remember what the movie was about, but apparently it had something to do with the Navy. Before the afternoon was out, I found myself at a Navy recruiter's office and I was seriously talking about joining the Navy. With my brother, Linton, having been in the Navy, I never thought of any other branch of the service. Linton and I had discussed joining the Navy and his only advice to me was, "Make sure you get a rate designation assigned to you before you sign up, as they have a way of forgetting unwritten promises once you're in." I wanted electronics and Navy Air. Now I found myself saying that I would join if they would give me that rate. The recruiter looked at his manuals and confided that I was lucky, as normally they required the recruit to have a prior history of Electronics, confirmed by an "EDDY" test (whatever that was).

For a 90-day period, they were suspending the test to see what kind of recruits they would get as a result. (This was the beginning of a series of flukes that seemed to follow me through my Navy life.) All I had to do was score well on their general tests and I was in. After agreeing to come back the following Monday for a physical and the battery of tests, I headed home to give Mom the "good" news.

I told myself that Mom would be OK. She really wouldn't be alone, as Granddad Smallwood and my cousin Richard (Uncle Rudolph's boy) were staying with us. Mom wasn't overjoyed at my decision, but after some persuasion, agreed to sign for me for a three-year enlistment. I told her of the great things I could learn in the Navy, especially electronics, which would be a start on a new life after I got out. To top it off, I told her of one of the sales point as given me by the recruiter. "Every year they take up to 160 sailors from the Navy and send them to the Naval Academy" (whatever that was). After a day of testing on the following Monday, I was pronounced physically fit for the Navy and mentally fit for the Naval Aviation Electronics school.

On February 2nd, I found myself standing down on the highway, satchel in hand, awaiting a station wagon to pick me up and take me to Washington, D.C. There I was sworn in, and along with ten or twelve others, put on a train heading for Chicago, transferred to the North Shore Railway for a final destination of Great Lakes, Illinois. This was peacetime Navy, and the Cold War was just beginning to influence the Navy's plans. I guess they had decided that the Utopia everyone had dreamed of as a result of winning World War II wasn't going to happen, and a modern Navy was on the horizon. Maybe the changes in recruiting rules were affected by this new term, "COLD WAR."

Whatever the reason, I was now at Great Lakes and learning how to say "Yes, Sir" and" No, Sir." Later on I would learn of an additional answer: "No excuse, Sir." Great Lakes, during WW II, trained a lot of sailors. They built a number of temporary barracks away from the main base, giving them such names as "Camp Downs." These buildings were weather boarded on the outside, no wallboard on the inside, and had many slits where the sunlight came through. On winter days, a small, sifted amount of snow would drift in. Now, this I could relate to. There were a large number of brick buildings, but it was my lot to end up in Company 49 going through boot camp at Camp Downs.

February at the Great Lakes Training Center was not quite the balmy spot that I had envisioned, where one might learn the ways of the Navy. The first day there, before uniforms and clothing were issued, we were out shoveling snow in our civilian clothes. In my case it was a light pair of trousers and a windbreaker.

Eleven weeks of basic training. That is what I faced at the Great Lakes. We learned to march, and march and march. And then march some more. The parade field where we marched was called the "Grinder." I'm not sure why, but I could have come up with a few reasons, none of them flattering.

I met young persons like myself from all over the East and Midwest. Those from the West went to San Diego for Boot Training. Some of the ones I remember were Bob Rockwell from Pittsfield, Mass, Henry

Rushing from Philadelphia, and Gordon Shockey, also from Philadelphia. There was Bill Testerman from West Virginia, Dominic Rittano and Walter Scott. Our bunks were assigned alphabetically and you can see the result of such an arrangement. I thought that I had broadened my world greatly after leaving the hills for the Shenandoah Valley, but I was unprepared for the differences I met in my basic training. There were a number of persons who had been in the service before (mostly Army), who had decided that the military was the place to be and had rejoined. They, of course, were older and "wiser" and were assigned the senior assisting roles. They also were instrumental in removing some of our youth and naiveté.

We learned to work together, even though we were many races and many creeds. We rowed "whaleboats," fought fires, and fired guns on the rifle range. We went to a lot of classes, from knot tying to aircraft identification. Boot Camp seemed like it lasted forever, but finally it was over and we took off on a two weeks leave.

Back after leave we went onto an "out going unit" to await assignment to schools or the fleet. Since I had been an "Aviation Electronics Technician Airman Recruit" with the word "recruit" changed now to "Airman Apprentice," I now sat and awaited the opening of the next class. I say "sat." We didn't do much sitting. Every day we mustered and were assigned work details. I learned how to operate an industrial floor polisher. When I first tried it, I ran into every wall in the place. After it was obvious that I wouldn't learn it on my own, and with a certain amount of fear that I was going to do permanent damage to the gym walls, one of the "ship's company" took time to show me the ease in balancing the unit to hold it in a stationery location as it rotated.

One of the never-ending chores was the unloading of sacks of potatoes from railroad cars. We took on the semblance of ants as we lined up to pick up the sacks, carry them so far that I would wonder why the spur track wasn't rerouted closer to the kitchen, and then get back into the line.

DIXIE

I wish I was in the land of cotton,
Old times dar am not forgotten,
Look away! Look away! Look away! Dixie Land.
In Dixie Land whar I was born in,
Early on one frosty mornin',
Look Away! Look away! Look away! Dixie Land.

Dar's buckwheat cakes and Injun batter,
Makes you fat or a little fatter,
Look away! Look away! Look away! Dixie Land.
Den hoe it down and scratch your grabble,
To Dixie Land I'm bound to trabble,
Look away! Look away! Look away! Dixie Land.

Den I wish I was in Dixie,
Hooray! Hooray!
In Dixie Land I'll take my stand
To live and die in Dixie;
Away, away, away down south in Dixie,
Away, away, away down south in Dixie.

Dixie

Some three weeks later, I was on my way to Memphis, Tenn. and the Naval Air Technical Training Center. The Aviation Electronic Technician Class lasted for 44 weeks. You became an "airman" after fourteen weeks and there were rumors that you could make Second Class Petty Officer out of school if your grades were high enough. Third class was assured by just graduating. But I was never to find out.

Memphis brought a lot of new friends. Ken Skillings became a friend to whom I was close for the next eight to ten years. Nelson Sonnenburg was the one who made it possible for me to do well on the Navy test to get into prep school for the Naval Academy. Ken Tice, from Empire, Ohio was another close friend. Ray Hanson, from Denver, became a friend and would be one who also went to Annapolis with us. Ken Skillings was the goer. Ken had an easy way with the girls and liked them in quantities. He became upset because many of the girls didn't care for sailors and he wanted to upgrade the quality of his girl friends.

He wrote his dad who ran a "fried clam" take-out cafe in Maine, near Old Orchard Beach. His father, who showed up and delivered to Ken a brand new 1948 Buick Road Master convertible, answered his plea. I should also add that it was bright red. Ken was not wanting for buddies before this event, and he certainly didn't lose his cronies afterwards.

The trips to Memphis through Millington and past the very smelly Wolfe River, took on a whole new life. No longer were we dependent on "Boss" Crump's municipal bus system. Now the only snag in the trip was the ever present Tennessee Highway Patrol who couldn't believe that sailors could be driving such an automobile, much less own one. So Ken spent a good part of his time proving his ownership. I was the only one who didn't drink, so I was always included in the group, one of the first designated drivers.

The Naval facilities at Millington (just outside Memphis) were broken into two bases: The Naval Air Technical Training Center and the

Naval Air Station. The Naval Air Station had runways long enough to handle the Naval Air traffic. The Technical Training Center had one runway almost in line with the main runway on the "Station" side, but separated by a state highway running between the stations.

In the summer of 1948 an Air Force B36 out of Barksdale Air Force Base made a forced landing at the Naval Station. The runway was long enough to get it landed but not long enough for it to take off. This event was the excitement of the summer. They had two problems, one being that the airplane didn't have self-starting engines. This, they could solve by bringing in jet starters from (I guess) Barksdale. The second problem, of course, was the length of the main runway.

Building a temporary connection between the two runways across the highway finally solved the problem of the runway length. At the time of take off, everything stopped. All sailors on the training side were ordered out of their barracks. (I suppose there was some question in the command's mind as to the ability of the plane to navigate the slight turn between the two runways, and they wanted us sailors to exercise an "every man for himself" maneuver in case the plane didn't make it.) I'm sure we would all have been out anyway to watch this giant six-engine airplane take off. It still had its wheels down as it came through our sight. The airplane was low enough for us to see the tread of the tires. It was an uneventful take off, but the sound and sight of that airplane taking off still remains with me, and, I guess, always will.

Summer came on and with it the oppressive heat and humidity of the South. We longed for the biting cold of Illinois in February, or so we thought. The Naval Academy came up in conversations. My first exposure to the thought was from the recruiter back home in Winchester. The second came in boot camp when everyone who had scored at a certain level in the general testing were pulled out the class one day and given a preliminary physical to the Academy. Of the companies in our boot camp group, I was the only one who passed the physical, and as such was accorded a certain amount of teasing. It didn't mean a whole lot to me, as I really didn't know what the Academy was all about. I was reintroduced to the idea at Memphis when the annual "All Nav" came out, inviting those interested in taking the test for the prep school at Bainbridge to show up at a certain time and place. Nelson Sonnenburg seemed to know more about the place than anyone. He talked to me of the requirements and he found out that I had no Physics in high school. Physics was one of the major parts of the exam. My Mom had always said, "When they offer you a school, jump at it," and this sounded like a school to me. Sonnenburg helped to solve the physics dilemma, taking me off to the library on a Saturday and Sunday to teach me Physics.

He must have been a good teacher, because when I took the exam I scored highest on Physics. I also flunked English. In previous years, failing one subject would have been enough to keep me out, but this year only, they were trying a new deal and they ranked everyone on the overall score and I ended up in the top number that was allowed to head for Bainbridge, Maryland and the Naval Academy Preparatory School (NAPS). As I mentioned, flukes seem to happen as I progressed along a path that was taking me toward a destination to which I seemed to have little control.

The last weekend before being detached from Electronics school, I ended up on duty with a watch to be stood. It was just my luck to get the "Ammo" dump area, which was in a remote section of the base. Along side the dump was a skeet range where officers could hone their shooting skills. It was usual for Memphis to have quick heavy rain showers and they normally were over by the time the officer of the day showed up with the rain gear. That night was no different as far as the rains coming. I took refuge in a skeet throwing shed. ("Left my watch station" was the legal term.) And would you know it, the Officer of the Day showed up and I was nowhere to be seen. He began his search and just as he stuck his head into the shed where I was holed up, I let one of the skeet throwers go with a "Sproinngg." The O.D. reacted and jumped back, landing in a puddle of water over his shoes. He was not happy. He threatened me with a court marshal and as many other thing as he could think of. I finally got to say my piece and told him I was scheduled to leave for prep school the following day and how I really wanted to be an officer and so on and so on. After awhile he began to see some humor in it and let me off with the statement that he didn't want me kept out of the academy by a "fluke." It was only later that someone told me that his name was Lt. Fluke.

N.A.P.S., Bainbridge, Maryland

It was "Goodbye Dixie" and "Maryland, here we come." I said goodbye to friends like Ken Skillings and Ken Tice, and boarded the train with Nelson Sonnenburg and Ray Hanson for the trip to Bainbridge, Maryland and the Naval Academy Preparatory School (NAPS.)

The train went from Memphis to Washington, DC, then on through Baltimore to Havre De Grace, Maryland. Havre De Grace is situated on the North side of the Susquehanna River where it empties into the Chesapeake Bay. The Susquehanna is a giant of a river at this point and the bridge across seems to go on forever. Bainbridge lies on a bluff overlooking the Susquehanna at a town called Port Deposit to the west of Havre De Grace. I don't remember the trip from Havre De Grace but my guess is that the Navy sent a bus over to pick up the Memphis contingent. My yearbook said that there were about 33 sailors with my same rate and since that was a school rate, I guess that was the size of the Memphis group. The same yearbook shows a total count of 534 sailors and marines. There were a few others from other branches who had congressional appointments to the Naval Academy and who were sent to NAPS as a part of standard operations.

Bainbridge was a large base during World War II, but had been cut back to the sole activity of acting as the home for the Naval Academy Prep School. The base, which acted as a boot camp and a training center, was shut down entirely with the NAPS students going to school in the Tome school buildings. Tome had been a prestigious private school in years past and the buildings were on par with any college in the country. We were assigned rooms with two or three persons each. This, of course, was quite different from our regular Navy days where barracks were the standards. Each of the dorms had been named after Presidents, and I remember some of them: Monroe House, Harrison House, Jackson House and Madison House. I ended up in Section 32 and the Harrison House, where I awaited the arrival of a roommate, one who would turn out to be a lifelong friend.

Don Upshaw came in from San Diego out of Electronics school there. Don had been born in Indiana but his family had moved to Scottsdale, Arizona because of his father's health, when he was in grade school.

After high school, where he was a three-sport athlete, he went into the Navy at San Diego. After boot camp there, he went to the Electronics Technician's school on the same base, through the same tests as myself and then on to Bainbridge. What brought us together as roommates I don't know, but I'll sure accept the results. He brought with him the love of a high school sweetheart who would become his wife after graduation from the Academy. They have four children and now after retirement from a second career at Penn State, lives in State College, Pa. (In 2006 Don and "Pete" moved to Littleton, Colorado to be near two of their children and the grandchildren,)

The Navy's system of bringing enlisted men into the Naval Academy involved the ALLNAV test. The test was administered in the summer time to anyone who met the age criterion, and passed the preliminary physical. Some 5000 (my guess, only) sailors take the test and the top four or five hundred are selected for the United States Naval School, Academy and College Preparatory, a long name shortened to NAPS. This school has been located at a number of Naval Stations over the years, and in 1949 was at Bainbridge. The prep school starts in September and goes to May, with courses in Geometry, Physics, English, Algebra, and History.

In May we were tuned up with some sample tests made up of questions from previous years' exams. Then we faced the reason we were there—the actual exam for the Naval Academy. The top 160 students who passed the exam were sent on to Annapolis. Any others who passed the exam (in 1949 that number was 26) were given open leave and shown the way to Washington, DC. There they were instructed to look for Congressmen, Senators, the Naval Reserve, and anyone else who had appointments to the Academy. All twenty-six managed to find appointments. Those who failed the test went back to the fleet to serve as before.

NAPS at Bainbridge had a full schedule of sports and extra-curricular activities. In sports they played other prep schools in the area, plus Navy and Marine Corps teams and the Navy Plebe team. In those days, freshmen (Plebes) could not play varsity college sports. Don Upshaw was a starting guard on the basketball team and played first base on the baseball team. This kept him busy in his spare time. I was not burdened with any athletic ability, so when liberty time came around, I was on my way to Baltimore, Washington, or home to the Blue Ridge.

The testing method at Bainbridge was the same method used at the Academy: a short test in every subject every day. Normally the quiz was four questions, three on current work and one on review. This was my kind of testing as I had a good short-term memory, but was not so good on the long term. So I usually aced the three questions and once in a while lucked out on the review question. Since a grade of 2.5 was passing, I sailed along with something above 3.0. If you didn't maintain a passing grade while at the school, you also went back to the fleet. I don't remember how often this happened, but the threat was there.

Bainbridge, I think, was probably my most carefree days in the Navy. Academics were fairly easy for my type of brain. Watches were easy to stand, and no girl friend to think about. I had a brother in Baltimore, half brothers in Washington, and a home some four hours away. To get home, I would typically hitchhike. This could take some time as I had two major cities to get through, plus all the outskirts. Many times this was solved by my "chicken hauler" friends from Harrisonburg, Virginia. They hauled live chickens to the New York and Philadelphia areas and were returning home along U S Route 1. Most hitchhikers would avoid this means of transportation, but I would wave them down and get a ride right to the path up to my house. This eliminated the hour or so getting through Baltimore and another one in Washington. Maybe the aroma of the chicken trucks was the reason I didn't have any girl friends, but Mom seemed happy to see me.

Since there was a deadline in returning, I normally rode the Greyhound bus to Washington, changed to another heading for Baltimore and points North. The only problem with the bus was staying awake during the last leg of the trip. The trip from Havre De Grace sometimes was by hitch hiking or at last resort, a taxi.

The mess hall was named "Tome Inn." Of course it wasn't long before it was nicknamed. "Ptomaine Inn." We did have to do one stint of mess cooking, which consisted of serving the food that was prepared by the regular cooks and clean up the mess after mess. The food was always pretty good in the service, although it did take some getting used to, particularly the baked beans and corn pone for Saturday mornings. Maybe that was their way of encouraging us to go on liberty. Of course, the sailors had some irreverent names for many of the dishes and a discussion of such is best skipped.

A Drum and Bugle Corps was established which formed the basic part of any parade. Some of the bugle players were selected to blow reveille and taps each day. Ray Hanson and Dale Size were two that I remember, I think also Ray Bright. Taps wasn't too much of an ordeal, but having to get up early, go out on the parade ground, and play reveille was a bit above and beyond the call of duty, or so one thought. This brought one of the three (I won't say which one.) to devise the scheme of raising his window, and sticking the bugle out the window and performing his duty in a slightly unorthodox manner.

The man raising the flag, who was forced by the logistics of his chore to be at the flagpole, was "standing by" awaiting the bugler, and his only warning was hearing a window of Harrison House go up. If his hearing was not acute, there was an unmilitary-like pause as the flag started up the pole just about the time the last notes were exiting the bugle.

This, no doubt, could have become a standard for the future, had it not been for the unfortunate presence of an officer one morning. He spent some time trying to identify the window that was the source of the sound of the dawning of another day at NAPS. Since the punishment of such ingenuity could be the loss of the chance to go to the Academy, the custom was curtailed. (The recognition of ingenuity is normally reserved for Admirals after they have survived a battle, one which no one expected them to win in the first place.)

Don and I had a two-man room until around December, when Jim Elfers showed up. As I recall, Jim had an appointment from some place and was assigned to NAPS as a result. Jim was from Texas and was more interested in roller-skating than studies and somewhere along the line didn't make the cut.

One of the more salty friends was John Roepke. John was a running back on the football team and had been telling us of a fancy new play they were putting in for the next game. He told us that when the play was going to be run, that he would let us know by scratching a certain part of his anatomy. We spent the game in the stands, awaiting the signal and were rewarded by a 75-yard scamper by Roepke. John was the elder in the group, having been in the Navy as a UDT man during the Battle of Okinawa. Later on, John had trouble explaining how a member of the Underwater Demolition Team ended up not passing the swimming test at the Academy and became a member of the "Sub" squad like many of us.

A couple of historical notes of interest. (At least, I remember them well.) The Navy desegregated the service during this time. No longer were blacks relegated to Steward's Mate ratings. At about the same time it was also decreed that persons in the military were subject to the income tax. Up until that time, officers and enlisted men had no income tax to pay. Now, they got it from the government in one hand and gave it back with the other. It didn't bother me, of course, as $66.00 a month is not a large base from which to start. The officers, however, were a bit upset.

The method of paying enlisted men is worth telling: On payday (twice a month) everyone lined up in a pay line. You had already checked the pay records, which were laid out on an adjacent table; found out how much you had available and filled out a receipt for any amount up to your total. The Paymaster, then, paid in cash, with the accent on two-dollar bills. I guess they thought we were going directly to the racetrack. You could sign up for an allotment to be sent to your dependents, and I had one for my mother. As I recall, fifteen dollars a month went out that way.

Travel on bus or train still carried the WW II 50% discount, and food was available at the mess hall, so we were able to get by and save along the way.

Navy
Blue
And
Gold

Now, college men from sea to sea
May sing of colors true;
But who has better right than we
To hoist a symbol hue?
For sailor men in battle fair,
Since fighting days of old
Have proved the sailor's right to wear
The Navy Blue and Gold.

Four years together by the bay
where Severn joins the tide,
Then by the service called away
We're scattered far and wide;
But still when two or three shall meet
And old tales be retold
From low to highest in the fleet
We'll pledge the Blue and Gold

So hoist our colors, hoist them high
And vow allegiance true
So long as sunset gilds the sky
Above the ocean's blue.
Just let us live the life we love
and when our voyage through
May we all muster up above
A-wearing Navy Blue.

PLEBE SUMMER

The shift from "Enlisted Man" to Midshipman 4th Class took about three days. It seemed like forever as we all wanted to get the swearing-in ceremony out of the way. This meant that we were really in the Academy. At Bainbridge another fluke came up: I overheard a ship's company sailor ask "What about sea duty? This man has no sea duty—" and was told that the sea duty requirement had been waived for this year.

After undergoing processing at Bainbridge, we packed our sea bags and piled onto buses and started on the next episode of our lives. It's about forty miles from Havre De Grace to Baltimore and another twenty-five to thirty to Annapolis. I don't remember the trip at all, but I do remember ending up alongside an old attack carrier, permanently tied up to a dock on the Naval Station side of the Severn River. Annapolis is located at the mouth of the Severn River as it enters the Chesapeake Bay. The Academy side is on the south side of the river, with the north side having an assortment of duties supporting the Academy and other duties such as a low frequency "round the world" radio transmitting station. A golf course and rifle range were also on the "station" side.

But at the moment, I didn't know any of this. All I knew was that we were taken aboard a ship and assigned bunks. This was a slight come down in expectations. I don't know what I had expected but it wasn't this. Later it was explained that we would be boated across the river each day during the processing and after it was all over, we would be sworn in as Midshipmen and assigned rooms at Bancroft Hall. Looking back, I suppose that there was a chance that some of us would fail the final physical or for some other reason, not be made a Midshipman.

The next few days were utter confusion on my part, but probably a well-run operation by the naval personnel involved. My first snag was that the physical was much tougher than the earlier Navy physicals. I made it through until I got to the vision testing. (I had a small problem with flat feet, but the corpsman doing the checking figured a way to get me past that one.) The doctor doing the finals in the eye check noted that I was 20–20 in both eyes. I thought that this was enough to pass the eye exam, but no, he spotted a condition called "lazy eye" or alternating vision. The net result is that I see out of only one eye at a time. This was enough to kick me out. I guess the look on my face was enough to touch the heart of the doctor, who excused himself and went over to a senior officer. After a discussion that seemed like ages, the doctor returned and said that if I understood that I could never be a pilot, they would give me a waiver. At that point, I would have agreed to just about anything, so another hurdle was passed.

The doctors were very sympathetic to physical problems that were borderline. One buddy, Del Smith, who was on the short side, ended up being measured at 1/8 inch too short. Since he had good results from all the other measures, they decided to postpone his measurement until the final morning of the exams. Meanwhile they gave him instructions on how to lengthen himself, and sent him back to the ship to do the exercises. On the appointed hour they sent corpsmen over to pick him up in a litter, carry him horizontal to the appointed measuring spot and helped him stand erect to full stature and re-measure him.

Yeah, you guessed it, he was 1/4 inch shorter. Again after conferences and the assurances from Del that he really wanted to be in the Academy, they let him in. (He graduated and retired as a Commander after a full career in the Navy.)

Another friend from NAPS, Tom Kent, had a problem with color blindness. He was the top student out of NAPS and the eye problem was his only hurdle. This really presented no problem as he had memorized all the color charts. All he needed was to know which series was being used. To solve this he would position himself behind a buddy and make sure that the numbers were called out loud enough for him to hear. Once he picked up the sequence, he knew all the numbers and passed the test with "flying colors," so to speak.

Finally, it was time to raise our right hands and be sworn in as Midshipman 4th Class, and we sailors from NAPS became the first of the Class of 1953. In a few days, we were joined by other candidates appointed from other sources (Congressional, Senatorial, Presidential, Naval Reserve and probably others). My first Plebe Summer roommate had a primary appointment to Annapolis and an alternate to West Point. After two days, he knew he had made a mistake. He resigned and ended up graduating with the West Point Class of '54.

Plebe Summer was a continuation of NAPS to a great degree. The classes, marching, rifle range, and the studying of material thought essential to start one on his way through the rigor of the oncoming Plebe year filled our days and evenings. Reveille was at 0615 (6:15AM) and Taps at 2215 (10:15PM). We began to make friends with those who would become a part of our lives, not only for four years, but also for the rest of our lives. Years later, some would die in yet unthought-of wars or training missions. One could pick up Time magazine and see on the cover someone you had known as a young sailor or marine at NAPS, or a midshipman at the Academy.

We were learning the ways of the Academy and some of us learned the hard way the different meanings that words can have between the military and civilian world.

The point was proven by one of my roommates who didn't understand the meaning of "cleaning" your gun. We had been issued M1 rifles for the summer, each his own weapon. When they weren't being used they were stored in Dalgren Hall with a cable laced through the trigger guard to keep them secure. On a particular Saturday morning, we had the M1's in hand and were readying them for inspection. The questioning of cleaning the gun came up and one of my "wise" roommates explained to the other that it meant "taking down" the gun and scrubbing its parts with soap and water.

Believing the words of his relatively newfound friend, he tore down the rifle and scrubbed the parts in the wash basin in the room. As inspection time neared, and in the haste to reassemble the weapon, one small, but essential, pin was missing. This pin held all the parts of the bolt action together. As the lost part was not to be found, we looked for a way out, finally settling on the use of a match stick to replace the pin.

It was found that the parts would stay together, but would not let the bolt be opened as was necessary during "Inspection Arms." This procedure occurred as the inspecting officer passed through the ranks and stopped in front of some or all of the Midshipmen and asked to inspect their weapon. Maybe my buddy would be lucky and be bypassed by the inspector. It was not to be. The officer, a Marine as I recall, stopped and put my roommate through the ritual. Thinking fast, he brought the rifle up to inspection arms and made a fast motion as if he was bringing the bolt to its open position. Of course, nothing moved and he stood there at attention with the rifle in a closed bolt position. The officer pointed out the incorrect position of the bolt and he made another fake pass at it.

A couple of times around and the exasperated officer grabbed the rifle and with the might only a Marine Infantry officer can exert, he hit the bolt. The bolt headed to the rear and finding no pin to stop it; it and all the associated parts went all over the ground.

The look on the officer's face was priceless as he was in a position never addressed in the training manuals. After a few feeble attempts at finding the pieces, and realizing that he was becoming the center of unwanted attention, he tried to give the weapon back to my roommate. Now, here, my roommate was on sure ground. He had been trained that if the weapon was not given back to you in the same condition as you had given it up, you were required to refuse the return of the gun. And refuse it he did. The two went face to face, with time on the side of my roommate, as this inspection was just before lunch formation.

Finally, the officer admitted defeat and finding out our room number, had the messenger (ever present) take the gun and leave it in the room. My roommate was instructed to find all the parts later on and return the weapon to the armory for repair. No one volunteered the presence of the matchstick and I'm sure the officer spent the rest of his days wondering how a faulty M1 had found its way into the hands of a Midshipman.

I remember vividly the day Don Upshaw showed up from Bainbridge. My section had been assembled at the water's edge at Dewey Basin to learn knot tying. We learned to tie such knots as bowline, bowline on a bight, square, granny, half hitch, sheepshank, and many others, the names of which I have forgotten.

As we were hard at our knotty task, we were interrupted by a group of sailors marching by. They turned out to be the lost contingent from Bainbridge, all of whom had somehow found an appointment to the Academy. My feelings were hard to contain when I recognized Don as one of the group. Up to that point, I didn't know how he was making out in his quest to find an appointment. As I recall, John Roepke was also among the group. I was ready to hold a celebration right then. The world was O.K. again.

PLEBE YEAR

As September approached, we all worked to be ready for the next hurdle: the return of the Brigade from summer activities. There is no way I can convey the fear we felt at this impending event. The return of the Brigade!! By this time, we had a full issue of uniforms. The uniform for the summer activities was called White Works. At first appearances, these looked like a sailor's white uniform, except that its only ironing was done by a "mangle." (To those unfamiliar with the modern conveniences of the "Fifties," a mangle was a sort of automated ironing system that was able to quickly press a quantity of clothes, but unfortunately ironed in permanent wrinkles into the clothes. And all this before permanent press!) The cap had a blue stripe around the top, and we had a neckerchief for dress occasions. We had been measured for our blue service uniforms and by the end of the summer we had them in hand. We learned how to wear them and the difference between "Blue Service Able" and "Blue Service Baker." (All uniforms of the day were rigorously defined and if one item of apparel differed, a new designation was made. As I recall, the only difference between "Able" and "Baker" was the color of the cap cover; blue or white.) Dress Whites and a "full dress" uniform would come later. We wore shoulder boards with no stripes on them signifying the lowest of the low: a Midshipman 4th Class. Before the return of the Brigade and the start of the academic year, we were assigned to a company. The Brigade at that time was divided into two Regiments, six Battalions and thirty-six Companies. Each Company was made up of a certain number from each class. The only thing in common within the company was the fact that they were taking (or had taken) the same foreign language. At that time, the choice of a foreign language was given to each midshipman, with some limitations on persons with ethnic backgrounds in that same language. (Since the Academy wanted to broaden your horizons, you could not take the same foreign language as your ancestry if they had emigrated within two generations.) Since I wanted to room with Don Upshaw, I asked him which language he wanted to take. Spanish was his choice, and thus Spanish became my choice, and we were assigned to the First Company.

Room number 1004. I don't remember them all, but the first room number sure sticks. It was a three-man room and the third man turned out to be Jack Jaynes. Jack had also been at NAPS, but I had not known him then. Jack was from Dallas, had been an ET3 (Electronics Technician, Petty Officer Third Class) in the Navy and had joined up before finishing high school. We roomed together for four years and have been close to each other ever since.

The Academy had a time-proven way to help Fourth Class Midshipmen (Plebes) get through that first year. They were assigned to First Classmen in the same company, who became their friends. All upper classmen were referred to as "Mister So and So", except for your "First Classman." Thus a room of First Classmen, comprised of Hank Hyatt, John Axe and Ken Gedney became our friends and mentors. It was their job to get us headed in the right direction (both mentally and physically), help us when we got into trouble, and keep other First Classmen from riding us too hard if we were struggling academically. Since Plebes could not have a radio or phonograph, their room became a refuge where we could relax and listen to their music. Hank Hyatt had a great collection of albums from Broadway shows, thus I had my first exposure to South Pacific and The Student Prince.

Meal formations were announced by the ringing of a bell that sounded for a period throughout the halls. It was followed up three minutes later by a "late bell" and two minutes after that by an "absent bell." Once we became familiar with the routine, we could do our mandatory "double time" run to our assigned spot, and line up on the bricks. (Plebes had to be at their designated locations before the formation bell rung or otherwise face the wrath of some First Classman in the company.)

Platoon reports "All ready or accounted for" were passed on to the company commander, then to the Battalion commander, on to the regimental commander and finally to the Brigade Commander, who gave the command to march off to the mess hall (or to any other activity involving the entire brigade).

That first meal formation with the Brigade meant finding where your company and platoon formed and being there before the bell rang. That part of my life is a blank. I don't remember how we made that first formation, but somehow we did and we were off to our first meal with the Brigade. We were assigned tables with others in our company by the Battalion Supply Officer. We had used the Battalion Bulletin Board to find our seat location. The First Classmen sat at the head of the table with the Plebes sitting next to them. Plebes had to "brace up" and sit at attention. No elbows on the table, eyes facing straight ahead. You could not look at the person addressing you (which probably was a good thing, since many of the stares would have revealed arrows that could have come back to haunt us). The First Classmen took this opportunity to find out who we were and observe our reactions to questions. The dining hall was the site where we were educated into the customs of the service and was as important in our development as any single place at the Academy.

Over the entire Plebe year, we were subjected to a barrage of questions, most of the answers we were supposed to know by heart, but some to be looked up and answered at the next meal. To this day I can do a "man overboard" drill, giving all the commands without hesitation. If we were asked "What time is it?" we could not answer just with the time. We were require to respond with "Sir, due to unforeseen circumstances over which I have no control, the hidden mechanisms of my chronometer are in such in accord with the great sidereal movements by which time is commonly reckoned, I cannot with any accuracy state the correct time, but I would estimate that the time is so many tics and so many minutes past the hour of—." We were issued a small reference book called "Reef Points," which contained the answers (but not all) to most of the questions. We were supposed to know it by heart.

Somehow we made it past that first meal and the Plebe year was underway. We started classes and became acquainted with the classmates, in our company, and the Second Company. We attended most of our classes with the Second Company. (They, too, were taking Spanish as a foreign language.) There were a few classes with the Third and Fourth Companies. We were divided into sections of twelve or thirteen students. Again, class formation times were announced by the bell, and we mustered at a certain spot, before marching as individual sections to the building where the class was being held. After class, we would either return to Bancroft Hall for "study period" or march to the next building and the next class. Mixed with the academic classes were training sessions in such things as small boat handling, or athletic sports. By this I don't mean the participation in a sport itself (That came after classes were over at 1630 (4:30 PM) and before dinner formation.) The athletic training sessions actually taught us the rules of most sports, from football to wrestling to golf. The idea was that as a junior officer you would most likely be named the Athletics Officer for your ship or group and you had better know the rules of the game.

The fall of the year brought about football season. This had it upsides and its downsides. The upside was that it diverted some of the upper class attention from the lowly Plebes. We also went to some of the football games played in Baltimore and the Army-Navy game in Philadelphia. The downside was that we had to be able to sing the fight song of the opposing team in the next Saturday's game. In addition, we had to draw a poster for the upcoming game and place it on our door by Thursday. That year I learned the fight song of Duke, Pennsylvania, Southern California, Wisconsin, Tulane, Princeton, Notre Dame, Columbia, and of course, Army. We did pretty well with all the songs except "Roll On, Tulane." This was the first year that Navy had played them and no one, including the upper class knew the tune of "Roll On, Tulane." In the end we had to sing it to the tune of the "Marine Corps Hymn," which irritated some ex-marines.

The Army game was (and continues to be) the football game of the season. That year, Army had the longest winning streak in its history, was ranked in the top two or three, but had played some pretty soft opponents, like Davidson. As we prepared for battle, we parodied the West Point song with words like: "We don't play Notre Dame. We don't play Tulane. We just play Davidson, for that's the fearless Army way." It was a cold day in Philadelphia but we played Army to a 7–7 tie in the first half. We were ecstatic. If we could beat Army, the Plebes could get to "Carry On" until Christmas leave. The second half started with our kicking off to Army; and Arnold Galiffa promptly started dashing our hopes by running it back for a touchdown. The game ended 42–7 and we were consigned to another month of "Brace Up, Mister" before Christmas leave. (Maybe an explanation of those two terms might be in order. "Brace Up" meant to stand or sit at attention with eyes straight ahead. "Carry On" meant that you could take on the momentary semblance of a human and talk at meals, walk anywhere in the corridors and not have to double time to every formation.)

I was an avid Navy fan and lived and died the games. (Mostly died, for Navy didn't have a great team that year.) There was a First Class-man in the company who was as apathetic about football as I was ecstatic. He was a foreign national from the Philippines. In those days, certain countries could send personnel to attend our Academy. They were mostly from Latin America and the Philippines. They only had to meet what physical standards set by their own country and some showed up with some limitations. This Midshipman had an eye problem; I don't know how bad they were, but his way of inspecting your shoes for shininess was to stick his shoe along side of yours and compare them. At a football game, he knew that after the game, he could go out and have some beers and this was the focus of his attention. The part he didn't understand was how the time was kept. It was beyond his comprehension how it could take three hours to play a one-hour game. Since his vision problems kept him from seeing the stadium clock, and since he always sat next to me, my time was filled with this First Class Midshipman squinting toward the scoreboard and saying, time and time again, "How much time do we have, Mr. Royston?" This would get particularly disconcerting toward the end of the game as timeouts and long passes would make the time creep. (This Filipino Midshipman died in 1970 as a Captain at the US Naval Hospital at Bethesda, Md.)

Sometime between the Army game and Christmas leave, I became pretty fed up with my status in life. In those days if you resigned from the Academy, after having been in the regular Navy, you would be discharged to civilian life. (Later on they changed that rule, after they found that some hot shots had figured a way to get out of their tour of duty, legally.) Had I been left to my own devices, I probably would have been out at that time and a whole life changed. The Navy had a little rule that said that you had to get your parent's permission to resign. Now they never gave their permission to get me into the place, but I needed it to get out. I wrote Mom and asked for a letter from her to do my thing. Now someone with any selfishness would have jumped at the idea. Mom was now all alone with Granddad who was in his late eighties and could have used a man around the house. The letter I got back, which I had to include in my resignation packet, gave permission, but she couched the letter in such a way that I appeared to be the biggest coward in the world. I don't remember the exact words, but I was so infuriated that I tore up the letter on the spot, and there I was left with no "permission to resign" letter. I settled down and stayed. Once I accepted that episode as history, the Academy became a way of life and the rest of my time there was enjoyable, including some five more months of Plebe year.

Academics, for the most part, were not a problem. I would say—for the most part—my choice of a foreign language cost me more study time than all the other subjects combined. Foreign language was a two year course and I could have taken such languages as Italian, Portuguese, French, German or even Russian. But no, I had to choose the easiest of them all, or so they said. The one little point that I didn't factor in was that most of the others had taken Spanish in High School. So when I showed up the first day and was greeted with "Como esta, Usted." and was expected to have an answer, I knew I was in trouble. The rest of the subjects slid while I tried to put my Blue Ridge Mountain accent around these unpronounceable words.

To top it all off, we rotated being Section leader, the one who was responsible for giving the marching commands to the group on its way to class. In foreign languages, once we entered the hall where the subject was being taught, the commands had to be given in the language we were taking. That meant I had to learn these commands in Spanish and speak them sufficiently well to herd my section of compatriots around. Since they already knew my limitations, they loved to pretend not to understand my commands and head off in a direction contrary to my desires.

Finally, I sat down and resolved the problem by memorizing the minimum number of commands needed to maneuver my charges. Let's see now—I needed to get them stopped —that's "Section Alto." Then I needed to turn them to the side before they were allowed to "fall out." That would be "left face" or "right face." I settled on "right face." That was "derecho-drea." Then I needed a "fall out." I memorized the pronunciation, "Ro-pon Feliz." Then I needed the command to present the Section to the Professor—"Senor, lo presento La

Section." (Now, if there are any Spanish aficionados reading this, those Spanish words are as I said them, and not necessary related to anything Castellan and yes, as I recall, for some reason the "section" took the feminine adjective.) It was sufficient to get the job done, even though on many occasions I could have used a "left face" to keep them from staring into a coat rack. The only solace I got out of this mess was that Don Upshaw was in my group of twelve and he had to endure my pigeon Spanish. After all, he got me into this.

Those marching affairs did serve to bring out professors from each room as they looked forward to my arrival. Foreign Languages weren't particularly captivating subjects, and I suspect that I afforded them the highlight of their day.

As the first term neared its end, I had struggled to get my Spanish up to a 2.8 grade point average. Exams were coming and "dailies" counted for 3/5 of the grade and the exam counted for 2/5. Some calculations showed that I needed a 2.08 on the exam to end up with a 2.50 passing grade. (Note how easily I handle the Math.) Should I fail the course, the Academic Board could either give me a re-exam, set me back a year, or toss me out. For a guy who, within the past month or so, wanted a way out, I now was trying to figure out how I could stay. A re-exam was out of the question. If I couldn't get a 2.07, there was no way I could pull out a flat 2.5 on a re-exam. My professor for this marking period was Prof. Sewell. (We were given new professors each six week marking period, and each one was responsible for having his class up to date when that time came to move to the next period.) To this day, I credit Prof. Sewell for my staying at the Academy.

My exam was returned. The first part had more red marks on it than black writing. My worst fears were coming true, but as I neared the back of the exam, the red marks began to become sparser. I turned to the last page that contained the score, a 2.07. I could have kissed Prof Sewell, an action that most probably would have accomplished the same thing as a failing grade. The final mark of 2.50 was posted on the bulletin board and a Foreign Language class standing of 1025 in a class of 1025 was official.

The period between Christmas leave and Easter was known as the "dark ages." It was aptly named. Annapolis gets cold and wet weather which curtails any outside curricular activities. It, of course didn't stop marching to class. We had dark blue ponchos that made us look like a formation of vampire bats on a search for victims.

The First Class finally tired of finding the limit of our endurance and began to toy with us. There was a signal for "brace up," that being the number "one." On the other hand, "two" meant we could carry on and pretend that we were normal human beings for a short period of time. As we sat at meal, we would tune in on the First Classman's words and actions, waiting to hear the word "two." Some would deliberately wink twice and if spotted in the same moment would cause the Plebes noticing it to thunder their elbows on the table. Even the word "to" or "too" used loosely by a "firstie" could produce the same result. The First Classman, caught this way, would generally go along with the alert Plebe and let us get away with it. Sometimes they would set us up with something like "I went "to" "one" where the two or "to" was followed by a one. "Aha, Gotcha." Meals became more of a game than an ordeal.

Once in a while we would get put in a catch-22 where there was no out. In the First Company, it was the question, "Who killed Magellan?" The only acceptable answer was, "The cannibalistic savages of the South Seas Islands." If you answered with the acceptable answer, the next words would be from a denizen of that area, that same Filipino Midshipman who set me up as timekeeper during the football game. "Come around tonight, Mister" was the order. This meant presenting yourself to the First Class Midshipman's room for interrogation at the appointed time and endure the questioning that would come. Not giving the acceptable answer would bring the same results at another person's room.

The Filipino Midshipman was a member of a three man room of First Classmen that you wanted to avoid at all cost. Each had his own fiendish way of getting to you. One of these Firsties was nicknamed "Moose." "Moose" had one of the most perverse sense of humor I have ever seen. Whether he ever slipped over the line into actual hazing, I don't know, but he sure came close to it.

One of his favorite tortures was to have all his "come arounds" show up in full uniform just after reveille. As they stood at attention on both sides of the corridor, he would take his morning constitutional down the hall towards the head. (For those land lubbers, the "head" is the Navy word for "toilet.") Once he was in the head, the Plebes were automatically dismissed to prepare for morning meal formation. Some of us, ones who had been found guilty of greater crimes against the realm, were sentenced to "toilet seat" duty.

Now the heads were unheated and the windows left open. On a cold winter night, the sitting down on the cold toilet seat was something approached very gingerly. "Moose" solved this problem for his own rear by assigning the real miscreants to warming the toilet seat. As always, a game was made of this and the rule was that the stool had to be warm when he sat down, but he couldn't see you at anytime during the operation. It was learned that one could hear his approach and quickly move to the next stall and be out of his sight when the king approached his throne.

As luck would have it, I was caught in his snare for some infraction and assigned the toilet warming duty for a week, a tour that I almost successfully concluded. On the last day of a particularly cold night, I overslept and came dashing into the head just as "Moose" plopped down on his supposedly 98.6 degree toilet seat. Needlessly to say, I got the duty for another two weeks, but it was worth it, as I would reflect on the scream of anguish that came forth from the enclosure from which "Moose" had suddenly leaped. I even gained a bit of renown myself as I could see or imagine that I saw myself being pointed to as the one who got "Moose". (Moose went into the US Air Force and retired as a Captain in 1954.)

Easter was on us, and Annapolis is as beautiful in late Spring as it is ugly in Mid-January. Tours begin to show up and young ladies are in the yard awaiting the release from formation of their upper-class drag (date). You could feel the admiration of the crowd and we marched just a bit taller as we headed to our appointed places. First Classmen became enamored with their new devotion, a new car. Many were making marriage plans. All were choosing their branch of service. At that time 25% of the class was commissioned into the US Air Force. (The Air Force Academy was not yet a reality.) Five percent were commissioned into the Marine Corps. (The Marine Corps was pretty well taken up by ex-marines or those whose parents were marines.) The rest went into the Navy.

Second Classmen dreamed of the upcoming June Week, the "ring dance" and becoming First Class. Third Classmen, "Youngsters," looked for increased liberties, duties and authority. The Plebes still wanted to keep a low profile, but were thankful for less attention paid to them. June Week and the Herndon Monument would come!!

June Week finally came. Exams were over and we looked forward to a week of parades, formal dances and, at the end, graduation of the First Class. As they graduated, everyone moved up a year. We were Plebes no more, except for one small detail. Some sadist in the past had decreed that a Plebe hat had to be placed on the top of the Herndon Monument, an obelisk statue in the yard. This involved the Plebes forming a human pyramid, growing higher and higher until someone was high enough to leave a cap on the top. I don't think the monument was over fifteen or twenty feet tall, but the task took a period of time. Looking back, I think the idea was to get the Plebes out of sight while the new officers basked in the attention of parents and girl friends.

Youngster Cruise

Shortly after June Week was over, we joined the new First Class and embarked on a cruise to various ports in the United States and around the world. The Academy issued a detailed set of instructions for this event, including what uniforms to take and what to pack in a large wooden crate, called a "Cruise Box." The Cruise Box was stenciled with your name and some other details and stored in the bowels of Bancroft Hall, awaiting your return from the summer's excursions. Typically the class was divided into two halves, with one half going on the first cruise while the second half went on summer leave. Then the roles were reversed. I ended up on a destroyer, the USS Barton, on the First Cruise. Don Upshaw was scheduled for the USS Missouri on the Second Cruise.

This was June, 1950 and the Navy was on short rations. Our cruise was limited to visiting two ports in the United States, and one in the Caribbean or Central America, all ending up at Guantanamo Bay, Cuba (Gitmo) for the firing of the big guns by the large ships.

The Barton's first stop was Portland, Maine. One of my classmates was from Portland and while he wasn't on the cruise, he had me call his family and his sister showed me the sights of Portland. My old Navy buddy, Ken Skillings, was from nearby Pine Point and I was able to meet his dad and have some of his famous "fried clams."

After Portland, we headed for New York City. My "watch" going into port was on the bow of the ship, where I was to report any oncoming vessels that might be a threat to the ship. It was a cloudy day but the water was filled with sail boats, motor boats, tug boats, garbage scows and barges. I reported so many impending dangers that the bridge finally limited me to reporting major vessels only. Apparently they didn't appreciate that the continuing safe voyage of the USS Barton was because of my alertness.

It did provide an unforgettable thrill. Coming into the harbor and seeing the Statue of Liberty for the first time is indescribable. New York sightseeing gave me a sore neck. Another Midshipman's comment, while staring up at the tall buildings, "It sure would hold a lot of hay," pretty well summed up the city.

A few days in New York and we sailed for the sunny climes of the Caribbean. The ships in the group split up and headed for different ports, ours being Colon, Panama. While we were steaming from one port to another, our days were filled with drills and training sessions. The two classes of Naval Academy Midshipmen (augmented with an equal number of NROTC Midshipmen from colleges around the country) had entirely different roles. The Third Classmen performed the tasks of enlisted men while the First Class took the jobs of "junior officers." The idea was to have the Midshipmen understand the duties of all the personnel aboard ship, so that they could better perform some years from then when they were a real part of the fleet.

Besides our routine training and "at sea" watches, (which were split between "engineering" and "deck" watches,) we were assigned "general quarters" jobs. The routine watches were boring enough to be forgettable, but my general quarters assignment left stamps on my memory. Among the weapons on the USS Barton at that time was what the Navy called a "five inch-thirty eight gun" mount. It was used as a triple threat against the enemy. They could be fired at another ship, used as shore bombardment or as an anti-aircraft weapon. The ammunition was in two pieces, consisting of a powder shell and a projectile. All of the gun crew was inside of an armor plated enclosure and, as I recall, consisted of projectile men, powder men, hot shell casement handlers, and "pointers and trainers." The Navy was sufficiently advanced to have the pointing and training actually done by radar, so the jobs of "Pointer" and "Trainer" were the cushy jobs. The handling of the ammunition was for the most part still a manual operation.

While the guns were able to turn 360 degrees, there was a stationary central part that delivered the powder cases and projectiles from below decks. The projectile, weighing about 58 pounds came up nose down in a fuse pot which kept changing the range at which the projectile fuse exploded until it was removed from the pot. The projectile was placed in the tray by the projectile man after the powder man had laid in a powder case. The powder case was capped with a cork pad to keep the powder from spilling out.

You might know who they picked to be one of the projectile men. Yep, you guessed it, skinny old me. My partner, the left projectile man, was Bob Cameron, a football quarterback who weighed in at about 205 and who could have picked up that pointed object with one hand. We went through training exercises with dummy ammunition that trained us to lift the projectile in a certain way, place it in the breech, and roll the fingers of the right hand a certain way to keep the 58 pound monster from mashing the fingers. The training projectiles had been reused so many times that the nose end had lots of burrs that tended to make the palm of the left hand like tenderized meat as the left hand's duty was to leave the projectile last, by sliding it away from its nose.

I dwell on the intricacies of this assignment as I believe that we came close to blowing up the entire mount because of my first firing assignment. I forgot to mention the chore of the hot case man, whose duty it was to wear asbestos gloves and "sort of catch" the spent case as it was ejected from the breech after firing, and direct it down through an opening in the bottom of the gun mount and out onto the deck below.

The gun used as an anti-aircraft weapon was limited in its vertical aiming only by the fact that the powder case and projectile had to lay in the open breech long enough for the projectile man to complete his cycle. It was necessary to hit a hydraulic ram switch that closed the breech, pushing the projectile and powder case into the chamber where the gun automatically fired. The breech then opened, throwing out the spent, but red hot, powder case. Let me say that we had practiced with the breech in a near horizontal position, which is the case during surface fire.

Our first live firing came out at sea on a day where the swells were pitching the ship pretty good, and our assignment was antiaircraft firing. I will leave it to your imagination as to how easy the chore was to plant one's feet, pick the projectile out of the fuse pot and place it in that ever moving breech that was now at an elevation angle of some 70 degrees. At the command to commence firing, Bob Cameron and I went about our task, he more successfully than I. My first round went into the tray at its precarious elevation and as I hit the switch to ram it home, the projectile hit a corner of the chamber and made an angle with the powder case, throwing the powder case out onto the floor and rupturing the cork pad that contained some fifteen to twenty pounds of powder. Bob's gun was firing and his "hot shell" man was trying to kick the smoking spent shells out of the hole and our side had powder spilling around the internals of the gun mount. It was not a sight that I'll soon forget.

While the mount was manned by a Midshipman crew, there was a Chief Petty Officer in charge. He managed to get a "cease firing" command out of his mouth. We cleaned up the mess and restarted the exercise with no further incident. I don't remember how many rounds I managed to fire successfully, (I know it was a lot) but it was that first one that I'll never forget. To this day, I will say that I have never hated a job as much as being the projectile man on a five inch-thirty eight caliber gun.

On to Colon, Panama. We tied up at a pier and the locals, peddling pineapples, bananas, trinkets and whatever, descended, like hordes, on the ship.

We were given liberty to visit the city. After walking the downtown area, we found that a Naval Air Station nearby was shutting down. The officer's club was selling drinks at some astoundingly low rate and thus was my introduction to "planter's punch."

(Some might ask how I turned from a non-drinker in the regular Navy to a drinker at the Academy. I don't remember the transition. I had nothing against drinking, and never was a heavy drinker. When we were protected from driving accidents by the Academy supplying the transportation, it was easier to have an extra drink, knowing that we didn't have to apply navigational skills to get home.)

The true memorable event was the start of the Korean War, which happened while we were tied up at Colon, Panama. Since no one knew the extent of the invasion into South Korea or the intention of the Communists, there was much confusion as to what to do with the USS Barton. We were tied up at a rather strategic location in the world: the entrance to the Panama Canal. There were some thoughts as to the danger to the Canal and any United States' vessels in the area. There was talk of issuing live ammunition to those on watch who carried unloaded weapons. Or should we move away from the pier and anchor out in the harbor? In the end, sanity prevailed; no ammo was issued and we sat tight until it was time to sail.

The start of the Korean War did have its effect on the second cruise. Don Upshaw was aboard the Missouri for his cruise when it was detached from the squadron after stops in Halifax and New York City, and sent to Korea for shore fire support. Don ended at Little Creek, Va. where he spent more time learning about amphibious operations than he ever wanted to know. This was after he had joined all hands in a thirty six hour nonstop loading of supplies and ammunition aboard the Missouri.

We ended our first cruise and I headed home for a month long leave before Youngster year started. I don't remember much about that leave except meeting a girl I would date for the next two years. This happened as I boarded a Greyhound bus in the front of Irvin Wiley's store. The only seat available was next to this pretty girl, so what else could I do but sit beside her. She was on her way to Washington, DC to get a part time summer job, before returning to Mary Washington College for her final year of studies.

Youngster Year

Probably the easiest year at the academy is the second year. For some reason, the Third Classmen are called Youngsters. (At West Point, they are Yearlings.) The academics were still on the easy side except for the ever threatening Spanish. By this time, I had gotten up to speed on the written and comprehension parts, but still had trouble wrapping my tongue around the words. The question of passing the subject had been settled in my favor, so I was able to concentrate on other subjects which were beginning to need more attention. We now had more freedom of movement, all within a seven mile limit of the Chapel Dome, of course, and I took every advantage of the added freedom.

The Brigade was changed in its makeup. During Plebe year we had 36 companies. At the beginning of Youngster Year, it was decided that a change was in order. The 36 companies would be merged into 24 companies. Since I was in the first company, it meant no change for me.

The Second Company was split and half were brought into the First Company and the other half, along with the Third Company became the new Second Company. Thus we had new company mates which included Bill Trueblood, Ross Perot, Lyle Armel, Sam Byrd, Jim Chesley, Ed Chase, Tom McCreery, Ray Crater, Bob Aller, George Apted,

Jim Burgess, Milt Rubb, Dick Clark and Chuck Carter. Surviving Plebe year from the original First Company were Bill Branson, Bill Holland, Randy Hanback, Mike Greeley, Joe Muka, J.D. O'Connell, "Scotty" Beat, Frank Martin, Arlis Simmons, Dick Martin, Bob Klee, Grant Millard, Billy Ray Clements, Mickey Flynn, John Gallivan, Tom McClean, Don Upshaw, Hal Lewis, Mel Holley, Don McAdams, Jerry Snuffin, Bob Lowell, Leroy Hebbard, "Jeb" Herndon, Ken Bocock, Bob Shaidnagle, Jack Jaynes, Dave Cannon, Ira "Killer" Kane and myself. Later on Randy Hanback, Dick Martin, Bill Holland and Bob Shaidnagle moved to the Fourth Company to balance out the companies.

So much for names. Our company was composed of a great group of guys, a fact that made it difficult to rate each other as we progressed through the Academy. A part of the leadership assessment was to rank your classmates in the company according to leadership abilities. We always complained that this was unfair in our company as all ranked high. (Looking back, many went on to achieve great things in their military and civilian careers. One, at the moment, 1992 is getting my vote as president of the country.)

Don Upshaw and Jack Jaynes continued as my roommates. We all struggled with certain academic problems. (My Spanish has enough press already.) Jack and Don had their problems in the math and physics areas. All of us managed to survive with a couple of re-exams thrown in to keep the tension high.

Jack and I had desks that faced each other. Every evening study hour went from 7:30 to 10:00, and we spent a lot of time facing each other. Jack developed study habits that apparently helped him to study, but which would drive us up the wall. One of his ways of concentrating was to perform a "mantra" as he studied, which consisted of "sea stories" which he made up as he went along. As he sat there immersed in a text book, out of his mouth would come the most ridiculous tales. He apparently didn't listen to his own stories and thus was not bothered by them. We, on the other hand, would first tune them out, and then find ourselves listening to them as he rambled on. "There I was at 40,000 feet in a motor whale boat. The sails luffed, the boat hit the water and became the "Good Ship Tuscahora," 52 decks and a straw bottom. The Captain brought a cow aboard. She ate the straw, the boat sank and we got six months submarine pay." And on it went for most of four years.

Jack kept a running score as to how he was doing. If he passed a test, it was one for Jaynes, if he failed, it was one for Navy. How he hated those "All Navy Days."

The fall season at the academy is almost as pretty as the spring. Throw in the football games and it really is the place to be (as long as you're not a Plebe). The crispness in the air, the turning of the leaves, pep rallies, and football games relegated the academics and discipline to a lower plateau. In those days only a few games were played at the Academy. Most home games were played at Baltimore and the liberty after the game was looked forward to with the zest of ones who had been cooped up all week long. The Lord Baltimore Hotel was the meeting place and a lot of parties were hosted on the nineteenth floor (as I recall) of the Lord "B." At the conclusion of liberty, we climbed aboard Academy buses which hauled us back to the Yard.

After one of these games, I ran into a Second Classman from the company who asked if I wanted a drink or two. Since I only had a few dollars in my pocket, I declined, giving that as a reason. "Two dollars should do fine for an evening of drinking," he said, suggesting that we pool our resources and put my trust in him. I did, then wondered at my decision making skills, as he proceeded to look for, and find, a shoe store. We went in and he bought the cheapest pair of women's shoes he could find, at somewhere about four dollars. After walking outside the store, he opened the box and threw one of the shoes away. "Now we're ready for some drinking." he said. I agreed, since no one wants to antagonize an obviously mad man.

We returned to the Lord "B" and took an elevator to the nineteenth floor. Party noises were coming from every room down the hall. We stopped at the first door and our knock was answered by a Midshipman. My partner in crime said that we had found this shoe out in the hall, pointing to the remaining new shoe we had purchased. He just wondered if it belonged to any of the dates inside. "Don't know," he slurred, "Come on in, have a drink and I'll find out."

We did, it didn't, and we retrieved the shoe and repeated the process at the next door. We worked our way down the hall and into a condition where I was glad the bus came to the Lord "B" to pick us up for the return trip.

Every year the Army game was held in Philadelphia. We took buses to Baltimore and boarded trains to Philadelphia. The trip took the better part of a half day and culminated in a "march on" to the field before the game. Both the Cadets and Midshipmen did this and alternated as to the "march on" order, depending on who was the home team. The previous year we had gone down to defeat at the hands of an Army squad that was ranked in the top three or four in the country. The current year looked like another repeat. Army was undefeated in their last 28 games; Navy had won two and lost six. We settled in for a long afternoon. At the end of the game, the scoreboard showed Navy 14-Army 2. Navy stopped them at every turn. Zug Zastrow, Navy's quarterback, ran for one touchdown, passed for another and fell in the Army end zone, giving them a safety. Whenever I hear someone refer to an "upset," I think, "You don't know what an upset is."

Once a week was parade day. All the companies would form and march to Worden Field, where we would go through a few exercises and then pass in review before the assembled dignitaries. Sometimes the reviewers would be Academy officials. At other times, we would be honored by some visiting dignitary from Washington who would usually prolong the agony by making a speech. The voice would cut in and out and was mostly unintelligible.

This was the time when French Premiers lasted from two days to two months. Every time one was elected, they would take a trip around the world, knowing that time was not on their side. Naturally, they would show up in Washington and, naturally, they would show up at the Academy for the review of the Midshipmen. Add to this the speech in French and the translation thereafter; it was surprising that their term of office lasted through the parade.

It was during these times that the Midshipmen in the ranks looked for a bit of respite from the standing at attention and the "present arms" that seemed to go on forever. We learned not to lock our knees, for to do so was inviting fainting and a trip to sick bay.

Some of the first class midshipmen looked for other ways to pass the time. One in our company would whisper to the Plebe in back of him, "Mister, tell me a joke."

The Plebe would whisper back a joke of questionable humor which might or might not be accepted by the First Classman. And so the process might be repeated. Only once did the tables get turned. When the whispered question came back to a certain Plebe, "Tell me a joke."

The answer came back, "Sir, I don't know a joke, but I know a riddle."

"OK, then tell me a riddle."

"Sir, what is brown and yellow and green and blue and has about a hundred legs?"

The First Classman growled back, "I don't know. What does have all those colors and all those legs?"

The Plebe replied, "I don't know either, but it's crawling up the back of your neck, Sir."

The entire brigade came awake as the First Classman's rifle went crashing to the ground, as he made wild swipes at his neck. No record was kept of the number of "come arounds" that were made by that Plebe as a result of the "caterpillar" incident, but it was well remembered by everyone within earshot.

At the end we would pass in review and march back to Bancroft Hall. All of our prayers were for a stable government in France.

SECOND CLASS SUMMER

Second Class summer was supposed to be a fun summer, consisting of an "air cruise," the CAMID Operations and a long 42 day leave. Have your fun now, for Second Class is the toughest year academically. We were now wearing our two diagonal stripes on the shoulder boards of our khakis and dress whites and the same on the left sleeve of our dress blues. We were almost in the big time.

The Air Cruise was made up of flights to various Air Force Bases and Naval Air Stations in the Continental United States. There we were treated to tours of the bases and dances where we'd meet the local "debutantes." To liven it up a bit more, Bill Trueblood was on my contingency and when we found out that Grosse Pointe Naval Air Station was on our itinerary, he was clicking his heels. At that time Bill was dating a girl from Grosse Pointe, who had been going to Margie Webster College. He was looking forward to seeing her in Michigan. Since we were buddies, he had to include me in the activities. It turned out that she lived in Pontiac, but "don't worry about that, we'll meet at "Ma-Ma's House in Grosse Pointe," she said.

Bill and I caught a taxi cab and found ourselves touring along the edge of a lake on our right, past very-very large homes on the left, which were set back some two or three hundred yards from the

"Drive." The "Drive" was a dual lane road with an unbroken grass median in the middle. We saw small roads going off to the right every once in awhile toward the lake, but nothing crossing the median to get into the houses which were all on our left. We figured that the cab would have to go to the end of the highway and turn around, so that it could enter the houses from that side of the road. We had our wallets out, checking our money supply as we imagined the meter running for the whole distance.

Soon the taxi pulled off on one of the roads to our right and to our surprise descended into a tunnel under the highway. Every house had its own tunneled entrance from the highway. Now how about that! The cab pulled under a large portico and we found ourselves staring at two of the largest doors I had ever seen on a house. Had I been alone, I would have most probably jumped back into the cab and high tailed it back to the Naval Air Station. Bill though, being of a stouter heart than I, rang the door bell and in time we were greeted by the maid. We were ushered in to await the arrival of Bill's girl. Spiral staircases and life size paintings of family members occupied our attention until Bill's girl came bouncing down the stairs. I remember the middle name as we were shortly introduced to her grandmother. Turns out that her late husband was one of the founders of General Motors.

The rest of the weekend included a visit to the Detroit Yacht Club and introductions to girls with names that were synonymous with the motor car industry in Detroit. That is a long way for a boy out of the Blue Ridge Mountains, who still didn't have electricity in the old house on the hill.

We left Grosse Point Naval Air Station and headed for Barksdale Air Force Base in Louisiana and off to more tours and more parties. After that, we ended up at the Pensacola Naval Air Station where we were exposed to the training facilities and given details on flight training that would be in the future of many of the Midshipmen. (But not mine, as I recalled the waiver that had allowed me into the Academy and the admonition that I could never fly.)

The air cruise ended with a week's tour on an aircraft carrier, where we observed flight operations. An entire cruise with no watches to stand, but CAMID cometh.

CAMID (short for Cadet-Midshipman) was a joint operation including the Second Class from West Point and the Second Class from Annapolis. It was held annually at the amphibious base at Little Creek, Virginia. The Midshipmen ran the boats and the Cadets took the beaches. Each of us was assigned duties that were supervised by regular Navy or Army personnel. My job was to run a LCVP boat which is a small craft normally used to ferry personnel and vehicles to the beach. Once the beach sand is contacted the front ramp is dropped and the soldiers rush ashore, getting wet from the knees down.

At the appointed hour we picked up the Cadets as they crawled down cargo nets from the troop ship and then headed for the beach. We hit the sand at a distance from the shore and the boat seemed solid onto the sand. At a consenting nod from the "Regular" aboard I dropped the ramp and the first tier of Cadets hit the water, only to sink in nearly over their head. I had landed the boat on a sandbar and there was deep water beyond. We pulled all the swimmers back aboard and made our way around the sandbar and repeated the process, this time without incident. The Cadets did not seem to see the humor in the situation and I made sure that I did not travel alone for the next few days. Notoriety has its pluses and its minuses, I guess.

Second Class Year

Second Class year brought Bill Trueblood in as a roommate; well almost. After deciding on having four of us in a room, it was discovered that no four man rooms were left. (The choice of rooms started with the First Classmen and worked its way down.) So we ended up having two "two man rooms" directly across from each other. Bill was from Indiana, had spent a year at Indiana University before the Academy, and had a brother in the First Company who had graduated the year before we arrived. Bill was by far the smartest of the four, so academics for him were a snap. He had a record collection that included every record cut by Doris Day. His soccer career was to be cut short by a broken leg during Second Class year.

At the Academy, the academics were divided into many departments with certain subjects assigned to each department. As I look at my diploma I see listed the Departments of Seamanship & Navigation, Ordnance & Gunnery, Marine Engineering, Aviation, Mathematics, Electrical Engineering, English, History & Government, Foreign Languages, Hygiene, and Physical Training. Some of these departments covered a two year period, others spanned the full four years. Foreign languages, fortunately, only lasted for two years.

Hygiene, by the way, is the only subject required by Congress to be taught at the Naval Academy. I wonder what they would say if we had spent four years learning that. Aviation was a "hands on" course taught for the last two years and was one where we were indoctrinated into flying using the facilities available. The most memorable facilities were Navy Bi-wing airplanes which had been built in the 1930's and somehow had been sent to the Academy to form their "Air Force." The planes were nicknamed "Yellow Perils," (The color was obvious, the peril part came from the midshipmen and pilots who had to fly them.) All Midshipmen were exposed to the flying, even though they knew they would never be flyers.

A brief description of the aircraft, before I tell you that they left me with some of the most memorable times at the Academy. They were two seaters with open cockpits, one behind the other. They had no radios and the only communication with the landing base was to fly over and "waggle" the wings. There was something called a "gospipe" which was an empty hose about seven-eighths inch in diameter, in which the pilot could speak and the midshipman could hear. Any response from the midshipman was to nod or shake his head, a motion which could be observed in a mirror mounted on the rear of the wing in front of the pilot's view. The plane had no wheels, only pontoons. They took off from a facility across the river from the Academy grounds and when airborne were prohibited from flying in an area where they couldn't glide to water in case of engine failure. Take off speed was in the neighborhood of 60–65 knots and cruising speed was around 85 knots.

Every second class midshipman was required to take a certain amount of "dual" flying in these planes which were piloted by young Naval Aviators who were assigned to teaching duties at the Academy. Most of these flyers had been flying the latest jets in Korea and did not take kindly to having to fly these ancient machines out of the Wright Brothers era.

On our "flying" days we would march to the boat dock and get aboard a small boat and take the trip across the river to be introduced to our pilot and plane of the day. We had flying gear mostly composed of a parachute and "Sky King" hat and goggles. The parachute was a necessary item, not to be used to jump out of the airplane, but as a seat as it sagged under our rear.

The midshipman and pilot would get into the plane while it was on a set of rollers on a ramp near the water. An enlisted man would hand crank the starting coil and when the button was pushed by the pilot, the propeller would spin and hopefully would start. We were then pushed down the ramp into the water and then would taxi to an area where the take off was made. Depending on the personality of the pilot, this was a time of silence or full of profane sayings. The plane would bounce around on the water, finally getting higher and higher on the waves to where the drag was lowered sufficiently to allow the plane to rise into the air. Once at flying stations, we were given rudimentary instructions in the art of flying, graduating to such maneuvers as shooting landings and formation flying. (Formation flying was done at such great distances between planes as to make it difficult to see the other planes in the formation. One of the smart things they did!)

One time out I was assigned to a Lieutenant who was shortly bored by the skills required to keep this modern weapon in the air. Through the gospipe, he said, "Have you seen the new Bay Bridge from the air?" I looked into the mirror and shook my head. He banked the airplane and we went out of sight of the other planes toward the new Chesapeake Bay Bridge. Once there he became more daring and inquired, "Have you ever been upside down in an airplane?"

This time the head shake was quite vigorous. "Make sure your seat belt is fastened," he said. I did, and acknowledged it with a nod of my head. Where upon, he turned the airplane upside down, a feat which violated all instructions we had received. As we flew along in this airplane which most probably had not been upside down since it was built, I noticed some liquid dropping from somewhere in the cockpit.

(Now, I was scared but not terrified.) To better investigate the leakage and perhaps being a bit disoriented, I stuck my head down into the cockpit, finding that the leak was from the liquid in the compass (which was built along the lines of an old Model "A" speedometer.)

While I had my head down in the cockpit, the pilot turned the aircraft back to its normal flying posture as he said, "Well, how did you like that?" and he looked up at me in the front seat. Well, "me" didn't show up in his view. I can only imagine the thoughts he must have had as he saw his career pass before his eyes.

Now, you can lose Naval Officers, but a lot of these Midshipmen are appointed by Congress and the President, and they don't take kindly to losing one of their charges. The shout in my eardrum, as he pled for a miracle reappearance of one Midshipman Royston, 2nd Class, was enough to do permanent damage to my ears. I reappeared before his eyes and he regained some measure of his composure as we headed back to a landing which would return me to my next class and, most probably, him to the bar at the "O" Club, where he could reconstruct his career and remove the ashen pallor from his face.

The very next week as I returned for my next flying lesson, guess who was my instructor? Yep, the same pilot. This time our job was to practice landings doing what they call "touch and go." A "crash boat" had been sent to a specified spot and we were suppose to practice landings on the water along side of the crash boat, following the plane in front of us. As soon as we touched water, we gunned the engine and took off, repeating the process until the exercise was over. We followed a routine that is used to land aircraft on carriers which involves sharp left turns until you line up the landing area, drop the plane down to very near the water and then cut the throttle and let the plane sink in. The first two or three went well. The next time I cut my turn too soon and found myself in the prop wash of the plane in front of us.

At some fifty to sixty feet above the water the plane continued to drop its left wing until the wings were about vertical with the water. The pilot pulled with all his might on the stick, I pulled with all my might on the stick and ever so slowly the plane came back to level flight as we flew off somewhat obliquely to the landing path.

No more landings were made. The pilot took the plane back toward Hospital Point and waggled his wings to indicate he was landing. After landing we alit from the plane and the pilot addressed me with words something like this: "Mr. Royston, I have been flying airplanes for nigh onto 'lots' of years. I've made over 'so many' carrier landings. I've flown 'umpty-ump' combat missions in Korea. And, Mr. Royston, that is the closest I've ever been to being in the "drink." (I wanted to reply that last week, I could have said the same thing.) "And you, Mr. Royston, I never want to see you again." And he never did. I had many more N3N flights, but that officer was never assigned to my plane again.

So much for the Aviation Department, which I will leave with only one comment. Every instructor I had (including the one above), complimented me on my good depth perception. (You might recall that I was granted a waiver when I entered the Academy. "You'll never be a flyer they told me, 'cause you have no depth perception." Apparently they had never heard of Wiley Post.)

The professors at the Academy were just about split between military officers and civilian professors. Each seemed to bring a uniqueness to the classroom that was only returned to uniformity by the fact that we changed professors every six week marking period. Since we took uniform exams throughout the Academy, it was necessary that each instructor have us up to date academically at the end of the marking periods. Sometimes we suffered through a professor with the knowledge that he only lasted six weeks.

In math, we had Professor Gallaway, who was renowned for his putting the "LL" scales on the slide rule. (For the younger generation, a slide rule, by the way, is a non electronic calculator.) Prof Gallaway was noted for scribbling math formulas on the board, and deriving solutions using steps only decipherable to him. He would reach a point, saying the answer is "obvious" and then move onto something else.

Jack Jaynes watched this maneuver one day and after some head scratching, ventured to the Prof, "It's not obvious to me." The professor then moved to another board (all of the walls had boards.) And with his back to us, scribbled furiously for five or ten minutes. He then left the room, was gone for a period of time, returned to the room, announced to Jack, "Of course it's obvious" and went on to the next problem.

Jack also had Prof Gallaway for another marking period, wherein we were reviewing for the end of year final exam in Calculus. When prompted by the Prof, "Are there any questions?" Jack raised his hand and inquired "Just what is dy/dx?" Apoplexy comes to mind as the Professor realized that Jack was serious, since Jack and the rest of us had spent an entire year using dy/dx, it being the first thing taught in Calculus. I did say that Jack had some re-exams, didn't I? This was at the end of Plebe year and Jack was as glad to get through that class as I was Spanish.

Second Class year brought forth some heavier physical training. We endured such things as jumping off of a platform into a pool of water. I don't remember the height, but it seemed like 500 feet into a wet sponge. I jumped because the person in front of me jumped and I was reasonably sure that the one behind me was going to. One of my company mates refused to jump. The swimming instructors tried to reason with him by suggesting that the deck of an aircraft carrier was some 80 plus feet above the water and if the ship was on fire and sinking, that he would jump. This elicited the reply, "Sir, I think I'd let it sink for a while." Not electing to jump put one on the "sub" squad and meant showing up three afternoons a week until the jump was made.

This was also the year of the "Dilbert Dumper." Some sadist came up with the idea of exposing the Midshipman to the crash landing of a fighter plane at sea. They had resurrected the fuselage of an old Navy "Avenger" torpedo bomber of early WWII fame and mounted it on a Disney sort of ride where it slid down a slope and hit the water. It then turned upside down after hitting the water. The Midshipman was belted in and equipped with a "Mae West" life jacket. Once the plane was upside down and the cockpit filled with water, the Midshipman was to unbuckle the safety belt, swim out from under the plane to the surface and inflate the life vest.

The only danger was getting the events in an improper sequence and inflating the life jacket before one swam out from under the plane. Being buoyed back into the cockpit made it impossible for the Midshipman to extract himself. Fortunately there were swimmers in the water watching the operation who would go in when necessary and remove an embarrassed Midshipman.

The jumping and the ditching were over in a moment. There was another test, however, that involved swimming the width of the Natatorium six times, using three different strokes. I don't remember the exact distance, but it had to be done wearing our "white works" uniform and had to be completed in six minutes. We practiced for this for an eon or two and finally the day arrived of the test. There was only one thing I was sure of, my chances of passing this test were about the same as coming away from Vegas a millionaire.

To make it worse, the timer handling my group was Lt. Cdr. Higgans who had been an Olympic breast stroke champion in some time past. He had little patience for someone who didn't have fins for feet. If we failed to complete the test in six minutes, onto the "sub" squad we went. That meant taking the test three times a week until it was passed. Ones who didn't pass would forfeit summer leave and continue taking the test.

The pressure was on!! Into the water we went and into the compulsive breast stroke. Once over and back, then into a back stroke. The last lap was of our choice, mine being a somewhat dismal interpretation of the crawl. (No one wanted to hear of my pact with the fish—"I don't swim in your water, you don't walk on my land.") As I ended my swim, and clutched the side of the pool, I looked up at Mr. Higgans and he said, "six minutes and fifteen seconds." The next sounds heard were the bubbles coming to the surface as I sank slowly to the bottom of the pool. I had given it my best; there was no way I could improve on that time.

But onto the "sub" squad I went, along with others including John Roepke, who had been a UDT (Underwater Demolition Team) enlisted man in the Navy. If John couldn't pass the test, what chance did I have?

Fortune smiles on us once in a while. My first "Sub" squad adventure meant taking the test again and there I stood on the edge of the pool counting the squares of tiles that covered the bottom. They and I were going to become great friends for an undeterminable length of time. The whistle blew and into the test I went. I swam my best, but without the intensity I had before. The test giver was Professor Gilley, who, when he wasn't drafted to be a swimming coach, was the music director at the Academy. As I finished my test and looked up at Prof. Gilley, he looked down with compassion on my drowned face and said, "Six minutes, even.") "Hooray and Hallelujah." Professor Gilley ranks right up there with Prof Sewell, my savior from my Spanish inquisition. Both are two of my favorite naval heroes.

Christmas leave of my second class year was notable. I arrived home to find lights all over the place. Electricity had finally arrived in the mountains. Mom had not mentioned it in any of her letters or visits, wanting to surprise me at Christmas. The old house was on its last legs, but Mom had an electrician, most likely, James Slack, put in the wiring. It was installed on the outside of the interior walls with "exposed" wiring. We had a great Christmas leave with the "good old days" being a part of the Christmas reminiscing.

Christmas leave also gave me the opportunity to enjoy one of my favorite sports, squirrel hunting. The years were gone when squirrel hunting was not a sport, but was necessary to bring meat onto the table. I always went to church on Sunday with Mom at Mount Carmel. Since services didn't start until late in the morning, I would sneak out and do a little hunting before church.

This particular Sunday I had hunted on the Mac Cornwell property up Wildcat Hollow. On my way back home, I stopped at Irvin Wiley's store. I was unshaven, dressed in some pretty old clothes, and wet from the morning dampness. As I went in, I sat the rifle in the corner and moved toward the welcome heat of the pot bellied stove.

I had seen a car with New York licenses outside and now noticed they were visiting with Irvin. Turns out they had stopped in for directions, but became enamored with some of Irvin's stories and were really eating up this exposure to mountaineers.

As I went in, Irvin, with a wink, led me into the conversation and we talked of how the winter was going to be a tough one because of the bushy tails of the squirrels. He laid it on pretty thick until I had to excuse myself to leave and get ready for church. Mom always insisted that I dress in my best dress uniform and in a half hour or so, I found myself going back by the store in my blue service uniform with white gloves, great coat, and silk scarf. The New Yorkers were still there and you could see the confusion set in as there was something familiar about this person in uniform, something they couldn't quite put their finger on. Finally, I think they made a connection between the mountaineer who had been discussing the lore of the mountain an hour or so ago and realized that they been "put on." It wasn't long before they were on their way with the realization that they would not be telling their friends about the mountaineers they had stumbled upon during their trip through Virginia.

Back at the Academy, the studying for first term finals began and it wasn't long until another term was over. I was doing reasonably well academically. The subject that was supposed to be the hardest, Electrical Engineering was perhaps my easiest, as the topic at hand was electronics. This, of course, was my specialty as an enlisted man, so I was standing pretty well going into the last term of second class year. Around March, I kept having stomach aches and not having any idea of what it could be, I finally made my way to "Sick Bay." The doctor poked around bit and in a short while I found myself at the Academy hospital going through a series of tests.

The diagnosis came in, Duodenal Ulcers. In those days, the treatment for ulcers was quite limited and was mainly comprised of a strict diet. The only way one could get a diet in the Navy was to be in the hospital. The Academy had a system to take care of teaching during an extended hospital stay, so I spent the next part of my academy life at the hospital. At the time, no mention was made of the effect this was going to have on my thoughts of a Navy career. I simply went to classes and stood at my bunk each Thursday when the supervising doctor came by, and after listening to the ward doctor read my chart, would push hard enough on my stomach area until it ground against my back bone.

His routine question, "Does that hurt?" was always answered in the affirmative. Heck, that process would have hurt, no matter what the condition of my stomach. Time went on until I became concerned as to whether I was going to get out of the hospital in time for June Week and the ensuing First Class cruise. My assignment for the cruise, the USS Wisconsin and the cruise ports of Portsmouth, England and Bergen, Norway had already been listed. I began a move to get the doctor to pronounce me cured so that I could get on with my life.

I managed to get out in time for June Week. Since I had recently broken up with a girl and my hospital stay had kept me from making any serious June Week plans, I would just settle back, maybe stand a few watches for others who had heavy June Week plans and keep a low profile. The week went pretty well like that. I almost ended back in the hospital as I found that the Parades in the hot late May-early June sun were somewhat difficult for someone who had been lying around for the past ten weeks or so.

The old girl friend showed up without announcement and we went to the big dance for this particular June Week. This was the "Ring Dance," the one where we were allowed to wear our new Class Ring for the first time. Of all the dances at the Academy, this was probably the most popular. There was an elaborate ceremony where the ring is dipped into a bowl filled with waters from the "Seven Seas" before being worn.

The ring has on one side the Naval Academy crest and on the other the Class Crest. The Class Crest is designed by a class committee during Plebe Year and is first given to you during Youngster year. Many of the crests were given to girl friends or mothers. The "One and Only" were pinned as a prelude to a formal engagement. When the ring is received at the ring dance, it is worn with the Class Crest side facing to the Midshipman, signifying that your class is closest to your heart. After graduation, the ring is turned around and the Academy Crest is worn facing you, signifying that upon graduation, the Academy is closest to your heart. Miniatures of the Academy ring are normally given as engagement rings with the wedding rings available from the ring manufacturer bent to fit around the Academy ring.

The ring dance was early in the week. Once that was over, I settled back into my self-enforced regimen of a quiet week. It almost turned out that way, except for a First Classman, who wanted to know if I would do him the favor of escorting his fiancée's sister to one dance. She was sort of chaperoning her sister from Minnesota and her week was pretty well filled by dates with Bill Tarpley, a classmate from the Second Company. And so I met this girl named Doris from Minnesota. *One dance, what could be the future of that?* I was definitely not in the mood for any lasting relationship. Minnesota seemed far enough away to assure that.

The dance went well enough. There were three couples, Bill Laux, his fiancée, Barbara, his sister, Pat, her Midshipman date, Doris and myself. Doris was a very pretty girl, and there was something about her easy smile and quick laugh and sparkling eyes that I found disturbing. We enjoyed an evening together and I gave her a fond farewell as I made plans for the First Class cruise to Europe.

First Class Summer

Fate is a word used to explain happenings that should, most probably, be credited to God's providence. As I look back, there were so many events that happened to allow me to get to the Academy and to stay there, that I can only assume there was a reason why God wanted me to be where I was, that week in June. And then I almost blew it. I met this girl who kept coming back into my mind. I was now on cruise and my chance of contacting her was lost. I knew her name and that was all. Bill Laux, who would have been my normal contact was graduated and out of my life. I was on a battleship headed for new adventures, Doris was headed back home, wherever that was.

Shipboard activities took over and occupied my mind. The USS Wisconsin was 40,000 tons of steel, armor plate, and heavy armament. We were assigned to engineering or deck duties and began standing the watches of a junior officer. Company mates aboard were J.D. O'Connell and Ross Perot. Our first port would be Portsmouth, England and there were lots of training exercises to learn on the way. The heavy armament on the ship were 16 inch 50 caliber guns. They fired a projectile weighing around 3800 pounds for a distance in excess of fifteen miles and would penetrate 35 feet of reinforced concrete before exploding. The USS Wisconsin had nine of these guns in three compartments. After my experience with 5 inch 38's during my first cruise, I was glad that I wasn't assigned to the big guns. (J.D. O'Connell did get the assignment. I wished him well.) The Wisconsin also had a number of "Quad 40" mounts and I was picked as mount captain for one of these. I guessed that if they had checked my past gunnery experience, this was a job in which I could do the least damage.

A "Quad 40" was four 40 mm. guns in one mount controlled by a single aiming and pointing system. They could be aimed manually using an "aimer' and "pointer" (One controlled the elevation, and the other the traverse or bearing.) In actuality they were controlled by a computer and radar. They were mostly used as anti-aircraft weapons but could be used against personnel or ships as strafing fire. After my previous gunfire experience, this gun mount was a piece of cake. The hardest part of the job was to haul the ammunition up from below decks before a firing exercise and return the unused, afterwards. (We found that a few extra rounds fired after the command "cease fire" did wonders in reducing the return work.)

It was on this cruise that I learned some of the unfairness of the Navy. As we progressed eastward across the ocean, we went through time changes. These were always executed during the night and the clock was set ahead an hour with the resulting loss of sleep. But that's ok, I thought. On the way back we'll get an extra hour of sleep. What a rude awakening! The time change as we headed west was done at noonday and we got to work an extra hour.

Portsmouth was an experience. We were given weekend liberty to go to London. We saw all the self guided sights, rode on the double-decker buses, and watched the "shows" at Piccadilly Square. (Or was it Piccadilly Circus?) We enjoyed the pubs and endured their mandatory closing each afternoon for a couple of hours in "honor of the Queen." We did have some trouble explaining that when cold beer was asked for, it didn't mean putting ice cubes in the beer.

We did come away with a profound respect for the English and their endurance, as we saw the devastation of London. This was 1952, only some seven years after the war. While much rebuilding was underway, there were few buildings standing that were more than three or four stories high. There were lots of rubble and vacant lots.

Somewhere along the way, I got this profound urge to write that June Week date, Doris, and thank her for the date. I figured that would only be common courtesy. My luck held. One of the midshipmen on the cruise was none other than Bill Tarpley, her date for most of that June week. Getting Bill to give me Doris' address was one of the greatest sales jobs I have ever done. Somehow I managed to convince him of a Midshipman's duty in regards to such things and I came out with an address. Bill was a "southern gentleman" in every way possible. Years later (in 1962), we mourned his loss in an airplane accident near Miramar Naval Air Station.

The letter to Doris was answered and the correspondence started that led me to invite myself to Minneapolis during my summer leave. But I still had a cruise to finish, even though it had lost some of its interest for me. We headed for Bergen, Norway and made our way through fjords that were so close on both sides that we could have reached them with a heaving line. The water underneath the ship was some 800 feet deep.

As we entered the Inland Passage toward Bergen, our attention was directed to the mountains on the starboard side of the ship. There were large holes which appeared to have been blasted out of the mountain at the waters' edge. These were German submarine pens which were a haven for the U-Boats as they preyed on shipping in the Atlantic during World War II. Later on we were to hear that "Heavy Water" experiments were conducted at the same locations.

The City of Bergen gave us a great welcome as the Wisconsin was the largest ship ever to anchor in its harbor. The anchoring itself was a chore as the harbor was so deep that the anchor chain was way short of its recommended length. As I recall, the Navy liked the chain to be about six times the depth of the water. We only had enough chain for one and a half times the depth.

After leaving Bergen we sailed for Guantanamo Bay, Cuba and the firing of the big guns. A few days there and back to Norfolk and the troop carrier to take us back to Annapolis where we left for summer leave.

Doris had agreed to my visiting her in Minneapolis and I decided to go the least expensive way. Had I kept a diary, that trip would have ranked right up there with the modern adventures of Lewis and Clark. One of the common ways to travel in the military in those days was to hitch a ride at a Navy Air Station or an Air Force Base. I looked at Anacostia Naval Air Station and Andrews Air Force Base as a place to start, settling on Andrews as it had a lot more flights. The process was to go on the base, sign in at "Operations" and wait for space available on an aircraft going in the direction you wanted to go. You were also ranked according to your "rank" with Midshipmen ranking somewhere below the Admiral's dog. After a long days wait, the only flight heading in that direction was a C-47 going to Wright Paterson AFB, near Columbus, Ohio. Not quite what I had in mind, but better than sitting there.

Wright Patterson was about as slow as Andrews, but finally I found a plane going to Glenview Naval Air Station near Chicago. Once there my flying luck ran completely out and I decided to hitchhike the rest of the way.

I was in uniform as was necessary when trying to fly on military airplanes. I got a number of rides, ending up in Madison, Wisconsin around two in the morning. And there the adventure began in earnest. I was picked up by a car full of beer drinking Indians from a reservation near Thief River Falls. Once in the car, wedged between a couple in the back seat, I got the ride of my life. The Dilbert Dunker and the N3Ns were child's play compared to this. They were celebrating the return alive of one of the group from the Korean War and were apparently trying to rectify this by killing him (and me) on the road between Madison and Thief River Falls.

As the driver passed the beer around, he would swerve the car from one side of the highway to the other running off the road, past the shoulder and up the embankments. About five of these and I was begging to get out, but to no avail. Somehow I had a glimpse of how Custer must have felt. Somehow we made it to Thief River Falls and I managed to get them to drop me off at the Greyhound Bus Station. I had learned my lesson and it was commercial travel the last hundred miles.

At the bus station in Minneapolis, I called Doris and she came downtown to pick me up. I'm surprised that she opened the door as I must have been a sight. I had no sleep during this ordeal, and my khaki uniform was a mass of wrinkles. Add to that the smell of the beer that must have permeated my clothes from the Indians (I had nothing to drink, myself; if I was going to die, I was going to die sober.) I would not have blamed her if she had let me out at the first stop light.

But she didn't and it's now forty four years later (This was written in 1997) and I still sometimes wonder why she didn't stop the car and suggest I catch the first bus back.

The Haugen family, Doris, her mother and brother, Bill, treated me well for the week I stayed at their house. Doris had learned from her sister that midshipmen are poor, and we did a lot of sightseeing. I reluctantly headed back to Annapolis after talking Doris into coming to the Army game in November.

FIRST CLASS YEAR

As we returned to the Academy and began our last year, we became a part of the cycle that makes the Academy a continuing process. As we were assigned as plebes to a group of First Classmen some three years before, we, too, had Plebes assigned to us. The room of Plebes we took under our wing included "Bud" Alexander and George Welsh. Bud remained in contact for a number of years, including his first assignment to a ship whose home base was Long Beach. At this time there was a TV series on, called "Men of Annapolis" and Bud was picked to be the "technical" advisor to the film crew. George, of course, went on to be a great Navy quarterback and a highly successful coach at Navy and the University of Virginia.

A few weeks into First Class year, I received a letter from General Motors, saying something to the effect that it had come to their attention that I was most probably not going to get a commission upon graduation and that they would like to have me consider a career with General Motors. That was the first inkling that I might have that my ulcer episode might have far reaching effects on my life.

I don't remember what I replied, but I recall wondering how in the world General Motors would be privy to my medical details. I then remembered that a girl I had met in Detroit during the second class air cruise, and with whom I had corresponded while she was going to Vassar, had a father who was an executive with General Motors. It was possible that she had put out the word. A month or so later I was called into the Battalion Office and advised that a medical "survey" would be necessary to determine my acceptability as a naval officer. They then explained that because I came to the Academy from the fleet, I would be allowed to stay and graduate. The point is that a Congressman or Senator could only have so many persons at the Academy at one time. If someone was there who would not get a commission, he would not be allowed to stay until graduation, since he would be keeping someone else from attending. The officer said that the survey would be sometime in the spring, but that from his past experience, I should be looking for a job opening on the outside.

The thought of my not being in the Navy was a bit scary in that it had been my life since I was seventeen. As I passed this information on to Doris, she didn't seem as concerned as I was about the loss of my naval career. Somehow more and more I was concerned about how Doris felt. As the fall went on, I was looking forward to seeing her at the Army game. She had made plans to have her sister, Barbara, and Bill meet us in Philadelphia to make a weekend of it. Trying to plan ahead to get more time with this girl, I again invited myself to visit her in Minneapolis during Christmas leave. In a weak moment she accepted, and now I had two "dates" to plan.

The Army game came and Navy won for the third straight year and we became the only class at the Academy who had lost to Army. Doris flew out during a blizzard in Minneapolis to come to the game. After the game, I met Doris, Bill and Barbara, and we spent the weekend in New York. Bill and I roomed together and Doris and Barbara roomed together. This cut the costs of the rooms and also gave Doris and Barbara a chance to visit for the first time in five or six months.

The plans were firmed up for me to visit Minneapolis during Christmas leave and the day after Christmas I caught the train out of Baltimore for Chicago, then on to Minneapolis. No more chances of rides with drunken Indians. A week in Minneapolis with Doris was more than enough to convince me of with whom I wanted to spend the rest of my life. We went to the Poinsettia Ball in St Paul and I asked her to marry me. To my astonishment she said yes, couching the response with a condition that I get her one of the balloons that were floating to the ceiling. I didn't get her a balloon, but the "yes" I heard, loud and clear.

Some fast thinking on my career possibilities made me think of living in the same city my future bride lived, so before I returned to the Academy, I went to Minneapolis-Honeywell and made an application for an engineering job. They said they would let me know.

Back at the Academy, the routine continued, but with less and less concentration on my studies. I had pretty well resigned myself to a civilian future and found myself liking the idea more and more. When the time came around for the medical survey, I was looking forward to getting it behind me and confirming my civilian plans. The doctors, not knowing my thoughts, said there were a couple of options. One was to have a "Reserve" commission and after an ulcer free period of four years, to apply for a regular commission. The other was to be discharged on the day of graduation. I was sure of my stomach conditions and the pressures put on it by the Navy and the absence of any possibility of a diet. I asked that the survey be written to recommend the discharge at time of graduation. My eyes had also deteriorated to a point where glasses were required so that a line commission would not be in the offing.

With this assurance from the medical department, I waited for a response from Minneapolis-Honeywell to cement my plans to be in Minneapolis come June. Some weeks later a letter came from Honeywell offering me a job as an engineer at the great sum of $315 a month. Sounded good to me, as an Ensign would have been paid $212 for the same period.

Toward the end of January brought the inaugural parade for the new President of the country. All Service Academies march full force in this parade which ran for at least three or four miles. Everyone, except Midshipmen on the staff, had to carry M-1 rifles. The staffers carried swords. Since it was windy and cold, the uniform of the day included wearing an overcoat and leggings. The president being sworn in, of course, was Eisenhower. And there was good natured grousing about having to march for a West Pointer. At that time I was on the Battalion staff (in a rather low position, but still on it), so I was able to carry a sword instead of having to tote a rifle.

After our return to Annapolis, some of us were gathered in my room discussing the events of the day and commiserating about "another West Pointer" becoming President of the United States. The subject turned naturally to whom we thought would be the first Naval Academy graduate to achieve that position.

We went through the names of the Admirals from World War II. (Remember this was only eight years after the end of the war.) Finally, the unanimous choice settled on Ross Perot. As I recall, I was going to be the campaign manager and we came up with slogans like "Perot, our Hero" and "Get Hot with Pe-rot."

We all knew Ross well as we had been friends for four years; had gone to classes together, and had watched his rise in the leadership roles at the Academy. It wasn't just his military leadership; there was a certain "get it done" attitude that exuded from him. He had not only been president of the class for two years, but was also the head of the Midshipman Executive Committee, a job that hadn't existed until Ross had chaired a committee to review the Midshipman honor code and this committee was a result of that reorganization.

Ross had great human values about him. He would spot a situation and move to make it better. I remember one time that my Mother came down to visit. A visitor to the Academy needed to sign in at the main office and await the system whereby the Main Office called the Battalion Office. The Battalion Office called the "Mate of the Deck" and he would go to the proper room and notify the Midshipman of a visitor. If the Midshipman was not there, a note was left.

This particular time it took maybe a half hour for me to make it to the Main Office and find Mom. There, to my surprise, was Ross visiting away with Mom. He had just passed by, noticed her waiting, and filled the void until I showed up. I remember Mom commenting what a nice young man he was, and that she thought that he would be going places.

The time came for the great lotto drawing that would help determine the career opportunities for the graduates-to-be. Everyone had their academic standing, something over which they had some control. The first tour of duty was to a great degree determined by lot. Everyone showed up at Memorial Hall and drew a number out of a hat. The number drawn determined the order wherein you could choose the billets that were published as being available. Many a career of a Midshipman ranking high in his class was slowed by a getting a bad ship or a poor billet. Even though I had to draw with the rest of them, I was quite unconcerned with the results. Bill Trueblood had a bad number with Don Upshaw and Jack Jaynes only a bit better.

Doris and I announced our engagement and everything was going well. Doris had some money saved and we used that to make the down payment on a new Pontiac which would be delivered in April or May. (The Academy had rules as to when First Classmen could have a car.)

Did I say everything was going well? Well almost. One day a message was put on my desk saying, "Report to the Superintendent's office at once." What in the world could that be about? I showed up and reported in, "Midshipman Royston, First Class, Sir." The super was Admiral C. Turner Joy, who was back from being in charge of the Korean peace talks (and which was unknown to anyone at the time was dying of Leukemia). He gave me a long stare and began with, "Mr. Royston, I hear the Navy isn't doing right by you." He went on to report that a personal plea from his sister to intervene in my case had been made and it was apparent that he cared about his sister's thoughts. Apparently his sister (as I found out from my mother later) had stopped in the store in Upperville, Virginia, where Mom worked, and after seeing my picture hanging up behind Mom, wanted to know about me and how I was doing. Mom told her that I wasn't getting a commission, and how much I loved the Navy, even though I seemed to be holding up pretty well.

It became immediately apparent that I was about to get reconsidered for a Navy career. By this time I had become acclimated to the idea of becoming a civilian and this new development presented a serious stumbling block to my plans. I had said before that the greatest sales job of my life was getting Doris' address from Bill Tarpley. Well, this had to rank as a close second. How does one tell an Admiral that you'd be better off outside of the Navy? Somehow I explained that the Navy really knew what it was doing and that I would have trouble passing a physical to get into the Cub Scouts. Explaining the possible need for a diet and the bad eyes and as many other ideas as I could come up with at the moment, left me breathless, but successful in convincing the Admiral of the wisdom of the Navy.

Jack Jaynes continued to provide the humor. When he was home on Christmas leave, he had obtained a pair of castanets. His sea stories were put on hold as he sat at his desk studying, and his elbows on the desk, with his forearms extended vertically, clicking these castanets until we were one league past sanity.

One evening during study hour, as Jack sat and clicked, we were interrupted by the "Officer of the Day." We jumped to attention and sounded off with our names and ranks.

The officer looked at Jack and inquired as to what those black things were hanging from his knuckles.

"Castanets, Sir," he answered.

"And what do you do with castanets?" the OD wanted to know.

"You play them, Sir." Jack responded.

"Well, play them." was the order. And so while all of us stood at attention, including Jack (except his arms were extended skyward), as he played the castanets. This went on for an eon or so as we tried to keep straight faces, knowing that if one of us cracked, the laughter would have been heard all over Bancroft Hall.

The Officer of the Day finally wearied of his cat and mouse game and left as we burst into hysterical laughter. That over, Jack sat back down and resumed his studies to the continued clicking of the castanets.

Our room during our First Class year was a corner on the top deck looking out onto the tennis courts on one side and Dewey Basin on the other. Right at the level of the bottom of the windows, a guttering system ran around the entire Bancroft Hall forming a ledge some eighteen inches wide. This was a favorite collecting spots for sea gulls, which became quite a detraction from the scenic beauty of the view. Chasing them away was a futile exercise, one of which we tired after a short while.

Jack, ever resourceful, pirated slices of bread out of the mess hall and went through a process where he would bait the sea gulls by leaving bread on the ledge. They would fly by and grab the bread, swallowing it as they flew away. Jack would keep this up for a while and then attach a string onto one of the pieces of bread. The gull would make his approach, gulp at the bread, and sail off, only to have his flight halted suddenly as he was brought up short by the string.

This was the only method that was successful in keeping the sea gulls away. They would stay away for a period of time, but would gradually drift back. Jack would repeat the process and the cycle continued the rest of the year.

That metal guttering also made a good antenna and even though it was against the regulations to have an outside antenna, my cheap radio made one necessary. I ran a couple of heavy wires out and with some screws attaching the wires to the guttering. The antenna wires were only obvious if one took a good look at the window sill.

One day we were inspected by a Marine Corps Major who was the Battalion Officer. He always wore a big smile on his face and carried the nickname of Mr. Friendly. He was noted for inspecting for singular infractions and because of this habit, saved me from a heavier tour of "extra duty." I came back to my room to find a dreaded form W-2 on my desk. (The star next to my name outside the room designated which resident was in charge of the room that week.)

The infraction: "Dust on window ledge," five demerits. I looked at the window ledge and you could see where the glove had rubbed on the window ledge, over the antenna wires and on the rest of the way. While I was nailed for "Dust on the window ledge," the antenna wasn't mentioned, (fifteen demerits.) It was said that if "Mr. Friendly" was inspecting for giraffes and you had an elephant in your room, he wouldn't see it. Up until that time, I didn't believe it. (These episodes of fourth deck mania have to be rewound to Second Class Year, as Bill Trueblood, always the guy with the good memory, reminded me that we lived on the First deck in the corner room during First Class Year. The episodes must have happened when Jack and I were in the two man room on the fourth deck.) (Now if you really want to be confused, the first deck was really the second floor and the fourth deck was really the fifth floor. All this because the Academy, following Naval tradition, named the first floor the "Zero" deck.)

Don Upshaw was making plans to marry his girlfriend, Darleen Sexton (better known as "Pete"). Jack Jaynes was marrying Fran Nagy. Fran was from Philadelphia and was going to Goucher College. They met on a blind date a couple of years before when she came to the Academy to sing in a combined Goucher-USNA Messiah production.

My wedding was planned for September. Bill Trueblood was dating but he had nothing serious going on. He later married Karen Wheland, whom he met a short time before he graduated. Karen was a "Navy Junior" whose dad was a retired Captain from the class of 1931.

We were all enjoying the last term of our First Class year. The Korean War was winding down and it looked like peacetime service for most of the graduates. The Navy Alma Mater, "Blue and Gold," began to take on a special meaning for us, but we said little about it, knowing that many of us would never see each other again. It was true that service duties would bring some together, but many would lose their lives in submarine, aircraft or shipboard accidents.

Looming over the horizon was Vietnam, a country we had hardly heard of, and it too would take its toll.

There would be nine of us out of the 925 graduates who would not be offered a commission. One of these was out of my company and he would later play a role in my life when I moved to Los Angeles. This was Hal Lewis, one of the greatest classmates one could have. Hal had gone to Pepperdine University for a year before he came to the Academy. He was an accomplished gymnast before he arrived and while at the Academy was the National High Bar Champion and second in the Flying Rings. He was quiet and reserved and couldn't understand why anyone would make a fuss over him.

Hal came down with stomach problems that the hospital couldn't diagnose. The pains became so acute that they discharged Hal without a commission. He returned to the Los Angeles Area and sometime during the next year went to Scripps Institute where they, after a battery of tests, found that he was allergic to wheat flour. Every time he would eat a sandwich or anything with wheat in it, he would get violent stomach cramps.

When graduation came, we threw our hats in the air and gave three cheers to those we left behind and were on our way into the next phase of our lives. Some rose to be commissioned into the US Air Force, others into the Marines and the rest (70%) into the Navy. Later on many would be attending Flight School or Submarine School.

Don, Bill and Jack would all become submariners, with Bill going on to becoming an "Engineering Duty Only" officer, retiring as a Captain. Don became a specialist in torpedoes and retired as a Commander. Jack spent some ten years in "diesel boats" and retired as a Lt. Commander. As many of my classmates later moaned about being "passed over," I would always remind them that I was "passed over" as a Midshipman.

We roommates have stayed close over the years and we see each other routinely. As Jack says, all of the wives are "original issue," making it easier to stay close. (Jack's wife, Fran, died in 2005.)

THE NAVY HYMN

Eternal Father, strong to save,
Whose arm doth bind the restless wave,
Who bidd'st the mighty ocean deep,
Its own appointed limits keep.
Oh, hear us when we cry to thee,
For those in peril on the sea.

Eternal Father, lend thy grace,
To those with wings who fly through space,
Thro' wind and storm, thro' sun and rain,
Oh bring them safely home again.
Oh Father, hear a humble prayer,
For those in peril in the air.

Oh Trinity of love and pow'r,
Our brethren shield in danger's hour,
From rock and tempest, fire and foe,
Protect them where so e'er they go.
Thus evermore shall rise to Thee
Glad hymns of praise from land and sea.

The Navy Hymn

As we packed and left Bancroft Hall for the last time, we knew that schooling was over. For nine of us, it was the entrance into civilian life that was faced with as much trepidation as the ones commissioned felt about their first duty assignments.

In 1953, 25% were graduated into the US Air Force. That's right, the US Air Force. The Air Force had become a separate branch of the service in 1947, but no service academy was in operation at the time. For a few years, West Point supplied the regular duty officers. This became a drain on their manpower and the solution was to commission officers from both Annapolis and West Point into the Air Force.

Since their uniforms was the familiar color of the color of our "sock bags" became after going through a lot of laundering holding the navy blue socks, it was common to refer to those going into the Air Force as "Sock Bag Blue."

Some years it was popular to go that direction and the Air Force would get an extraordinary number of Midshipmen with high academic standings. At other times, the reverse would be true. To solve this, the 25% were taken from a cross section of the class.

Five percent went into the Marine Corps. Priorities were given to those who had previously been in the Corps or who had a parent in the Marines. As a result, the quota filled up fast and it was unusual for a Midshipman with no Marine connections to make it into the Corps. The exception out of our company was Don McAdams. Don had been a petty officer in the Navy prior to the Academy, but decided on the Corps as a career. Maybe standing in the top fifty of the class helped.

The remaining 70% or so were commissioned into the Navy. After their first assignment, they could apply for specialty branches such as Navy Air or Submarines. Bill Trueblood headed for the USS Mount McKinley. Don Upshaw for the USS Seminole, and Jack Jaynes for the USS Hazelwood. Later all three would get their "dolphins" and spend time on "Fleet Boats" (Non Atomic Submarines.)

Ray Hanson, a buddy from as far back as Aviation Electronics School in Memphis, had resigned during his second class year and returned to Denver. Nelson Sonnenburg, who had been instrumental in getting me past the first Navy hurdles went into the Navy and resigned in 1958.

The "Shipmate" magazine, published by the Alumni Association, was, and still is, the lifeline that connects the Naval Academy graduates. Each issue has a class section and a report on the doings of many of the individuals. While class reunions are held each year with accents on the five year mileposts, it is the Shipmate to which we turn. Many times the news is great. First it was marriages, promotions and assignments. As the years passed it became news of our own Navy Juniors also going to Annapolis. Then it was and is about grand kids and cruises (without the benefit of watch standing.)

But it was, and continues to be, the obituary columns to which we turn. A death is first reported in the class news and then in the "Last Call" columns. The Navy Hymn began to take on a different meaning when it was a classmate, friend or pal who had lost their life. Most of the first ones reported were aircraft accidents, either in training or on patrol. Occasionally, it was an automobile or shipboard accident. The loss of the USS Thrasher in April of 1963 took the life of Mike Di Nola. Bill Tarpley, the gallant Southerner, and Doris' date during June Week, 1952, lost his life in an aircraft accident in June of 1962.

When the Korean War started in June of 1950, there was an up swelling of desire to get into the war. It had been common for the Academies to graduate their classes a year early so as to provide replacements for fallen warriors. And our pleas were loud enough to be heard all the way to Washington and in due time brought the Chief of Naval Operations to visit us. He called us into Mahan Hall and delivered a lecture, the details of which have long passed into memory. I do remember his parting words. "There has never been a graduating class from the Naval Academy who did not get the opportunity to fight in a war and I doubt that yours will be the first."

For my class it was the Viet Nam war. And it took its toll, especially on those in the Marines, or the Navy and Air Force Aviators. Lyle Armel survived the war, only to die from "Agent Orange" effects many years later. Bill Leftwich, a brigade commander during his Midshipman years, was killed in action on his second tour in Viet Nam as he tried to save those under him with a helicopter rescue team.

These are just some of the names who come to mind as I wander through my memories. Bill Branson, Hal Lewis, Randy Hanback, Ken Bocock, Bill Holland, Grant Millard, Jerry Snuffin, are all company mates who died early. As we grow older, the deaths are occurring with a rapidity that makes one turn again to the words of; "Eternal Father, Strong to Save," knowing that the years are shortening until the notification at the class heading will be: "Any news of the class of 1953 should be sent directly to the Alumni Association."

Fortunately, we have a classmate who prays for us daily. Jim "Pappy" Walker came out of the fleet with us and being older, acquired the name of "Pappy." He was a wild type that was known for his battles with the bottle. He was a Southern Baptist from Georgia who somehow married a Catholic girl. I don't know all the details, but after his wife died he turned to the Catholic Church and became a priest. Now he is pastor of an inner-city church in Georgia and his biggest battle these days is to find the funds to keep his school going. (Father Jim Walker died in 2000 from Cancer)

It is not my intention to turn this into a funeral dirge. Only that the thought of how much we wanted to graduate and get on with our lives was paramount, with no thought for, "You are now entering the real world and this is not a drill." The results of the failure of this "test" could and did cost one his life. School was out.

FAITH

OF

OUR

FATHERS

Faith of our fathers! living still
In spite of dungeon, fire and sword;
O, how our hearts beat high with joy
Whene'er we hear that glorious word!
Faith of our fathers! holy faith!
We will be true to thee til death!

Our fathers, chained in prisons dark,
Were still in heart and conscience free:
How sweet would be their children's fate,
If they, like them, could die for thee!
Faith of our fathers! holy faith!
We will be true to you til death.

Faith of our fathers! We will love
Both friends and foe in all our strife:
And preach thee, too, as love knows how,

By kindly words and virtuous life:
Faith of our fathers! holy faith!
We will be true to you til death.

Faith of Our Fathers

Mom and Dad had started us kids in our trip through faith when we were just babies. Mom would love to tell about me lying in a crib under the front church pew, imitating the preacher as he preached. (Just in case you might get the idea that it was the "crib" experience that headed me in a certain direction, I must tell you that as an infant, I also spent some time in a jail cell. Granddad Smallwood was sheriff of the county and Mom would many times drop me off at the jail for Granddad to "baby sit." The word has it that he simply put me in the holding tank and closed the door. There I could crawl around to my heart's content.)

I grew up going to Mount Carmel, a historical Methodist church, about a quarter mile from home. We felt we were a part of the church, with Dad as the Sunday School superintendent, and Mom playing the organ. Dad was a bit of a fanatic. (Or, so I thought at the time.) Mom's faith was sure and resolute. She never wavered, no matter what problems she went through. She never confronted us with "church or else." She simply got ready and somehow you knew that you were joining her.

We learned some of our early self assurance as we participated in "All Day Services" and Christmas Programs. We played on the huge boulders around the church and ruined the knees of our "Sunday" clothes as the rocks and grass took its toll. The church was a meeting place where gossip was exchanged, as there were only one or two telephones in the mountains.

We came to know persons who had lived in the mountains and after having moved, would return for visits or special occasions. Some are still vivid in my mind's eye. I recall persons like Mr. Will Elliott, who kind of took over the organ when he returned. I remember his energetic pumping of the foot pedals, as he leaned back from the organ and with his arms straight out and his head cocked to one side, he would fill the church with his voice and music. (It's possible that his rearing back from the organ had something to do with farsightedness.)

When I enlisted in the Navy, I went through a period where my only church attendance was when I returned home on leave. The only group of sailors who seemed to attend church regularly were ones who professed to be "Catholics." Upon my admission to The Naval Academy, I found that everyone had to attend church services. As they said "There are no Atheists in foxholes or at the Naval Academy."

They tell the story of one Midshipman who thought that church going was not the thing to do. He finally came up with a way. He decided that he was a Muslim, knowing that the closest Mosque was in Washington, DC, some thirty five miles away. He reasoned that they wouldn't make a trip to DC just for him.

Well, he had them snookered—for a while. Then, one morning the Officer of the Day knocked on his door before sunrise and provided him with what appeared to be an authentic prayer rug; took him out on to the assembly area in front of Bancroft Hall, pointed toward the East and said "Have at it."

A few days of this and he decided to become a Christian and joined the others in the Sunday services.

There were several choices as to what service you could attend. In the Yard there were Protestant, Catholic and Jewish services. In addition, you could sign up for a "Church Party" and march out into Annapolis and attend a specific church at their services.

The Yard services were very popular with the visitors as they were moved by the men in uniform and the very fine choirs that all groups had. In addition, the Catholics had St Andrew's Chapel in the basement of the main chapel for daily mass.

The Navy was very practical about the handling of the Catholics and Protestants. The Cross was a Protestant symbol, where as the Crucifix was the Catholics'. The Navy made sure that the body of Christ didn't extend out beyond the sides of the cross. When the Protestant service was held, the cross side was turned facing the worshipers; when the Catholics showed up, the cross was turned around so the crucifix was showing. Very practical, but I often wondered what the Protestant

Chaplain thought as he viewed the crucifix from his side as he led the service.

The first year I went to the Protestant services at the chapel. The rest of the time, until nearly the end of my Academy days, I went to a Methodist Church out in Annapolis.

While my tradition was all Methodist, it was a tradition only. I didn't feel driven toward a personal relationship with God. One of the most impressive things I saw as I watched my fellow Midshipmen show their faith, or lack of it, was that one group seemed to stand out; these being the Catholics. I first dismissed it as the discipline from their youth, but as classmates like Don McAdams (if you were up at the time) were seen heading out to daily mass, it was apparently more than that. The attraction to this somewhat mysterious religion was there, but I didn't act on it.

When I met Doris, lo and behold, this gal with the Norwegian name was a Catholic. After I became more and more interested in Doris, I made a conscious effort to find out more about what she believed, and visited the Catholic Chaplain. The Catholic Chaplain didn't seem to be overly anxious to spend a lot of time with me. Perhaps he had seen a number of persons who showed interest in the Church because they had met a sweet young thing that came with the baggage of the Catholic Church.

I kept showing up and finally Chaplain Michaels started giving me instruction. After some three or four months I made my decision and with Bob Klee as my Godfather, (Rear Admiral Robert Erhart Klee, deceased 1995) I was conditionally baptized into the Church on my birthday, May 20, 1953. (I had most probably been baptized as a Methodist but didn't have the written records to prove it. It just seemed easier this way.) I now have been a Catholic for lo these many years and can't imagine being of any other faith. Mom wasn't too happy about my change, but grew to accept it as time went on.

As I look back on the ethnicity of my forefathers, I'm sure that becoming a Catholic, was returning to "The faith of my fathers," albeit hundreds of years ago.

There have been many changes in the Catholic Church, especially in the area of discipline. The discipline of the Church was always a strong point with me as I had come to it from the very disciplined atmosphere of the military. But like the other areas of our lives where discipline was rejected for the easier way of life, the church followed suit. (A strange thing happened; the church relaxed the rules in response to complaints of being too strict but those who wanted change left anyway.)

I have come to believe that I will be judged on how I treat my fellow man, especially those who need my help, and not by the brand of religion that conducts my funeral. (I was hungry, and you fed me; I was naked and you clothed me,....). On the other hand I feel that the discipline put on us by the church, whether it be silly rules, such as no meat on Friday or fasting for all of Lent, help us to be mentally and spiritually strong when temptation rears its ugly head. Maybe our life is meant to be one long Plebe Year, a time where we went through some ridiculous rules in order to make one a better potential Naval Officer. After all, a lifetime "Plebe year" is short compared to eternity. Going through life marching down the center of the corridor and squaring corners morally might not be such a bad idea after all.

978-0-595-47688-6
0-595-47688-0